THE HOODED MAN

Best wishes
Charles Searle

Charles Searle

The Book Guild

First published in Great Britain in 2025 by
The Book Guild Ltd
Unit E2 Airfield Business Park,
Harrison Road, Market Harborough,
Leicestershire. LE16 7UL
Tel: 0116 2792299
www.bookguild.co.uk
Email: info@bookguild.co.uk

The manufacturer's authorised representative in the EU
for product safety is Authorised Rep Compliance Ltd,
71 Lower Baggot Street, Dublin D02 P593 Ireland (www.arccompliance.com)

Typeset in 11pt Adobe Garamond Pro

Printed and bound in Great Britain by 4edge Limited

ISBN 978 1835743 096

British Library Cataloguing in Publication Data.
A catalogue record for this book is available from the British Library.

To Carolyne, for keeping the faith.

PROLOGUE

Dommiers, Aisne, June 1917

HE WAS SUBMERGED in a balmy dream of early childhood and the days when he collected the cows for milking up on the high pastures of the Cantal, when he was ripped from his sleep by someone grabbing his shoulder and giving him a rough shake.

'Get up, Corporal, and report to the divisional headquarters in five minutes flat.' By the time Antoine had opened his eyes, cleared the fog from his brain, all he could see was the retreating back of Captain Duprais, his section leader.

He pushed himself up from the thin straw bedding that was all he had been able to find when they had arrived at their latest billet in the early hours of the morning. He looked around him at the rest of his section, most of whom had not even managed to take off their boots before collapsing onto whatever was to hand before falling into a deep sleep. All of them were still unconscious, physically obliterated by the miles of forced marching back from the front. He peered out of the ragged hole in the wall of the stables across what remained of the farmyard. The dawn was only just breaking as he heard a cockerel away to his left heralding the start of the day.

He felt exhausted as he shuffled across the yard, pulling on his tunic, with his two corporal chevrons on his sleeve. He settled a cap over his hair, which was lank and greasy after their weeks in the trenches. He headed for the main farmhouse. It had survived relatively unscathed from the artillery barrage that had demolished most of the rest of the farm's outbuildings. He knew that the general and his staff would have commandeered the farmhouse as they always took the most comfortable lodgings when the regiment came out of the line.

He passed by two guards on the main door and entered the hall that was full of the clutter of a battalion on the move. Captain Duprais was waiting for him. He gave him a quick once-over to make sure he was presentable and then knocked on the door. They waited for what seemed like a minute, before they could hear boots crunching across the floor, and then the door swung open to reveal the general himself. He was a short, stocky man, in his mid-fifties, with a florid face that was offset by a large, greying moustache that hung down both sides of his mouth to below his chin.

'Come in, Martinet,' he said as he turned into the room. 'Duprais, you can leave.' The captain saluted the general and closed the door behind him.

'Before we start, Martinet, I need to introduce you to this gentleman,' he said, gesturing across the room at a man, dressed in civilian clothes, who was sitting at the dining room table, draped languidly over his breakfast coffee. He had long, dark hair that was swept back over his forehead and came to rest on his shoulders. He wore a white silk shirt underneath his dark-blue tunic jacket, with the top buttons undone, revealing a pale, hairless chest and what looked like a small Star of David.

For a man used to giving orders, the general appeared unnerved in the presence of this civilian. 'This is Monsieur Gallopin. He is from the Renseignement Généraux and has come down especially from Paris. Do you know what they do, Martinet?'

'No, sir.'

'Well,' went on the general, looking around the room in search of the right words, 'they look after the internal security of the fatherland.'

'You mean they are spies, sir.'

Before the general could respond, Gallopin held up his hand. 'No, not spies, that sounds too monarchical, as though we are back in the ancien régime and not servants of the Republic. No, no, we are here to make sure that nothing disturbs our unwavering mission of beating the Germans and driving them back over the border, but not before we take back Alsace and Lorraine. You would agree with that, wouldn't you, Martinet?'

'Yes, of course. I signed up in August 1914 and have fought for three years solid to bring about that end.'

'Excellent. Your general said that you were the most steady and patriotic man in this division and that you would do whatever it takes to protect and advance the cause of the fatherland. Which makes you exactly the right man to give me the information I need.'

Antoine looked across at the general, who was struggling to return his gaze.

'So, Antoine, I can call you that, can't I?'

Antoine gave a curt nod.

'You know about the mutinies that have taken place among some of the regiments over the past few weeks, with men refusing orders to leave the depots and go up to the front, and others deserting the trenches and running from the enemy?'

Antoine tried to remain composed as the memories and sensations of that day on the frontline came rushing back to him. He wanted desperately to suppress them, particularly the sight of the face of his younger brother Philippe as the life drained out of him. His platoon had been caught up in the mass frenzy that had gripped whole regiments during the latest campaign on the Chemin des Dames. He had witnessed men from the regiment turning around and running. As a result, the platoon had had to dig in, waiting for the bombardment to stop and darkness to fall, so they could make their way back to the start line. Along with Philippe, he had lost two other men. Their shallow foxhole had taken a direct hit from a shell. He would not forget the sight of one of them somersaulting headless through the air before coming crashing down in front of where he had been huddled. When they eventually retreated that night, they passed the burnt-out stores in the depot that had been looted by the mutineers as they ran amok behind the lines. Due to the chaos of the retreat, he had had to leave Philippe's and the other men's bodies in no man's land.

'Yes, of course I am aware of the mutiny and the mutineers. They put me and my men in great danger. I lost my bother Philippe because of their cowardice.'

'Good, I am glad we agree on that.' Gallopin paused

before going on, staring directly at Antoine. 'So, I want you to give me the names of those in your regiment who turned tail and ran.'

Antoine took his time before giving an answer. He was a corporal, in charge of no more than thirty men, in a division of thousands. Surely, this was the responsibility of someone much more senior than him. He turned to the general, who was still not giving him eye contact.

'Sir, why have I been chosen? I am surely of too low a rank to be asked for this information.'

Again, before the general could muster a response, Gallopin interjected. 'First, you are a patriot, and we are finding those thin on the ground. Second, you have an exemplary service record. You may not have many men to command, but you lead by example. And finally, and to be as direct as I can, we cannot ask someone whose reputation and career might be damaged by such a request.'

Antoine thought about the men from his regiment who had deserted their brothers in arms at the very time when they should have stood by each other. He had seen some of them, the socialists and the pacificists, handing out their leaflets calling on the soldiers to defy orders. They had been joined by colonial troops from Algeria and Indochina, who wanted France to be defeated, so they could advance their quests for independence. They had shown no loyalty to him or to their country, so why should he show them any loyalty, just because they were from the same regiment? Above all, he blamed them for the loss of his beloved brother.

'Barthas, Lalaque, Vidal, Sévérac, Tanty and Vacher. The colonials' names I don't know, but they included Annamites and Algerians. I am sure you can find some that fit the bill.'

'Yes, yes, we have had our eyes on the colonial agitators from the moment they arrived in the country, so don't worry about them.'

There was a long pause as Gallopin continued to stare at Antoine, like some hungry bird of prey circling for the kill.

'Can I go, sir?' Antoine directed his remark towards the general, who still could not meet his gaze.

Gallopin again interrupted before the general could say anything, not that he looked like he was going to engage in any part of this conversation. 'No, Antoine. I am not finished with you just yet. I think that we have just struck up a very fruitful relationship, you and I.'

'If you say so, sir.'

'I do. So, one final request. Or, should I say, order. I am giving you the honour of commanding the firing squad that will administer justice to these cowards.'

Antoine ignored Gallopin and turned to the general.

'Sir, have these men been charged and found guilty following the correct military procedures?'

The general spoke quietly and without much conviction. 'Yes, Martinet, these men were all charged and found guilty.'

'Are you ordering me to carry out this command, sir?'

'Yes, I am.'

'Well, I'm glad that is all sorted,' Gallopin said impatiently. 'Now, let's get down to some practicalities. These men will be shot by firing squad at dawn tomorrow. We have chosen a location not far from here, out of sight of any encampments or civilian settlements. We have selected the men who will make up the firing squad. You, and they, are sworn to secrecy about when and where the executions will take place. After the event, we will publish the fact that it has happened, to ensure that the right message gets through to the rest of the troops. You will receive a reward for undertaking this commission, either in additional leave, extra pay, or a citation, or maybe all three, we haven't made up our minds yet. Do you understand, Martinet?'

'Yes, I understand. But you, and the general, need to know that I am only doing this because I have been ordered to by my commanding officer and because I too believe that the mutineers have let down their fellow soldiers. But I don't see why they need to be shot.'

'Pretty little speech, Martinet. Now, leave and await further orders about tomorrow.'

In the early evening, Captain Duprais entered the stables and ordered Antoine to follow. They went across the farmyard and through a gate at the side of the farmhouse into a small walled orchard behind the house. At the back of the orchard, out of view of any passers-by, were a group of ten men. Antoine's heart sank when he saw them. He could tell from their uniforms that they were all from the African Light Infantry. To serve in that regiment meant that they would have been released early from military prisons to swell the ranks or they were petty criminals who had been convicted in France and were commuting their sentences by serving in the army. They were brutalised by a regime of discipline as harsh as that found in the Foreign Legion. They repaid that brutality in kind by meting it out to anyone who crossed them, friend or foe.

Captain Duprais called them all together.

'OK, men, this is Corporal Martinet, from the 97th Regiment. He has a proud war record and is in charge of you lot tomorrow.'

This announcement was met with derisive whistling and slow handclapping from the assembled group. Antoine slowly took them in. He was used to some rough-and-ready types in the infantry platoons he had served in, but this lot looked like they didn't give a damn, for authority, for themselves, or for each other. Some had faces disfigured by badly healed broken noses or being sliced open with a razor. Their hands betrayed their favourite pastime of bare-knuckle brawling.

One of them, a particularly imposing man, standing over six feet tall and with powerful shoulders, detached himself from the group and stuck his face in Antoine's. He spoke in a thick Provençale accent that Antoine struggled to understand. 'My name's Thierry Sandoz. I boss this group. They do what I say. We have signed up for this jaunt tomorrow because we get to quit the army the day after we shoot the mutinous bastards. So, any orders for them come through me, understand?' With that he turned away and spat on the ground.

'OK,' barked Duprais, 'we assemble here at four-thirty tomorrow morning. We then march to the execution site, where you will receive your rifles and carry out the orders given to you by Corporal Martinet. As a token of our goodwill, we have provided you with some refreshment for tonight.' Duprais turned to point at several flagons of red wine and bottles of absinthe nestled up against the trees. The men gave out wild catcalls and whistled in appreciation.

It was still dark when Antoine pushed the gate open into the orchard early the next morning. He was met with the sight of men slumped in heaps with their arms wrapped around the trees. Antoine strode across to Sandoz and shook him roughly by the shoulder.

'Get up immediately, you drunkard, and fall in your men.'

Sandoz squinted up through bleary eyes. He lurched up, swaying. He took a wild swing aimed at Antoine's head. Antoine ducked and then drove his fists into the man's stomach. Sandoz collapsed onto his knees, throwing up what remained of the cocktail of red wine and absinthe he had consumed overnight.

'Fall in!' commanded Antoine.

The sun was starting to rise as they turned into a small, secluded field that had a derelict barn in the middle of it. Antoine could see that there were several regimental gendarmes standing guard over ten men who were crouched on the ground. As he got closer, he could pick out their faces. It looked like a few of them had received some heavy treatment while they had been questioned in detention. One or two had burst lips and closed eyes, disfigured by huge red and blue swellings. Of the ten men, two were *tirailleurs* from African regiments, maybe Senegalese and Saharan; one was from Indochina; and the rest were French infantryman. They all looked up apprehensively as the column of men marched towards them.

One of the gendarmes took Antoine around the back of the barn, which was shielded from the road, and showed him where the firing squad would take place. There were ten wooden stakes driven into the ground in front of the wall, with pieces of rope tied to them.

'This is where the poor bastards are going to die. Just make it quick. Then get those scum of yours to dig a mass grave and dump the bodies in there. Others will come back later, dig them up again and remove them until they decide what to do with them. Understand?'

Antoine nodded. He took a couple of deep breaths, sucking in the early morning summer air, and then walked round to the other side of the barn.

'All right you lot, pick up these captives, march them around the other side of the barn and tie them to the stakes.'

The members of the squad grabbed the condemned men by their arms and frogmarched them roughly around to the other side of the barn. They did not resist or make a sound. They were resigned to their fate.

Once they were tied to the stakes, Antoine took pieces of red cloth from his tunic pocket. He then worked his way down the line. He stood in front of each man, pinning the red cloth strips to their chests. He grabbed hold of the regimental insignia on their collars and ripped them off, before putting them in his pocket. The men's head and shoulders jerked backwards and forwards as he did this, but none of them protested. Finally, he stuck a lighted cigarette into the mouths of those who could still open them. Whilst he did this, he leant forward and asked each of them whether they had been tried and sentenced to death by a military court. Most of them shook their heads. The Ammonite from Indochina stared at him with calm defiance and said that he had been marched here from prison without any trial. Behind him, he was aware of Sandoz observing his every action.

He then turned and walked to stand alongside the members of the firing squad.

'You will aim at the pieces of red cloth that I have pinned to their uniforms. You do not aim anywhere else. The sequence of my commands will be come to attention, present arms, load, aim, fire. Do you understand?'

The men grunted their assent. Antoine gave them a quick once-over and could see that some were swaying a bit, with others starting to sweat. He knew he had to do this quickly before they started to lose their nerve or pass out from the previous night's indulgence.

'Firing squad. Come to attention!'

The order was followed in a desultory fashion as the men brought their heels together and straightened up.

'Present arms!'

There was the slapping sound of ten Berthier rifles being removed from the men's shoulders and brought to the ground.

'Load!'

The men snapped the three round clips into the rifles' magazines.

'Aim!'

After ten seconds, Antoine shouted, 'Fire!'

There was a ragged volley of shots, followed by a roar that reverberated off the walls of the barn. This was met by a cacophony of cawing from the crows that took off from the trees surrounding the field. As this sound died away, it was echoed by the groans of the dying men. Antoine ran across to the line of captives who now hung from the stakes. Most of them had died instantly, but a couple had not received clean shots and were writhing in agony, their bodies swaying. He unholstered his revolver, pressed the muzzle against the back of their heads and pulled the trigger.

Antoine spent the rest of the day stretched out on his straw mattress trying to blot out what he had done. Those men were mutineers. They had betrayed their comrades in arms and their country. His brother had been killed because of their cowardice. But they had not received due process.

They could have been imprisoned, given hard labour, not shot like dogs.

Later that evening, after the platoon had had its paltry evening meal that consisted of tiny morsels of some indecipherable meat, Antoine could see Captain Duprais' silhouette filling the doorway of the stables. Lurking behind him were two other men, one of whom was Thierry Sandoz. Antoine went outside to meet them.

'Your platoon has to go back up to the line for reconnaissance duties tonight.'

'But we've only just got back from the line and are due our rest,' Antoine protested.

'Too bad. We are short of men. Talking of being short of men, your platoon is down two, so Sandoz here and Gaston have been assigned as replacements.'

'I thought they were going to be given dispensation from service after what they did this morning.'

'No, they volunteered to stay on, like true patriots, didn't you, Sandoz and Gaston?'

'That's right, like true patriots.' The two men grinned.

It took the platoon three hours of hard marching to get back up to the frontline, carrying their full packs. Once they reached the first trench, the officer in charge, whom Antoine didn't recognise but who was wearing the uniform of the African Light Infantry, took him to one side.

'As soon as it is fully dark, you need to go up to the observation point and look out for any enemy movements. You will be in charge, and I am assigning Sandoz and Gaston to go with you.'

'No disrespect to your regiment, sir, but I don't trust those wastrels. They are ill-disciplined and unprofessional.'

'No offence taken, Corporal, but those are your orders.'

Just after midnight, when the sky was inky black, the small party set off, crawling in single file with Antoine in front. After thirty minutes of moving forwards on their hands and knees, they arrived at the terminus of the trench, where there was a small periscope that they could use to observe the enemy. They were so close, they could hear the Germans' chuntering, muffled laughter and clinking of canteens.

'Right, I am going to do two hours on periscope watch. Sandoz, you are first relief, and Gaston you are second. In the meantime, you can get some sleep. I will wake you when it is your turn.'

He placed his knees on his pack to keep them off the ground and raised the periscope. All he could see were the sandbags lining the top of the opposite trench and the coils of barbed wire in front of them. There was no other movement. After half an hour of this inactivity, he started to doze, drifting in and out of wakefulness as the events of the past two days caught up with him.

Suddenly, he sensed a rapid movement behind him and before he could turn round, a massive weight had pinned his body to the side of the trench. He could feel and smell warm, fetid breath washing over him. His assailant had his hands around his neck and was squeezing hard. Antoine bucked his back as furiously as he could. This momentarily dislodged his attacker. He rolled to one side and then sprang to his feet. In front of him was Sandoz armed with a bayonet, and Gaston with a trenching tool.

'Why are you doing this, you bastards? Who put you up to it?'

'You know too much. We cannot rely on your silence anymore. So, we are going to end it here.' Sandoz, whose thick Provençale accent had disappeared to be replaced by that of an educated Parisian, crouched low in front of Antoine.

They started to close in. Antoine thought his best chance of escape was to get round them and run down the trench to get some help. He threw a feint, which unbalanced Sandoz, and then plunged at the gap. He was almost through when he felt a crushing pain in his knee as Gaston wielded the trenching tool. He went down, scrabbling at the mud, and then felt the bayonet thrust into his back, followed by one in his side.

As Antoine slipped in and out of consciousness, all he could hear was his brother Philippe calling his name and the plaintive sound of the herd as they returned from the high meadows of the Cantal.

PART 1

Indochina

CHAPTER 1
Marseille, April 1926

ANTOINE LOOKED DOWN at the gangway as passengers boarded the *Aramis*, one of Messageries Maritime's largest ocean-going liners. They were a cross-section of the colonial society he was about to call home for the next few years. There were married couples of varying ages, still bundled up in winter coats despite the early morning spring sunshine. They were accompanied by their Chinese servants, who followed behind balancing hand luggage with various hatboxes. There were single Frenchmen, dressed in tropical whites or military uniforms, who were on their way to take up roles in the empire's civil service and army of occupation. Bringing up the rear, there was a very small group of young Vietnamese men, whose haughty posture and smart tailoring marked them out as students returning from their studies at Paris's elite universities.

Shortly before lunchtime, the liner cast off its moorings and headed out into the Mediterranean. As it did so, Antoine took a last look at Le Vieux Port as it slid from view. This would be the first time he had left the shores of his native

France. The voyage to Saigon would take thirty days, with stops at Djibouti and Colombo. It would give him plenty of time to reflect on what had brought him to this point.

Sandoz and Gaston had left him for dead after they attacked him in the observation trench. He had lain there, face down in the mud, his wounds pumping blood until a reconnaissance party had stumbled on him the next day. He had been patched up and discharged from his infantry regiment. General Pétain wanted to draw a line under the outbreak of mass disorder as fast as he could, so it was considered best to get Antoine out of the way so he wouldn't talk about his role to anyone else in the army in identifying the mutineers and commanding the firing squad. Not that Antoine wanted to dwell on that. At the time he had thought he was following his duty, even if he had doubts about how justice was dispensed. He still believed that. But the way he had been treated by the authorities, sent home with just an ill-fitting demob suit and a paltry disability pension, left a sour taste in his mouth, after the promises that had been made to him of extra pay and promotion.

He had returned home to his family's small farm in the Cantal. It soon became obvious that the farm could not support an additional mouth to feed. While he had been away, his youngest brother, Gerard, had grown into a strong and capable young man, whom his father had increasingly begun to rely on to carry out the hard graft involved in looking after the dairy cattle. So, Antoine joined the exodus from the countryside to the surrounding towns to find work. This had led him to Clermont-Ferrand, where the factories and workshops were booming as they switched from war work to domestic production.

He quickly found employment in the Rodin tyre factory, one of the largest employers in the town. He started at the bottom, folding bicycle tyres as they rolled off the assembly line. He was soon identified as a hard worker and someone whom others looked up to. He gained promotion to the role of line supervisor. Then he was given charge of a whole workshop. Not long after that, he was called into the director's office and made the factory's head of security. This was to prevent the endemic pilfering from the workplace, whether it be of tools, raw materials or even spoons from the work's canteen. As the workforce grew, he was tasked with keeping an eye on the growth of labour militancy in the factory. Although the owners did not recognise trade unions, organisations like the CGT were sending activists into factories to agitate for strike action. In the trenches, Antoine had seen how socialists and communists spread pacifism and defeatism. He had come to loathe them. That was one of the reasons he had named the mutineers. He recruited a network of informants, drawn from the many veterans working at the factory, to tip him off about the militants. When necessary, he had identified them to the director, who promptly sacked them. The factory remained union and strike free.

One day early in 1926, the director had asked him to attend a meeting with the company's owners. The meeting was in the boardroom, in a part of the factory complex that he had never seen before, tucked away at the top of the administrative block. On arriving, the director introduced him to the two brothers who had founded the company, Édouard and André Rodin. Although they were both in their late sixties, Antoine could see from the way they held themselves and spoke to him that they still had the vitality and drive of much younger men. They explained that the company wanted to expand into new products, particularly the tyres needed for cars and trucks. To do this, they had to secure supplies of rubber that they controlled themselves, rather than be reliant on other producers of this vital raw material. They had identified an opportunity in Cochinchina, one of the three provinces in colonial Indochina. The colonial administration was awarding concessions to anyone who was prepared to clear the land and plant trees. To his surprise, the brothers asked Antoine to be part of a small team to go out to Cochinchina to set up the new operation. His role would be to recruit and oversee the labour force to work on the plantation.

Antoine did not need much encouragement to agree to the offer. He had done well at his time at the factory, but, in truth, he was bored. The routine tasks of frisking people for stolen spoons were not compensated by the occasional drama of unmasking a communist militant. He missed the camaraderie of his infantry platoon and, he had to admit, the excitement of combat. He had never found the war frightening. Yes, there had been the mud and rain, the infestation of lice and plagues of rats. But he had never felt as alive as when he went over the top, leading his men into the maelstrom of battle. This new venture could provide him with a simulacrum of those experiences and sensations.

That was the reason he was now steaming towards Saigon on the *Aramis*. He was accompanied on the trip by two other company employees. Pierre Jouvin was the oldest of the three. He had already done a stint in Cochinchina, setting up and running a small rubber plantation for an absentee landowner. The Rodins had hired him to do the same for them, but on a much larger scale. Jouvin had already made it clear that he had a very low opinion of the colonial class of planters, describing them as arrogant and lazy. He also didn't hold much truck with the indigenous workforce, saying that they had to be treated harshly if you wanted to get any work out of them. Then there was William Demotte, who was younger than Antoine. He was an agronomist, who would test the soils and select the strains of rubber tree they would plant to maximise production. Jouvin informed Demotte that there was very little science needed to run a successful plantation. In his view, you simply stuck the trees in the ground, drove the workforce hard and waited for the liquid latex to make your fortune.

The three of them had been booked into first-class berths by their employer. The rhythm of onboard life was dictated by the rituals and routines of the French colonial upper classes. The ship's entertainment officer had devised a programme of on-deck competitions and indoor quizzes to fill up the daylight hours. The evenings were devoted to formal dinners, dancing to music played by a light orchestra and, for those inclined, of which there were many, a visit to the casino for some serious gambling. After one day of this, Jouvin made it clear that he would rather spend his time with the soldiers and minor civil servants in second class. Demotte was paralysed with shyness, so hardly ventured out of his cabin. Although Antoine felt out of his depth in this social milieu, he was determined to embrace it. He wanted to learn as much as possible about the society he was going to be a part of before he got there. Although he was clearly from a lower social class than the rest of the passengers, many of those he mingled with on the ship appeared to suspend their metropolitan prejudices on the grounds that he was going to become one of them, a colon in Indochina. He was, in their eyes, first and foremost, a Frenchman, and therefore part of a superior race.

As was the custom, Antoine was assigned to a table for dinner, with the same set of dining companions for the whole voyage. During the first evening, his attention was monopolised by a middle-aged couple, Vincent and Louise Bonnet, who were sitting on either side of him. They took it upon themselves to chaperone him for the duration of the voyage and give him an entrée into colonial society, or at least that part of it travelling first class. Vincent arranged to meet Antoine in the bar for a drink before dinner the following evening so he could give him, as he put it, 'the low-down on our delightful dining companions'.

Antoine arrived at the cocktail lounge to find that Vincent had already ensconced himself at the bar. He looked as though he had made a good start on his pre-dinner drinks. Vincent beckoned him over, asked him what he wanted to drink and then ordered the same for himself.

'I really should tell you a bit about myself before I launch into a character assassination of our fellow passengers.' He chuckled.

'I am an old Saigon hand. I've been there over twenty years. I got in right at the beginning when the colony was being set up. Those were the days! You could make your mark quickly, and there wasn't the stifling government control that there is now. I started off as a low-ranking civil servant but soon got bored of that. I had always fancied myself as a writer. So, I started writing gossip articles for one of the monthly journals that had sprung up in Saigon. People seemed to like what I wrote, or at least the editor did, so he hired me as a full-time journalist on the weekly paper he had, *Le Journal de Saigon*. And I have been pretty much muckraking away as a hack journalist ever since.'

He pointed at their empty glasses and got the barman to fill them up. 'With that job, you have a pretty good idea about what is going on in the higher echelons of society. Who is in. Who is out. The scandals and the gossip. Who's sleeping with whom. The business deals. That sort of thing. So, I can let you in on what I know about everyone sat around the dining table tonight, for starters.'

Antoine reciprocated by ordering another round of drinks, even though he was already beginning to feel light-headed. Vincent seemed unaffected by the volume he was drinking, although he was becoming more expansive with every cocktail he downed.

'Take the very haughty-looking gentleman sitting opposite you. That, my friend, is René Thion de la Lacaze. He is the managing director of the Banque de l'Indochine. The bank basically runs Cochinchina. Not the governor. Not the military. The bank. Every major company in the province is in hock to them. They decide which industries get loans. They decide who gets land concessions. And if they don't like you or you can't turn a profit, then they just call in your debt. Most of the time, you don't even know you are in debt to them as they use a network of Chinese and Indian compradors to act as their middlemen. You will no doubt have to deal with them if you are going into the plantation business, so beware!

'Now, the gentleman sitting next to Lacaze.' Vincent paused for a moment to collect his thoughts. 'Paul Bernard.' He paused again. 'Nasty piece of work. Head of the Police Spéciale de Sûreté. I've had my run-ins with him when we have published something he doesn't like. Sends round one of his thugs to try and intimidate you. I get that we need to keep an eye on anyone who wants to undermine or overthrow French control of the colony, but his lot go in for torture and summary executions. His problem is that there are too few French ruling over millions of Vietnamese that he thinks he must use every resource at his disposal to keep them down. So, he tries to rope everyone in as informants or accomplices. Don't be surprised if he approaches you to become one of them, especially if you are heading up country to set up a plantation. Perfect place to harbour insurgents.'

Vincent's mood lightened as he moved on to his next pen portrait. 'Now, I saw you taking in our female dining companion. She is difficult not to stare at, even for an old stick like me. Madame Janie-Marie Marguerite Bertin Rivière de la Souchère, to give her full title. One of Saigon's true beauties. Came over with her husband, who worked for the very company whose ship we are sailing on now. He died tragically young, a victim of the debilitating tropical climate. She then branched out on her own and bought a rubber plantation in a province just north of Saigon. Single-handedly she has turned it into a thriving business, and she is now a recognised authority on how to run a successful plantation. Although, there is a rumour that she has financed most of the expansion of the business through the Banque de l'Indochine. She is also a renowned philanthropist who looks after her workforce well, building a school and a clinic for them to use. Apparently, she has stayed faithful to her dead husband and does not even have one lover, which everyone thinks is a great waste.

'And finally, our last companion. Our native friend. You might find it strange that he is sitting at our table in first class, seemingly on equal and friendly terms with his colonial masters. He is from one of the ruling Cochin families, who ran the province before we got here and has now been co-opted by us to provide some semblance of indigenous input into how the province is run. His father is a famous mandarin, whose scholarly works are held in high regard by his compatriots. As is the custom among his class, he has sent his son to study in Paris, so he can learn something of our language and culture before becoming part of the local ruling establishment, even if in a subordinate role.'

'Does he have a name?' enquired Antoine.

'Yes, Nguyen Den Hieu.'

At that point, Vincent was joined by his wife as the bell for dinner sounded.

CHAPTER 2

The Red Sea, April 1926

LIFE ON BOARD proceeded at a leisurely pace. Days were taken up with light-hearted games, evenings with promenades around the decks and night-times with dining, serious drinking and gambling. Antoine made a point of dragging young Demotte from his cabin, so he could get some fresh air and exercise. Jouvin was nowhere to be found. He appeared to have abandoned his cabin and moved into second class.

Over the course of the journey, Antoine had several encounters with the other dining companions on his table whom Vincent had so ably introduced him to. One night after dinner, the young Cochin, Nguyen Den Hieu, asked him to join him for coffee. They repaired to the ship's smoking room, which was exclusively reserved for male passengers. As well as coffee, brandy and cigars, some of the other men were playing a game of billiards on a table at the side of the room.

Den Hieu was dressed in his usual elegant, but understated, style, in a light beige linen suit. For a Cochin, he was tall and very slender. He wore his straight hair quite long, to just over the back of his collar. In one hand he languidly held a black ivory cigarette holder, from which he would take the occasional puff but without ever really inhaling the smoke into his lungs.

'Is this your first trip, Monsieur Martinet, to my beloved country?'

'Yes, it is. I have been sent out by my employers, the Rodin brothers, to set up a new rubber plantation in the province.'

'Ah, yes. They own a big tyre-making company in France, no?'

Antoine nodded.

'And do you know where this plantation will be?'

'No, not yet. When we arrive, we will meet with the governor's office and see where the land concessions are being made available and then work from there. We have an agronomist with us, who will help us select the most productive soils. Our employers have already written to the governor, expressing our interest, so we expect to be received favourably.'

'I'm sure you will be. Everyone wants to encourage rubber production, just so the province can diversify from its dependence on rice. Being exclusively reliant on the produce of our paddy fields just makes us into eternal peasants. Nothing but beasts of burden,' he ended dismissively.

'You are returning from university in Paris, I believe.'

'You are well informed, I see. No doubt Monsieur Bonnet has been pouring his scurrilous gossip into your ear. You need to watch him. Like all journalists, most of the information he uses is ill-informed and inaccurate. But, yes, I have spent the last three years at the École Normale Supérieure in Paris. My father sent me there to prepare me for a life as a member of the local ruling class. He wanted to give me a grounding in the classics of Molière, Montesquieu and Racine, so I can become a Cochin version of a French *gentilhomme*. Instead, I spent most of my time reading Voltaire and Jean-Jacques Rousseau and listening to Vietnamese students from other parts of the country, such as Tonkin, talking about how we should follow the Chinese road to independence.'

He stopped and smiled. 'Don't tell Monsieur Bernard that, or he will whip me off to one of his dreadful jails as soon as we arrive in Saigon.'

Antoine felt a bit out of his depth with all these references to classical French writers and thinkers. Like all the children in his commune, he had left school after his compulsory primary education and gone straight into working on his father's farm before the war intervened. His knowledge of France's colonies was minimal, made up of scraps of information he had gleaned from the patriotic textbooks at school and his brief interactions with colonial troops in the trenches. He still remembered the defiant look and proud bearing of the Annamite soldier just before he was executed by the firing squad.

'So, how do your countrymen feel about French rule?'

Den Hieu looked at Antoine, considering his response. 'Well, that would depend on who you asked. My father is resigned to French rule. He is a proud member of a long line of mandarins, who were the ruling class of the province before the French arrived. Although his status has been reduced, he is grateful that his years of learning have been recognised, and he has been given some place in the administration of the colony. The great mass of people in Cochin are peasants who toil to produce enough rice to feed themselves and their families. Any surplus is removed by the French tax collectors, or their Chinese agents. Who knows what they think, if they think at all. They temporarily flare up in revolt. Are savagely repressed. And then return to toiling in the fields. It is the growing group of middle-class intellectuals you need to watch out for. They are few in number, but their influence is growing. Currently, most are republican nationalists, like those behind Chiang Kai-shek in China. But some are starting to spout more radical ideas, like the Communists. Those you need to watch out for.'

With that, Den Hieu extinguished his cigarette. 'What I do know, is that irrespective of my social standing, my breeding and my education, I will always be considered a social inferior because of my race. Goodnight, Monsieur Martinet.'

The next day, the ship docked in Djibouti on the Red Sea. Antoine was leaning against the handrails watching the stevedores as they loaded new supplies onto the ship, ready for its departure, when he felt a shadow fall across him. He turned to find Paul Bernard standing a few feet behind.

'Dommiers,' exclaimed Bernard.

'Pardon.'

'Dommiers. You heard me.'

'What of it.'

'Well, that was where you named the mutineers and took charge of the firing squad that executed them, including, I believe, an Ammonite soldier. That's true, isn't it?'

'Where did you get that information?'

'I am the head of the Police Spéciale de Sûreté. It is my job to know about any new arrivals in the colony. I have been in Paris for the past month, exchanging intelligence with my colleagues in the metropole. I had an interesting conversation with a Monsieur Gallopin about you. Remember him?'

'Of course I do,' snapped Antoine. 'That was nearly nine years ago. I was following orders and doing my duty.'

'Yes, you were. It is good to come across patriotic citizens such as yourself who understand what duty means.'

Bernard paused, observing how Antoine reacted to these statements. Antoine said nothing.

'We can always do with men like you in the colony. I hear that you are planning to set up a plantation in one of the provinces north of Saigon. I also hear that you are responsible for recruiting and overseeing the labour force. This means that you will have to travel up to Tonkin to secure indentured labourers and bring them back south. Among them will be some subversives, who will stir up strikes or, worse, bring communist ideas into the province. It would help us greatly if you could report any of these people and their activities to us, so we can nip it in the bud.'

Again, Antoine said nothing. He made to walk away from Bernard, who reached out and firmly grabbed his arm. Pulling Antoine close, he said, 'Before you go, I see that you had a pleasant post-dinner chat with the illustrious Monsieur Nguyen Den Hieu. Did he have anything to say that might be of interest to me?'

Antoine shook himself free and walked rapidly away down the deck.

That evening, they left Djibouti. Antoine noticed at dinner that the members sat around the table had changed. Nguyen Den Hieu was no longer in his usual place. He had moved across the dining room and was now seated at a table that was exclusively made up of Cochinese and Vietnamese people. His place had been taken by William Demotte, who had finally ventured from his cabin.

Antoine found himself sitting next to René Thion de la Lacaze, the managing director of the Banque de l'Indochine, for the first time.

'Ah, I see you have noticed that the dining arrangements have changed,' stated de la Lacaze.

'Yes, have we offended Monsieur Den Hieu?'

'No, no. It is just the natural order being restored.'

'How do you mean?'

'Well, at about this point in the journey, fraternisation between the French and the natives pretty much ceases. They return to their lot, and we stick with ours. Nothing is said; it just happens. I gather that you work for the Rodin brothers from Clermont-Ferrand and that they have sent you over to set up a new plantation.'

'Yes, that's right.'

'Well, members of the bank's board, who represent all the great financial houses in France, do regular business with the Rodins. So, once you've got your land concession from the administration, come and see us. We can fix you up with all the capital you will need to clear the land, plant the trees and cover your running costs until they start producing.'

With that, he slipped a card across to Antoine and turned to talk to the dining companion on his other side.

CHAPTER 3

The South China Sea, May 1926

THE SHIP WAS one day away from entering the mouth of the Mekong Delta and arriving in Saigon. The atmosphere on board had become more excitable as the old hands yearned to return and the new arrivals nervously looked forward to their new lives in an unknown country. For first-class passengers, the end of the voyage was to be marked by a gala dinner dance on the last night.

Antoine spent the morning trying to contact Jouvin, who had not resurfaced since he had exiled himself to second class at the beginning of the voyage. Antoine eventually found him in the bar, snoozing on a banquette, surrounded by a mountain of empty beer bottles.

It took a couple of rough shakes to rouse him from his stupor. He looked up at Antoine through bloodshot, bleary eyes.

'What do you want?'

'I am just checking to see that you are alive. I didn't want you sleeping through our arrival in Saigon tomorrow. I need to update you on some contacts I have made, particularly with the Banque de l'Indochine that will come in useful when we land.'

Jouvin swung his legs from the banquette, coming to rest in a sitting position.

'Don't worry about me. You'll see, I will be ready to go tomorrow morning. It will make a welcome change from sitting on this tin can for the past thirty days.'

With that he waved a hand to dismiss Antoine and slumped back down onto the banquette.

Antoine met up with the Bonnets for a farewell cocktail in the bar before dinner. They had just started reminiscing about the highlights of the journey when they became aware of Madame de la Souchère hovering in front of them.

'Can I be as rude as to ask if I can join you? It is not the done thing for a single woman to drink on her own, and I would so like one of those colourful cocktails that you seem to be enjoying.'

Antoine and Vincent both shot to their feet, with Vincent gesturing to Madame de la Souchère to join them.

'Of course, my dear, we would be delighted for you to join us,' gushed Vincent. He waved to the barman to get a drink for their guest.

'Thank you. I have really been looking forward to this. I have enjoyed the wine at dinner, but it was these fancy cocktails I really wanted to try.' She took a small sip and puckered her lips in delight.

'Please don't stand on ceremony with me. Call me Marguerite, which is the *prenom* that I prefer. I do so dislike it when people try to address me by my full name. It can take all week!'

While their new guest engaged in some small talk with

Vincent and Louise, Antoine took the opportunity to look at her. Although they had sat across from each other at dinner, he had not spoken to her nor really absorbed her appearance.

She looked to be in her mid- to late-thirties. The skin on her face was tight, but weather-beaten, showing the signs of her outdoor life as a working plantation owner. Her hands were brown and strong. She was tall and broad for a woman, radiating physical vitality and confidence. Although she was dressed in a white satin ballgown, it did not sit easily on her, as though she was not accustomed to wearing such finery very often. She only wore an unostentatious set of pearls around her neck and a small silver broach on her left breast.

After a few minutes of talking to the Bonnets, she turned to Antoine.

'I don't think we have had a chance to chat, have we, despite being dining companions. The rules of engagement of those formal dinners can be very stuffy, can't they?'

'No, and yes.'

She gave a light laugh in response.

'My name is Antoine Martinet, a blessedly short name.'

'So, Antoine Martinet, of the blessedly short name, what is your business in Saigon?'

'The same as yours, I believe. I am here to help set up a rubber plantation for the Rodin brothers.'

'Ah, the big boys. My enterprise is minute compared to what they will want to have.'

'Maybe. But I am sure we can learn a lot from established planters such as yourself. You can help us with advice and prevent us from making any mistakes.'

'Yes, well, it is not as straightforward as putting some trees in the ground and waiting for them to grow, I can assure you.' She laughed. Antoine noticed that her eyes were a light brown, which matched the colour of her hair.

'I lost the whole of my first plantings to a forest fire, so I had to start all over again. But times are on the up now. The demand for rubber is growing, so there are good profits to be made.'

'And where is your plantation?'

'It is at a place called Long Thành, about fifty kilometres north-east of Saigon. Not so far from civilisation that you feel too isolated, although I am not really one for the bright lights of the big city.'

'Would you say that is a good area to look for land concessions?'

'Yes, it has fertile red soil and is close to the river to transport the rubber. I also grow some coffee, which also does well there. Now, let's not just talk business. Tell me, Antoine, are you a good dancer?'

Antoine could feel a slight flush spread across his face. The only dancing he had done was at his commune's fetes, where the emphasis was very much on picking up your partner and hurling them around the room rather than anything more decorous.

'No, I wouldn't say that is one of my strengths.'

'Well, if you can put one foot in front of the other, and not fall over, then I am marking your card for a dance. After a cocktail, what I have most looked forward to on this trip is some dancing.'

Most of the dinner conversation passed Antoine by as he fretted about his imminent humiliation on the dance floor.

He looked forward to spending more time with Marguerite, but just not in that way.

When the moment arrived, she made it easy for him.

'Don't worry, I will tell you what to do. We will start with the most straightforward dance, the waltz. Place your hands here and here.' She guided Antoine's right hand and placed it gently on the small of her back, taking his left hand in her right hand. 'Now push off with your left foot into mine, and bring your right foot forward, and then bring them together. Then repeat.'

They started slowly and then started to speed up as Antoine got into the rhythm of the movement. The only tricky bit was when they came to a corner, where Marguerite pulled him round a couple of times, until he got the hang of the sideways glide that made the manoeuvre more effortless.

As the dance went on, Antoine became more aware of Marguerite's physical presence. She was only slightly shorter than he was, so their faces were close together. He could see a faint bead of sweat on her top lip. The warmth radiating from her skin combined headily with the smell of her perfume. He could feel the muscles moving under his hand on the small of her back.

'Antoine?'

Antoine broke from his reverie.

'Yes?'

'Antoine. I must stop now, as we disembark early. I need to make sure that my servants do my last-minute packing properly. Will you please escort me to my cabin?'

They walked together along the deck, saying nothing. They could feel the slight swell of the Mekong under their feet. The surface of the water was inky black.

When they got to the door of her cabin, she paused.

'Thank you, Antoine. I did enjoy that enormously. I wish you well with your new venture in Saigon. I do hope that our paths will cross again.'

With that she lightly pressed her hand against his chest, turned and entered her cabin.

CHAPTER 4

Saigon, May 1926

ANTOINE STOOD AT the rail on deck as the *Aramis* proceeded slowly up the eighty kilometres of the Mekong Delta before arriving at the Messageries Maritime's pier in Saigon harbour. On the riverbank to his right were serried ranks of dark-green paddy fields, splayed out across the flat delta plain. Within the fields were the stooped figures of peasants, with their trousers hitched up to their waists and their faces hidden by the shade cast by large conical straw hats. Travelling in the opposite direction to the liner were legions of junks and sampans, sailing out to the South China Sea on their way to the ports of Annam and Tonkin, to deliver cargoes of rice, pepper, rubber and coffee. As they drew nearer to Saigon, the paddy fields gave way to clusters of houses on stilts on the banks of the riverside. Behind them were settlements of straw huts that housed the poorer labourers and their families who serviced the needs of the largest city in Indochina.

As soon as they disembarked, Antoine, Jouvin and Demotte each commandeered a rickshaw to take them and their luggage to the Grand Hôtel de la Rotonde, where their employers had booked them in. The rickshaws made their jerky progress up Rue Catinat, a wide shaded avenue that led from the port into the centre of the city. To begin with, the avenue was lined on either side by shops of all types that conducted most of their business on the pavement. As you got closer to the centre of the city, the shops gave way to more imposing government and civic buildings, surrounded by small parks. In the centre was the Place du Théâtre, where the cafés were already starting to welcome their first customers of the day, many of whom were sitting outside under large awnings that swept across the pavements. These were more to protect the clientele from getting a soaking than to give them shade, as the wet season had just begun and would run until November.

At dinner that evening, Antoine laid out the timetable and process for securing the land concessions and capital funding for the plantation. They agreed to meet after breakfast the following day and pay a visit to the Hôtel de Ville on the Boulevard Charner, where the colonial administration was housed.

The Hôtel de Ville was an exact replica of those to be found in cities and towns across France. It had a tricolour flying from its belfry and a monument to those from the colony who had served and died in the war in a garden in front of the steps that led up to the reception area. After some initial enquiries, the three men were shown into the office of a Monsieur Aynard, who was responsible for administering land concessions.

Antoine handed over the letters of introduction that the Rodin brothers had given them. Aynard gave these a perfunctory inspection.

'Yes, *messieurs*, I have been expecting you. The bush telegraph that operates in the colony had already alerted me to the fact that you would be on your way. Of course, we would welcome such a prestigious organisation as the Rodin Tyre Company to set up a plantation here. Do you have a particular area in mind?'

Demotte responded that they would sample the soils of any areas that they selected before making a final decision, but to narrow the decision down, they would be looking at the red soil areas where there were already successful plantations in operation.

'Well, then. You should be looking at Long Thành and Xuan Luc.' Aynard got up from his desk and led them to a map of the province on the wall. He pointed to an area north-east of Saigon. 'We have concessions in both places. There are some established planters doing good business there.'

Antoine registered the name Long Thành and its association with Marguerite but said nothing to the others. Instead, he directed his next question to Aynard. 'We are looking for a substantial plot, in the region of five thousand hectares to begin with. Is that available?'

'It's a lot, but I am sure we can find something to fit the bill.'

'So, how does this land concession work? Do we have to make a down payment and then further instalments as we develop the site?'

'No, no. The provincial government gives you a long lease, with a peppercorn rent. That is in recognition of the fact that you have to put up all the capital to clear the site – and it is essentially a jungle. You have to invest in buying and planting all the saplings. You will have to build accommodation for yourselves and your workers. Once you are up and running and producing rubber, we will, of course, then tax your goods in line with our current policy. After ninety-nine years, we renew the leasehold, and then perhaps look at a one-off payment then.'

'What's the next step?'

'Well, before we sign over the concession, we must see proof that you have the capital in place to start investing in clearing the site. Do you have that?'

'Not yet, but we know where to go for that. We shall return with the proof as soon as we can. In the meantime, please start drawing up heads of agreement for a concession in the two areas you mentioned. Monsieur Demotte will visit them both to assess their suitability. Once we have done all those things, we should be ready to proceed.'

CHAPTER 5

AFTER AYNARD HAD given them a more detailed map of the area showing where the concessions were in Long Thành and Xuan Luc, Antoine sent Demotte and Jouvin to survey them and take soil samples. He also told them to speak to local planters about the challenges they might face in taking on the land. He did not direct them to pay a visit to Marguerite, for reasons that he could not explain to himself.

Antoine sent a message through to René Thion de la Lacaze at the Banque de l'Indochine requesting a meeting. He received a prompt reply inviting him to attend the bank's main office at 9am the next day.

The bank's headquarters were in an imposing, colonnaded building on Quai de Belgique, on the banks of the Mekong River. The steps leading into the entrance were flanked by two granite lions with magnificent manes. Antoine looked up at the rows of gargoyles perched on the top of the building, who fixed him with a lapidary stare. If the aim of this architectural grandeur was to impress on the visitor the financial might of the bank, then it had succeeded.

Antoine was escorted by a white-coated concierge up the sweeping staircase that led from the reception area to the main offices on the first floor. He was waved into the anteroom outside the director's office. The room was furnished to reflect the status of its main occupant, with a mixture of classical French furniture and carpets and wall-hangings representing the bank's reach across south-east Asia. A fan in the ceiling rotated slowly as it tried to animate the humid air.

The door to the main office opened to reveal de la Lacaze. He beckoned Antoine to enter. Lacaze's office was furnished in the same style as the anteroom. It was dominated by a huge desk behind which Lacaze sat down, after indicating to Antoine that he should take the chair in front of it. As Antoine walked across the office, he noticed that there was another person in the room, sitting on a sofa to one side of the desk. This was a middle-aged Chinese man, dressed in an expensively tailored, if ill-fitting, suit. As their eyes met, the man smiled, revealing a mouth that had several gold teeth interspersed with a few black stumps. Smoke wafted around his head from the smouldering cigarette that was clamped in the side of his lips.

'Can I offer you a drink, Antoine?'

'No thank you, it is a bit early in the day for me.'

'A sensible decision when conducting business. Too many of our compatriots in this country are slaves to drink. So, you are here to take up my offer of a loan to finance the establishment of the Rodin's plantation. Have you found a suitable plot?'

'Well, we have been offered a five thousand-hectare concession. My men are currently surveying some land in the Long Thành area to see if it meets our requirements.'

'Ah, Long Thành. Yes, we already have some investments up there. Madame de la Souchère is one of our clients. I think you met her on the crossing, didn't you?'

'Yes, briefly.'

'A remarkable woman. Pioneering. Set up and runs that plantation all on her own. Won the respect of the other planters, even the crusty old colons, who don't take well to women assuming what they see as male roles. But she's proved herself. They even made her a member of the Chambre d'Agriculture, for God's sake. First female ever.'

Lacaze left a pause for Antoine to make a comment, but he stayed tight-lipped.

'Down to business, then. It is at this stage that I leave you in the very capable hands of Monsieur Hung here.' Lacaze pointed at the man sitting on the sofa. 'He is one of the bank's most reliable compradors to whom we entrust a lot of our financial arrangements. He can also help you source a labour force for the plantation through his contacts in Tonkin, so he will be worth talking to about that as well.'

With that, Lacaze got up, came round the desk, shook Antoine's hands and left the office.

As soon as the door had shut behind Lacaze, Hung uncoiled himself from the sofa and came towards Antoine. When he was in front of him, he gave a short bow.

'Monsieur Martinet, I am Yip Pak Hung. I represent one of the largest trading houses in Cholon.' Even in the short time that he had been here, Antoine knew that Cholon, a few kilometres upriver from the centre of Saigon, was the main trading hub for rice. It was dominated by forty powerful Chinese families, of which the Hungs must be one. As well as being the primary traders in rice, they also acted as the main intermediaries between French businesses in the colony and the indigenous population.

'We are honoured to be doing business with you and the illustrious Rodin family. Once I know your requirements, I am sure I can come up with a financial package to meet your needs. I heard that you want an initial loan to cover the costs of clearing five thousand hectares and the capital to set up the plantation, complete with a labour force. Is that right?'

'Yes. But, of course, any loan that you offer will have to be agreed with the Rodins.'

'Of course, of course.' Hung smiled broadly, revealing again the glints of gold in his mouth.

'You can tell me your exact requirements once you have surveyed the land. But based on our extensive experience in financing operations like this, we would nominally allocate one million piastres for every thousand acres, so an overall loan of five million piastres. For this, we would require 6% interest per annum over twenty years. I think you will find that very competitive. Of course, the loan would be subject to all the normal conditions. Any default would result in us reclaiming the land, including all the capital improvements that you had made to it up to that point.'

Hung waved his hands reassuringly in the air. 'I am sure that situation would never arise. Rubber is booming now. The demand for it is being driven by the worldwide increase in the demand for automobiles and trucks. I am myself the proud owner of one of your country's Citroën cars. You and the Rodins will be printing money!' Hung gave out a delighted laugh.

Antoine told Hung that he would get back to him as soon as he had telegraphed the Rodins and received the reports on the suitability of the land from Jouvin and Demotte.

'Excellent. Once we have sorted out the loan, then we can look at getting you a labour force. We have all the contacts in Tonkin that you will need for that and can act as your middlemen. I look forward to doing business with you.' With that, Hung lit up another cigarette. He clamped it into the side of his mouth and left with smoke streaming out behind him.

CHAPTER 6

ANTOINE FOUND HIMSELF with a couple of days to kill before Jouvin and Demotte returned from their fact-finding mission. He decided to pay a visit to the offices of *Le Journal de Saigon* to catch up with Vincent Bonnet and check with him what he knew about the reputation of Yip Pak Hung. The paper was housed in a small office tucked down a side street off Rue Mac-Mahon, near to the Palais de Justice. The tamarind trees on Rue Mac-Mahon were just entering into full bloom, so overhead there was a blaze of red and orange petals.

Antoine's eyes had not adjusted between the bright outdoor light and the dark interior of the office, before Vincent had grabbed him by the arm and propelled him back onto the street again.

'Come on, let's go and have a drink. All that muckraking has left me parched.'

They sat down at an outside table at the nearby Café de la Musique under one of its large bright orange awnings. This protected them from the bright sunshine but did little to counteract the humidity of the air. Antoine felt the sweat start to collect around the band of his trousers.

'Right, Antoine, tell me what you have been up to then.'

Antoine spent the next ten minutes updating Vincent on his dealings with the provincial government and the bank. When he had finished, he asked Vincent about the integrity of both the provincial administrators and, more importantly, Yip Pak Hung and his trading house.

'The administrators at Hôtel de Ville just do what they are told. If they say there are concessions available and where they are, then that will be the truth. They just want to get the land cleared and more tax revenue coming into the coffers. Pak Hung, like all the heads of Chinese trading houses, is a spider in the centre of a web. You have just become another fly he has ensnared. He will consume you if he has to. But if you pay up your interest on time, then he will just leave you dangling there until you are ready to do more business with him. The trading houses are first and foremost business enterprises, interested in turning a handsome profit. However, some of their methods are unorthodox, to say the least.'

'Such as?'

'Well, it is difficult to prove but is well known in the business community. Hung's clan originated in Guangzhou in southern China. They have brought with them some of their Chinese customs from the mainland, such as the use of Triads. There is one group that is associated with Hung in particular. I think they are called something like the Society of the Sky and the Earth, or some such mumbo jumbo. Or is it the Society for Duty and Concord? Who knows. But they are essentially enforcers. If you are not paying your debts on time, you might find your warehouse going up in flames, or the junk carrying your products being boarded by pirates in the South China Sea.'

Antoine remained silent.

'Don't look so worried. You are working for the Rodins, for God's sake. You are not going to fall behind with your payments. Anyway, I must be off to an assignment, some social function with the province's bigwigs, where there's bound to be some juicy gossip. Any time you need any further information, just call in.'

After Vincent left, Antoine stayed sitting in the café, considering the information he had been given and whether he should let the Rodins know. He thought best not. They had entrusted him to get on with the job, so that is what he would do.

He was just about to leave, when the chair opposite him was pulled back.

'May I?'

This did not sound like a request.

Antoine looked across to see that the chair that Vincent had recently occupied was now filled by Paul Bernard. Bernard was dressed in a creased white linen suit. There were yellow stains under the armpits of the jacket.

'Monsieur Bernard. I am terribly sorry, but I am in a bit of a rush and must go.'

'I am sure that you will have time to listen to what I have to tell you.'

'Get on with it, then.'

'I told you that I had had an interesting conversation with Monsieur Gallopin from the Sûreté when I was in Paris. He informed me all about your illustrious war record.

Apart from what you did to quell the mutinies. I hear that you were quite the hero at Verdun.'

'What of it?'

'Well, I am here to remind you that all ex-soldiers who served in the world war can be conscripted by the colonial authorities should they be needed for military, or more likely, police, operations during their time here. You look surprised, Monsieur Martinet.'

'I have never heard of that.'

'Nevertheless, it is true. I can show you the regulation if you want.'

'You said "should they be needed". Are you saying they're needed now, because I have business to conduct that would make it impossible for me to join up now.'

'No, not now. But I am putting you on notice that you may be needed in the not-too-distant future. There is trouble brewing in the north, particularly on the border with China. Insurgent bands are starting to form. We have heard of attacks on Catholic missionary outposts. Don't worry, we will be in touch when we need you.'

With that, Bernard pushed back his chair and left. The two men did not shake hands.

CHAPTER 7
Long Thành, May 1927

A YEAR HAD passed since Antoine and his colleagues had first set foot in Saigon. Jouvin and Demotte had returned from their trip upcountry to confirm that they had found some substantial, fertile plots where they could establish the plantation. Antoine signed the agreement for the land concession with the provincial administration. Pak Hung released the loan. He followed up, as promised, by securing the labour force to clear and plant the land. The workers were all indentured peasants from Tonkin. This arrangement was the standard practice on all the large plantations in the colony. It tied the labourers to the plantation. They could not leave before the end of their term of three years. If they tried to escape, Pak Hung's Triads would track them down and bring them back, but not before administering rough justice. All their pay was sent home in remittances to the families they had left behind in Tonkin.

As rubber trees took six years from the moment they were planted as saplings to produce useable latex, Antoine had bought more mature trees from local planters to speed up the process. It would still be two years before the land was fully cleared and the trees became productive. During this time, Antoine oversaw the building of his own and Jouvin's accommodation and the housing for the workforce. Demotte was sent back to France, having completed his work for the company.

Antoine left Jouvin in charge of the day-to-day running of the plantation. Jouvin was, as he had declared on the crossing over, a hard taskmaster. He drove the workforce forward relentlessly. Sometimes Antoine had to step in to prevent him from inflicting beatings to those he considered were not working fast enough. He also had to stand in for him on the weekends when Jouvin went on one of his benders, which left him insensible for a few days. Despite these shortcomings, Antoine came to trust and rely on Jouvin for his dedication to the goal of getting the plantation up and running as fast as possible.

Antoine tried to distract himself with work, but since his arrival in Long Thành he had thought constantly about Marguerite and when he could visit her. He told himself that she had said that he could ask for her advice. She was an experienced planter, while he was a novice. So, it would only be normal, even polite, to go and see her to talk through how the business was going. But he resisted for as long as he could. In truth, Antoine had very little experience with women, especially more mature women such as Marguerite. Of course, like all adolescents in his commune, he had fumbled around in haystacks with girls during harvest time and after dances. When on leave during the war, he would seek out the hotels doubling up as brothels in some provincial town and pay for a few minutes of unsatisfactory coupling with women of an indeterminate age. He knew that those experiences did not prepare him to court a woman like Marguerite.

Antoine's resolve not to visit Marguerite lasted six months. The rainy season had just ended. The daily heavy deluges of rain had been replaced by the heat of the dry season. The tracks that criss-crossed the province were now passable by automobiles, so Antoine took the plantation's one truck and drove towards Marguerite's plantation. When he arrived, he swept through the stone portals with an arch between them with the words 'Plantations du Tan Loc' emblazoned across the top in bold red lettering. He drove up a long curving avenue, surrounded on either side by rubber trees. After a kilometre, he came to a stop in front of a large green lawn ringed by beds of colourful tropical flowers. Behind it was an imposing colonial-style bungalow that had verandas running along its front and round both sides.

As soon as Antoine parked, a servant in a stiff white jacket and black trousers, with the letters PTL stitched on the front pockets, came out of the house to greet him.

'Is Madame la Souchère in? I am Antoine Martinet from the Rodin plantation.'

'Yes, Madame is here, but she is currently overseeing some work on the plantation. I will send someone to find her and tell her you are here. Please, come in.'

They went into the hall of the house, which had rattan chairs and a small sofa ranged against one of the walls.

'Would you like a drink, Monsieur Martinet?'

'Just cold water, if possible.'

Antoine was left to take in his surroundings. The room was refreshingly cool compared to the heat outside.

Apart from the chairs and the sofa, the room had minimal furnishing. The floors were wooden, with a simple rug in the middle. On one of the walls was an exhibition case that housed samples of different rubber plants, with explanatory labels against each in Latin text.

After ten minutes, Antoine could hear some footsteps coming along the veranda outside the front of the bungalow. At first, they had a quick tempo, as though they wanted to get somewhere fast, and then they slowed down to a more measured pace.

Marguerite entered the hall. Antoine stood to greet her. There was a silence as they took each other in. Marguerite was dressed in tropical white workwear, complete with a pair of shorts that came down to her knees. She wore long socks that reached up to the top of her calves. She appeared more at ease in this outfit than she had in her ballgown on the boat. She was trying to control her breathing after her rapid walk up from the plantation.

'I was beginning to think that you were never going to call.'

'Apologies. But we have been very busy.'

'Of course. Come, we shall go and sit on the veranda out the back and you can tell me all about it.'

Antoine followed her through the bungalow, entering a large sitting room that had some patio doors leading out onto the veranda. Taking up one corner of the sitting room was a piano, on which Antoine could see arrayed a group of family photos. One was of a young couple dressed for their wedding. The bride was smiling radiantly.

The garden at the back of the house sloped down a small hill, giving the bungalow a panoramic view of the plantation as it swept towards the foothills of the highlands that eventually led to Cambodia.

'So, how has it been going since you took on the plantation? It is quite a size, isn't it? It completely dwarfs mine.'

Antoine explained the ease with which they had acquired the plantation and the progress they had made in getting it up and running since then. He knew that she had taken out loans with Pak Hung to finance her operations, so he asked her whether there had been any problems in her dealings with him.

'No, no. If you pay the interest on time, he leaves you alone. I have had no problems with him at all. In fact, I have increased my loans with him to take on some more land. The market is booming right now, so I feel that I can extend myself a bit more.'

She paused while one of the house servants brought out a tray of iced drinks and left them on the table.

'You know, you should think about getting your own piece of property that is separate from the Rodins. Pak Hung would give you a loan as he now knows who you are. I could vouch for you if you need. Get something like five hundred hectares and build from there. Now is the time to do it.'

'I had never really thought of that. I will look into it the next time I am in Saigon.'

'Are you living permanently on the plantation? Some managers stay in Saigon and get an overseer to do the day-to-day management.'

'Yes, I have built myself a small bungalow. Nothing like this.' Antoine swept his arm around him. 'It meets my needs.'

'You have a couple of servants to look after you?'

'Yes, a cook and a housemaid.'

'Ah,' she laughed, 'you have your own *con-gai.*'

Antoine looked puzzled.

'It's what the Cochinese call a "little girl". Someone who meets your every need.'

Antoine could feel the heat rising from his neck across his face.

She laughed again. 'Don't be embarrassed. It is what is expected of a red-blooded Frenchman in the colonies. To have one or more native mistresses on hand. Everybody out here thinks that I am very strange, the way I have stayed single since the death of my beloved Charles. I have had plenty of suitors, to be sure. But none of them could measure up to him.'

'What did your husband do?'

'He came over initially as a river boat pilot for Messageries Maritime. By the time of his death, he was managing all the company's shipping in and out of Saigon. He was an ambitious man.'

'And what did he die of, if you feel able to tell me?'

'Malaria. This was a time before we could all dose up on Nivaquine to protect us. Mercifully, it was a quick and relatively painless death.'

Marguerite finished her drink and stared across the lawn at the two gardeners weeding the flower beds.

'Enough of that maudlin stuff. Let me give you a quick tour of the plantation. We can take your truck.'

Once they were both seated in the front of the vehicle, Marguerite told him to drive back up to the main track and then turn left to take them into the heart of the plantation. At first, they passed rows of rubber trees, some of which bore the scars of where they had been cut to drain the latex resin. Marguerite gave a running commentary on when they had been planted, the different varieties of plants she had experimented with over time and what kind of arboriculture practices she used to get the best out of the trees. Antoine realised he still had plenty to learn about the industry.

Eventually, they came to a large clearing that contained a range of buildings of different shapes and sizes. She told him to stop, and they got out of the truck.

'Now, this is what I am most proud of,' she said, sweeping her arms in a circle.

'All the labourers are accommodated in these bunkhouses. They all have washing and toilet facilities. I don't use indentured labour, only free labourers. If you have indentured labourers, you are essentially treating them like serfs. I have built a school for the children and employ two teachers. And I have just started a clinic, where we have a nurse to provide basic health care.'

'It is very impressive. I must admit that we have indentured labourers that Pak Hung sourced for us. I don't think Jouvin, my site manager, would go with free labourers, who could come and go as they please without any ties.'

'What I have found is that if you treat them like human beings, then they repay you with hard work and respect.'

Antoine wasn't sure whether he was being rebuked. He knew from his short time in the colony that Marguerite's philanthropic efforts were applauded in public but frowned upon in private whenever other planters got together. For some, what she was doing was bordering on communism.

After returning to the bungalow, they sat in the cab of the truck for a while.

'It's a very impressive set-up, Marguerite. You must be proud.'

'I am. But it's been bloody hard and, yes, lonely, work.'

She turned to face Antoine.

'Well, now you know where I am, I hope you won't be a stranger. Please feel free to drop in at any time, whether it be for advice or for a drink.'

'I would like that.' Antoine hesitated. 'Would you like to go into Saigon one evening for a meal or a visit to the theatre? I think the season at the Municipal Théâtre has just started.'

After a slight pause, she responded with an emphatic, 'Yes, let's do that.' She then got out of the truck and walked back into the bungalow without a backward glance.

As Antoine drove back to the Rodin plantation, his head was full of contradictory thoughts and feelings about Marguerite. She was still in mourning for her husband, even though it had been nearly ten years since his untimely death. At the same time, she was clearly lonely. There was an age gap between them, but she appeared to treat him as though that did not matter to her. For the first time in his life, he was struggling with feelings that he didn't recognise or understand. What he did know was that he wanted to see her again, and soon.

As he drew up in the yard, he saw that there was a black Citroën Traction Avant with a tricolour pendant attached to the bonnet parked outside the steps to his bungalow. Sitting on the veranda, as though he lived there, was Paul Bernard. Rather than his normal white linen crumpled suit, Bernard was dressed in his gendarme uniform. He had placed his kepi on the table next to him.

Antoine approached him slowly. 'I wasn't aware that I had invited you here.'

'You hadn't. But I gave you fair warning when we met last.' With that, he held out some papers to Antoine. These contained authorisation from the governor general of the province stating that Antoine was being conscripted as part of the reserve and that he had to report for duty to Bernard.

'I am seconding you to the Sûreté for the duration of this mission. You will travel north, setting off tomorrow, and report to the Sûreté headquarters in Hanoi. You will be in charge of a colonial infantry unit. Your orders are to track down and capture a Chinese insurgent and bring him back for interrogation.'

'What has this Chinese insurgent done to warrant this attention?'

'Apart from butchering countless innocent Catholics, French and native, he is also spreading communist propaganda among the peasants in the province. His name is Chen Geng. By all reports he is a capable guerilla leader.'

'And what am I supposed to do with all this while I am away?' Antoine pointed at the plantation.

'You've got men that can take care of that. Jouvin knows what to do in your absence. Besides, we have cleared it with the Rodins. They are fully supportive of the mission and have sanctioned your involvement. They understand that we must crush this before it starts threatening their business interests.'

Bernard stood up and placed the kepi on his head.

'I want him back alive, Martinet. He is no good to me dead. Understand?'

Antoine did not respond. He turned his back and entered the bungalow.

CHAPTER 8
Hanoi, January 1928

IT TOOK ANTOINE two days of travelling to reach Hanoi, the capital city of French Indochina. The first leg had been on an armed navy junk from Saigon to the port at Hue. Here he had transferred to the newly completed railway that snaked up the coast to Hanoi. Now he found himself in a rickshaw on his way from his hotel to the headquarters of the *tirailleurs tonkinois*, based in the city's citadel, which also housed the gendarmerie and the central prison. On the way, he passed the offices of the Banque de l'Indochine, set back off Avenue Gambetta in its own grounds. He was reminded of Vincent Bonnet's observation that it was the bank that was all powerful in the colony. He made a mental note that as soon as he returned to Saigon, he needed to contact the bank, or go straight to its representative, Pak Hung, to sort out a loan for the purchase of the land for his own small plantation.

The rickshaw drew up at the checkpoint leading up to the barracks of the *tirailleurs tonkineis*. The *tirailleurs* were a colonial infantry regiment, with French officers and NCOs leading indigenous troops who had been conscripted from the province. They, along with troops from the other provinces in Vietnam, Annam and Cochinchina, and France's North African colonies had fought bravely in the trenches during the war. Antoine tried to dispel from his mind the memory of the Ammonite soldier staring into his eyes with proud defiance before he had been executed by the firing squad he had commanded after the 1917 mutiny.

Antoine was directed to the office of the regiment's commanding officer, Colonel Pierre Rannou. As soon as he saw him, Antoine knew that he was in the presence of another veteran of the war. Although a tall man, immaculately turned out in his starched khaki tunic and shorts, his body was hunched inside his clothing, as though he was flinching from the threat of an artillery barrage. He could not hold Antoine's gaze for more than a few seconds before he reverted to staring at the wall behind him.

'Captain Martinet reporting for duty, sir!' Antoine snapped to attention as he saluted. He found it unnerving how quickly he had fallen back into the routines of the army.

'At ease, Martinet. Welcome to the regiment. We are very honoured to have someone with your war record seconded to us for this mission. We are all aware of what you accomplished at Verdun.'

'Thank you, sir.' Antoine hesitated before going on. 'You should know that I didn't volunteer for this role but was conscripted by the security services to undertake it.'

Rannou dismissed this remark with a wave of his hand. 'Yes, they are a bunch of thugs those Sûreté men. Unfortunately, they are a necessary evil given what we are up against in this province. Tonkin is a huge area that is constantly being infested by the Chinese, who slip across the border or come up the river estuaries. They range from out-and-out bandits, who are here to smuggle goods, normally opium, or those of a more ideological bent, who want to stir up the peasantry to revolt against us.'

'And where does Chen Geng sit on that spectrum?'

'Chen Geng is an opportunist. In my view, he is a mercenary, who will sell his services to the highest bidder. If someone wants to hire him to smuggle, he will do that. If someone else wants him to terrorise Catholics, then he is up for that. Lately, he seems to have added to his repertoire offering protection to the Communist Party activists who are brainwashed in China and then sent across the border to spread the word in the villages in the river delta area. He isn't a communist himself, of course. He is just interested in who pays him the most for his services. But, for us to suppress the spread of communism, we will need to remove him from the picture.'

'How many men does he command? What kind of training have they had?'

'Based on our latest intelligence, he has about eighty men. The group he leads call themselves the Yellow Flags, for some reason. I think the colour denotes their allegiance to a warlord in China. There are black and blue flag groups as well. They are well armed with weapons they have received from the Communist Party and the Kuomintang, although they don't have any artillery. As to their training, I think they pick it up as they go along. But they are merciless bastards. They don't take prisoners, and they happily butcher civilians, as our Catholic communities have found to their cost.'

'So, what information can you give me on where I can track him down?'

'Our latest intelligence is that he is holed up in a fortified village just outside Cao Bang, which is in the north-east corner of the province, close to the Chinese border. You can get most of the way up there by road and track, but the area between his camp and Cao Bang is mostly jungle, so you will have to go on foot.'

'What resources are you allocating to me?'

Rannou briefly gave Antoine an apologetic look, before his eyes slid over his shoulder and fixed on the wall behind him.

'Look, Martinet. We are under a lot of pressure here. The province is facing multiple threats. So, all I can spare you is a couple of companies of men, who will come with their machine gun and mortar squads. I can also let you have some scouts recruited from the local hill tribes, who know the area around Cao Bang well and are vicious little fighters to boot.'

Antoine didn't see any point in haggling with the colonel. A squad of that size, properly equipped, should be enough to take on eighty men. It would just depend on how well trained they were.

'So, sir, when do I get to meet my men, and when do you propose we set off?'

'You can have them straight away, Martinet. I suggest you have a week knocking them into shape and getting used to you. Then you need to set off before the monsoon season starts. Any more questions? No, good. Dismissed.'

As Antoine reached the door to leave the office, Rannou called out, 'Captain.'

'Yes, sir?'

'Good luck.' Antoine could not help but hear its valedictory tone.

CHAPTER 9
Hanoi, February 1928

ANTOINE SURVEYED THE troops as they started to fall in on the parade ground. They looked more like a group of irregulars than the disciplined soldiers he was used to from the infantry regiments in the war. None of them were wearing the standard uniform of khaki tunic and matching puttees. Instead, they were clothed in a mishmash of colours and styles, some with shorts, others with loose black trousers. Many wore *salaccos* on their heads, the conical hats made from bamboo cane favoured by peasants working in the paddy fields. Most of the native troops were barefoot. Standing apart from the soldiers were a group of five men, crouched on their heels, taking in what was going on in front of them but showing no obvious signs of joining in. They were unlike the native troops in that they were dressed in loin clothes, were shirtless and had necklaces of beads strung round their necks. Their skin was a dark, mahogany brown.

Gesturing towards this group, Antoine turned towards his NCO, Corporal Antony Tardy.

'Who are they?'

'They, sir, are our scouts. Chen Geng is holed up in the T'ai hills, so we need them to track him down. Most of our patrols go through the hill country so we rely on them a lot. The T'ais hate the people from the deltas, the Vietnamese and the Chinese, who have oppressed them over the years.'

'How do we communicate with them?'

'Through me. I speak several hill dialects, which I have picked up over the years. I am also married to one of the head tribesmen's daughters, so they are loyal to us, well, at least, me.'

Antoine could not hide his amazement at this last statement.

'Is that allowed?'

'Well, it is not disallowed. The high-ups turn a blind eye to it, as they know it strengthens our alliances with the tribes. And we cannot operate in the high country without them.'

Antoine gave Tardy a sideways glance. Now that he had revealed his unorthodox marital arrangements, Antoine could also see that this was no regular army NCO. He wore a bandana under his forage cap and appeared to have a succession of bracelets and bangles on his wrists and up his arms, some with feathers tied to them.

'Tell me a little bit about yourself, Tardy.'

'Well, I am originally from the French Ardennes, which is why I feel at home in the hill country, although it is a lot hotter and wetter here, of course.' He chuckled. 'After the war, I stayed on in the army. Got transferred out here.'

'As you have a good understanding and rapport with the hill tribes, I will be relying on you a great deal for this mission. Get the men to fall in.'

'Yes, sir.'

After Tardy had given the order, Antoine carried out a brief inspection. This was more so that the soldiers under his command could get a good look at him as he went up and down the lines, rather than any attempt on his part to inspect their kit or clothing. He realised quickly that this group of men were more familiar with fighting in the local conditions than he was. He was not going to impose normal regulations, but he did need to make them see that he was in charge.

'All right, men. At ease. Now, I am going to tell you about our mission. We have been selected to track down and arrest a Chinese gang leader, one Chen Geng. He leads a group called the Yellow Flags.'

At this, there was some murmuring among the soldiers.

'They are responsible for massacring groups of Catholics. We also think they are spreading communist propaganda among the peasants. We need to liquidate them. But we also need to capture Chen Geng alive and bring him back for interrogation. Is that understood?'

There was a slow swell of assent from the soldiers.

'We are going to spend a week training on the tactics I want to use before we leave on the mission. Essentially, I am going to split you up into different groups for different roles and drill you in how I want you to operate and combine. There will be a machine gun squad, a mortar squad, a reconnaissance team, which Corporal Tardy will command, and several groups of storm troopers who will spearhead the assault. I will lead the group who will be responsible for capturing Chen Geng. Training will start in an hour. Dismissed!'

CHAPTER 10

Red River Delta, March 1928

ANTOINE WAS QUIETLY pleased with the way the training had gone. The men may have been irregular in the way they dressed, and their parade ground discipline was sloppy, but they grasped quickly how he wanted them to fight when they eventually encountered Chen Geng and his group.

The first stage of the journey towards Cao Bang was relatively straightforward. They used a combination of trucks and pack horses to make their way towards the hill country, first along tarmacked roads, and then along established tracks. A gang of conscripted Vietnamese workers carried most of the heavy equipment and supplies. As they got nearer to the hills, the weather changed. Night-time temperatures dropped. When they woke, they were greeted by low-hanging mists that shrouded the hills around them. Their clothes felt damp and clammy until the daytime heat dried them off.

They skirted around Cao Bang, leaving the main road and tracks behind them, and started to ascend into the hills.

Antoine sent Tardy and his group of scouts ahead to try and find the location of Chen Geng's fortified camp. The lower slopes of the hills were covered in dense vegetation and elephant grass, which had to be hacked through with machetes before progress could be made. Eventually, they would reach the upper summits before descending into the next valley, where they would have to start again with clearing a path through the undergrowth.

On the third morning after they left the main road, Tardy returned on his own, just as they were breaking camp to start the day's march. His face had a haunted look.

'You need to see this. Follow me.'

Antoine and the rest of the company set out after Tardy at a fast pace. After a couple of kilometres, they came across a path that had been cleared from the encroaching jungle. It led up to a small hamlet. It was shrouded in smoke. Antoine could pick out the scouts, who had taken up their customary position crouched down on their heels. They were all staring down at the ground and did not acknowledge the new arrivals.

All around the clearing were scattered dead bodies. Men, women and children. Most of them had been shot in the back, presumably as they fled. Some had been hacked down with machetes. The blood from the wounds had congealed, attracting hordes of buzzing flies. The smoke was rising from the remains of a building to one side of the clearing. Inside were the charred figures of what looked like people who had been caught in prayer. Melted and warped communion cups and other religious artefacts betrayed the building's function as a church. In the middle of the clearing, someone had erected a makeshift crucifix. Nailed to it, head slumped and torso sliced open to leave his entrails hanging out, was a priest, still clad in the remains of his vestments.

Antoine had seen slaughter before. Slaughter on a mass scale. But that was the impersonal killing of industrial warfare. This was far more intimate and personal. He felt the vomit rise in his gorge as he looked around. Controlling himself, he turned to Tardy, who was standing silent by his side.

'How long ago do you think this happened?'

'A day at most. We got here late afternoon. The blood was fresh at that point. The fire in the church was still going.'

'Right, your scouts should be able to pick up their tracks. We will follow them and hope that they lead us to their camp. Then we will strike.'

It had not taken long for the scouts to pick up Chen Geng's trail. They reported back through Tardy that the gang had been slowed by the captives they had taken from the T'ai village, most of them young women, who they would turn into concubines, and a few young men, whom they pressed into service as conscripted Vietnamese workers. They also reported that they had seen riding alongside Chen Geng, a young man dressed all in black, whom they did not recognise but who seemed to be issuing orders to the gang leader and his men. Towards the end of the day, the gang had arrived at their fortified encampment. It nestled into a secluded valley surrounded by steep, wooded hills, making it hard for any air reconnaissance to spot. The encampment was more like a fortified village, with its own rice paddy fields that doubled up as a moat. Submerged under the water within the fields were walls topped by sharpened bamboo stakes, which added a further line of protection.

When Antoine and his men caught up with the scouts, they took up a position on one of the hills overlooking the encampment. Antoine knew that they would have to act quickly or the captives the gang had seized would be abused and possibly killed. Dusk was beginning to gather. Soon, it would be pitch black as the night descended. Surveying the encampment through his binoculars, Antoine decided his plan of action. Gathering the men around him, he issued the orders for the attack.

'We are going to implement the plan we rehearsed during the week of training. First, the scouts need to identify and take out, as silently as possible, any guards they have posted on the perimeter of the fence. They need to then signal, using the flashlights we have given them, when they have successfully eliminated the guards. Tardy, can you make sure they understand those orders? When they do, you can set off, as by the time you get there it will be night-time.'

Tardy left, followed by his scouts.

'When we receive the signal from the scouts, the mortar team, which will be based up here, will then aim to demolish the walls around the encampment. Once that has been achieved, we will then put some shells into the camp, just to stir them up. The machine gun team will deploy around the back of the camp, because my bet is that most of the gang will try and flee that way. Your job is to take them out. Is that understood?'

The men nodded their assent.

'I will lead the assault group. We will access the camp through its main gate, which should have been blown off its hinges by the mortar attack. My task is to find and capture Chen Geng alive. Your task is to provide me with cover by taking out the gang members who have not fled. We need to be as careful as we can not to kill the captives. They should be unarmed, and they are hill people not Chinese renegades, so you should be able to tell the difference.'

The men let out a nervous laugh, more to relieve their own tension than in recognition of Antoine's feeble attempt at humour.

'Right, all except the mortar squad should follow me to the foot of the hill and prepare for action. I would estimate that the signal will come through from the scouts in a couple of hours' time, when it is nightfall. My hope is that the gang will be in a celebratory mood and may get themselves nice and drunk, making it easier for us to take them by surprise. *Bonne chance!*'

It took them an hour of quick marching to descend the hill to their jumping-off point. The men in the machine gun unit peeled off at the bottom of the hill and then set off for the back of the encampment. The rest settled down to wait for the signal, maintaining a strict silence. Some of them spent their time blacking up their faces. Others checked and double-checked their weapons. The familiar sensations caused by nervous tension and the flow of adrenaline Antoine experienced before going into combat returned to him now.

After what seemed an eternity of waiting, but in fact had only been the couple of hours that Antoine predicted, the agreed flashlight signals briefly lit up the inky darkness. After a few seconds, there was a thudding noise as the first mortar shells were launched into the night sky. This was followed by the sound of large splashes as the shells fell short into the waterlogged paddy fields. Antoine prayed that the men firing the mortars would use these sounds to help them find their range. Again, there was the thudding noise of the next round of shells being fired. This time, they landed right on top of the encampment's gate and walls. There was a loud crashing sound of falling masonry, followed by shouts and screams from within the encampment. Antoine signalled for the men to fall in behind him in single file. In the meantime, further shells were being lobbed inside the camp, resulting in further shouting and screaming.

Suddenly, the night air was rent by the staccato rattle of the Hotchkiss machine gun that was starting to pick off the first gang members as they fled out of the back of the camp. Antoine could not hear any return fire. This suggested that Chen Geng and his men had been caught by surprise. As they raced up the track leading into the encampment, several dark shadows appeared from behind what remained of the walls and opened fire. Antoine heard the groans as some of his men were hit, followed by a splash as they fell into the paddy field. His troops instantly returned fire, enabling him to pass through the gate and into the heart of the encampment. Around him, he could see the bodies of the gang members who had been killed by the initial mortar attack.

Now that he was inside the camp, he could make out that in the middle there was a circle of straw huts built on stilts. Most of these were ablaze, as the sparks from the exploding shells had set them alight. Even in the swirling smoke, Antoine could see that there was one hut that was bigger than the rest in a prominent place within the circle. Signalling to his men to follow him and unholstering his pistol, he climbed up the wooden ladder that led up to the hut's front door and kicked it down. As he burst through the door, he rolled across the floor, as a burst of machine gunfire passed over his body. He reached the side of the room and hid behind what looked like a large, teak chest. The inside of the hut was lit up by the light coming from the flickering fires outside. Antoine could see that there was only one other room in the hut, whose door was ajar. It was presumably from there that the shots had come. Using his hands he indicated to his men, who were crouched on either side of the main entrance, that after a count of three he wanted them to fire into the doorway and then give him time to get through it. He counted the numbers down, waited for the following fusillade to end, and then sprinted into the room. As soon as he passed the doorway, he felt a glancing blow down his left side, followed by the warm feel of blood from a cut to the top of his shoulder. In one movement, he swivelled rightwards and punched out. His fist crunched into the attacker's nose. There was the sound of smashed bone and cartilage, followed by the thump of someone hitting the floor. Antoine gave the prone body a savage kick in the stomach.

His men came racing into the room behind him. They quickly tied up the attacker's hands and legs, so he was in no position to get up again. Antoine used his boot to roll the man over, so he was facing upwards. Although the centre of his face was a bloody mess, Antoine could see that he was Chinese. Across his tunic he wore a yellow silk sash, the uniform of the Yellow Flags. Antoine bent down and shouted into his face. 'Chen Geng!' The man stared up at him in mute defiance.

'Yes, that's him.'

Antoine swivelled round to find where the response had come from. Crouched in the corner, unarmed, dressed all in black, was a young man with a familiar face.

'You don't remember me, do you, Monsieur Martinet, or should that be Captain Martinet? I can understand as we met in very different circumstances previously.'

'Nguyen Den Hieu, isn't it?'

'Well remembered.'

'What are you doing here, with this lot?'

'I am the brain. They are the brawn. To be honest, I am sick of them… him.' Den Hieu pointed towards the prone body trussed up on the floor. 'They are nothing but cold-blooded murderers. You saw what they did to those harmless tribespeople in that village. Now, this evening, they have been systematically raping the women and making their menfolk watch while they do it. That is no way to win their hearts and minds, which is what I have been sent out to do.'

Antoine winced as he felt one of his men put an antiseptic swab on the gash on his shoulder and started to bandage him up.

'So, you are telling me that you are the one who has been spreading communist propaganda among the peasantry, while this lot have been butchering Catholics and smuggling opium?'

'They are a vehicle for us to reach the masses, although I can now see not a very efficient one.'

'What's happened to you? The last time I saw you, you were returning from an elite Paris university on the way to a top job in the colonial civil service.'

'Yes, well. I told you on the ship that even with a pampered post in the colonial administration, I would always be a poodle with no power. I couldn't stand it. I went off to China to one of the Communist Party's training schools. After seeing the light through a schooling in Marxist-Leninism I am now back to spread the word.'

'But you are not, are you? I am going to have to take you back to Hanoi and hand you over to the security services. I cannot guarantee what will happen to you there, but it won't be pleasant.'

'Don't worry about me. I am expendable and the first of many who will eventually drive you out of the country.'

Antoine gestured to his men to take the two prisoners away.

The convoy set off back down from the hills to the main highway that would take them through the delta and then onto Hanoi. The prisoners were put in leg shackles, with their hands bound behind their backs, to prevent them from escaping. Antoine reflected that he and his men had come off lightly from the skirmish. His wound was skin deep and was already healing fast. They had lost two men, killed as they tried to enter the encampment, and a few had minor wounds. The real casualties were the hill tribeswomen who had been assaulted and raped by Geng's gang members on their first night in the encampment. Antoine cast a glance at the women as they brought up the rear of the column. They were all petite in size, dressed in the customary T'ai clothing of tightly draped skirts, white blouses with silver clasps and large conical straw hats, which hid their faces. Antoine could not see their expressions but could tell from their defeated postures that they had been traumatised by their recent ordeal. Standing a few feet away from them were the T'ai scouts, who provided a protective presence.

Antoine's plan was to drop off the T'ai women and the young men whom Geng had used as conscripted Vietnamese workers at the nearest hill village they could find, so they could be assimilated back into their own community. Tardy said there was a village over a day's march away, so they would need to camp out for one more night in the jungle before reaching it.

The next morning, Antoine woke to the cacophony of animal and bird sounds that heralded the start of a new day. The low-lying mist had left a warm spray of water coating his hair and increasingly straggly beard. He looked up to find Tardy standing over him, his hands on his hips.

'The T'ai have gone.'

'What do you mean gone?' Antoine scrambled to stand up.

'And it's not just them. They've taken Chen Geng and his other gang members with them. They've left Den Hieu with us.'

'Do you know where they will have gone?'

'They look as though they left in the early hours of the morning. They will have put some distance between us and them by now, even with the women alongside them.'

'Well, we better get after them. My orders were to bring back Chen Geng alive for questioning. Get the men fallen in, Corporal.'

'Sir,' Tardy hesitated, 'we've got what we need in the black-shirted communist. That's who the Sûreté are interested in, not some common thief. Anyway, I doubt we will catch them, not with their head start. And, by the time we get to them, they will have administered their own form of rough justice to Geng and his men.'

Antoine looked hard at Tardy, who returned his stare.

'You knew this was going to happen, didn't you?'

Tardy said nothing.

Antoine knew that Tardy was right. Bernard would give him a hard time for not returning with Geng alive, but the real prize was Den Hieu. He was the one spreading propaganda and the one who would know something about the Communist Party networks in the area. Antoine, like Tardy, was comfortable with the T'ai dealing with Geng in the way they saw fit.

'OK, Tardy. Get the men fallen in. Next stop Hanoi.'

CHAPTER 11
Hanoi, April 1928

WHEN THEY RETURNED to Hanoi, Antoine took his prisoner straight to the prison *militaire* in the citadel. He had not exchanged another word with Den Hieu since they last spoke in the encampment. Den Hieu had not asked him what had happened to Chen Geng. For someone who was about to be delivered into the hands of the Sûreté, he looked remarkably composed, betraying no hint of fear.

When they reported to the guardhouse in the prison, they were directed into a side room. Antoine opened the door, to find Bernard sitting behind a small table, with another man standing behind him. This man was dressed in military fatigues that bore no discernible markings to show his regiment or rank. He was wearing a Basque beret, which sloped over the front of his forehead, shielding his eyes.

'I ordered you to bring Chen Geng back alive. Where is he?'

'Dead, I presume. Most probably garrotted by the T'ai and left to rot out in the jungle. You didn't want him, in any case. This is who you are really after.'

Antoine pushed forward Den Hieu.

'Ah, Monsieur Hieu. I wondered where you had got to.' Bernard could not hide his relish at who had fallen into his hands.

'The last we knew, Monsieur Hieu had left on a boat for China to enlist in some Communist Party training school. We will have a lot of catching up to do, won't we, Monsieur Hieu?'

Den Hieu did not dignify this with a reply. He simply stared back defiantly at Bernard.

'Martinet. That's all for now. You can return to Saigon. But we might call on your services again, particularly given the successful outcome of this mission.'

With that, he dismissed Antoine.

In the early hours of the following morning, Antoine returned to the prison. He entered the guardhouse, which was only manned by one prison warden.

'I am here to see Den Hieu, the prisoner I brought in yesterday.'

'Apologies, sir, but the Sûreté left strict orders that he was to receive no visitors.'

'I am the Sûreté. Now, come on, take me to his cell.'

The warden got up reluctantly and asked Antoine to follow him. They proceeded through the main body of the prison, along the wings that housed hundreds of criminals. Antoine could hear his feet ringing against the metal stairs as they walked for what seemed an eternity. Eventually, they exited through a side door that led into a yard. In one corner was a small building. The warden searched through the keys on his ring, before finding the right one to open the door. As soon as he entered, Antoine had to press a handkerchief to his nose to combat the fetid stench of human faeces and dried blood that assailed him. The warden, who seemed unperturbed by the smell, pointed at a cell door.

Antoine looked in. It took some time for his eyes to adjust to the gloom of the cell. In the corner, lying in a foetal position, he could see Den Hieu.

'Open the door!'

Antoine walked slowly across the cell and knelt beside Hieu. The warden locked the door behind him.

Antoine recalled what Bonnet had told him about the Sûreté's methods. How they frequently administered electrical shocks and systematic beatings as part of interrogation, sometimes concluding with summary executions. Antoine could see that Hieu's hands were blackened and that the tops of his fingers were covered in blood where the nails had been ripped off. His face was swollen, and his eyes were so puffed up that they were closed. His bare feet were also covered in blood, where his toenails had been smashed.

Antoine pulled a bottle of water out of his pocket and tried to dab some moisture on Hieu's lips. But Hieu was unconscious.

'Don't waste your sympathies on him, Martinet.'

Antoine turned to find Bernard's silhouette filling the door to the cell.

'There was no need to do that to him, you sadistic bastard. If you were any good at your job, you could have got the information you needed without beating him to a pulp.'

'Careful, Martinet. Remember that you are under military orders, and I am your commanding officer.'

'No, Bernard. You are Sûreté. I was under orders to Colonel Rannou.'

'Read your sign-up papers. You were seconded to us for this mission. Which, by the way, has not finished yet.'

Antoine glared at him, fearing what would come next.

'You will escort this prisoner, along with some others we have locked up here, and ensure that they arrive safely at Poulo Condor. You know what that is?'

Antoine understood by now that Bernard always answered his own questions.

'It's our penal colony out in the South China Sea. That's where we stick these politicos, some place so remote they can't cause any trouble and hopefully rot away.'

CHAPTER 12

Poulo Condor, South China Sea, May 1928

THE SWELL AT the bow started to slacken as the navy junk transporting the prisoners approached the harbour at dawn. They had set off from Saigon the evening before to cover the 250 kilometres to Poulo Condor. As Antoine peered through the early morning mist, he could see the peaks of the three small islands that made up the penal colony clustered close to each other. Behind him, he could hear the clanking of chains as the prisoners bestirred themselves to take in their new surroundings. A small groan of despair rose from the men who were huddled in the middle of the junk, overseen by a couple of armed guards.

When they docked, the prisoners were formed into a chain gang and marched the short distance from the port to the prison. As they approached, the main gates swung open to reveal a parade ground surrounded by squat concrete detention blocks. Antoine ordered the prisoners to assemble in the middle of the square to await the arrival of the prison governor. The prisoners were struggling to remain standing as they shuffled into line. Most of them had received a beating or worse as part of their interrogation.

After half an hour, the governor eventually arrived to take charge of the prisoners. He was a large, overweight man, sweating hard into his uniform as the heat of the day started to take hold. As soon as he opened his mouth, Antoine could smell the alcohol on his breath.

'Right, I will take these off you. What have we got? Twelve politicos from the north?'

'Yes, all arrested as suspected members of the newly formed Revolutionary Youth League. Infiltrated from China.'

'OK, don't worry, we will soften them up a bit. I always chuck the politicos into a cell with the common crims. Nothing like a close brush with your average murderer, smuggler or rapist to disabuse you of the nobility of the peasantry, or whatever these fellows believe.'

'Can I ask a favour, Governor? I want to have a few words with that man there before I leave.' Antoine pointed at Den Hieu.

'Don't see why not. Guard, take the officer and this prisoner to one of the segregation cells.'

Den Hieu was grabbed by the arm and hustled off by a guard. Antoine followed. They entered one of the main prison blocks. The walkway bisected the cells. These were dug into the ground with steel meshes across the top of them. Antoine peered down to see groups of men huddled together in the cells. The cells were not high enough to enable the prisoners to stand up. Most of them squatted or lay down. The smell of urine and faeces was so intense that Antoine had to pull his vest up to cover his mouth and nose.

The heat inside the block was sweltering. At the end of the prison block, there was a small cell. The guard pushed Den Hieu inside and then ushered in Antoine behind him. The guard slammed the door shut behind them.

Antoine studied what he could see of Den Hieu's face, which was partially covered by the lip of his large conical straw hat. The marks of his beating were still evident around his mouth and nose.

'I am not going to apologise to you for the fact that it was me who arrested you. That was my duty as a French army officer. But I don't believe that you should be subjected to the treatment that Bernard gave you. Do you want me to contact your family when I get back to Saigon, so at least they know where you are and maybe can do something about getting you released?'

Den Hieu raised his head so that Antoine could see his full face. His eyelids were partially closed and puffed up with red and black bruising.

'That is very gracious of you, Captain.' His words were slurred. He pronounced each one very slowly and deliberately.

'I have been disowned by my family. So, no need to contact them. I renounce them anyway for their bourgeois lifestyle. I hold no grudge against you. As you say, you were just doing your duty. But you need to know that you are now a marked man. Information has been circulated to my comrades about your role with the Sûreté. At some point, there will be a reckoning.'

Antoine waited to see if Den Hieu had anything else to say. He remained silent.

'Guard! We are finished here,' barked Antoine.

CHAPTER 13

Saigon, October 1928

WHILE HE HAD been away, thoughts of Marguerite had been constantly in Antoine's head. Before he left, he had written her a brief note explaining why he would not be able to ask her out as he had suggested at the end of their last encounter but promising that he would do so on his return. As soon as he had got back from the north, he sent her a message inviting her to join him at the opening of the new season at the Municipal Théâtre. He waited impatiently for her reply. It came after a week. She had a reserved box at the theatre that she could use throughout the season. She suggested that they attend the opening night together, the premiere in South East Asia of Puccini's new opera, *Turandot*. This, she informed him, was 'always a grand affair, with everyone who is anyone in Saigon society in attendance'. She asked him to meet her for a light supper in the nearby Café de la Musique before the start of the performance.

Antoine booked himself into the Grand Hôtel de la Rotonde for the week of the opening night, as Marguerite said she would be staying on in Saigon, to take in some of the season's other shows and to catch up with her acquaintances in the city. On the evening of the performance, he arrived at the café to find her already seated at a table on the terrace, overlooking the Place du Théâtre. From here, they would have a good view of the early arrivals at the performance.

Antoine made a few last-minute adjustments to his white dinner jacket, which he had rented especially for the occasion. Approaching her from behind, he gave a discreet cough to indicate his presence. She turned slowly to acknowledge his arrival. Antoine took her right hand and brushed his lips against it. His head filled momentarily with the heat and perfume it gave off.

'It's lovely to see you again, Antoine. I was beginning to think that your promise to take me out had been an idle one.'

'My apologies. I got called away rather unexpectedly after our meeting. I was away longer than I thought.'

'And where was that?'

'Just a military mission in the north, as part of my duty for the infantry reserve.'

Antoine was relieved that she seemed happy not to explore the matter further.

This brief exchange of pleasantries had given him time to register again what a striking and handsome woman she was. Unlike most upper-class French colonial women, who tried to keep their skin as white as possible by cowering inside to protect themselves from the sun and heat, Marguerite's arms and shoulders were a dark brown, which were enhanced by the pale-yellow silk evening dress she was wearing.

'So where are you staying, Antoine, while you are in Saigon?'

'At the Rotonde, just round the corner.'

'Very grand. I have a townhouse on Rue Mac-Mahon, which I use when I am in town. It was the first house that Charles and I bought when we arrived here, and I kept it on after his death.' She briefly looked away. 'I hope you won't be bored tonight. They always do an opera on the first night. They can drag on a bit.' She laughed.

'Well, I can't honestly say that I have been to many operas. In fact, I haven't been to any. It will be the start of my cultural education.'

After a short pause in the conversation while they started to eat, Marguerite asked Antoine whether he had done anything about buying himself some land for a small plantation.

'No, not yet. But, while I am in town, I will contact Pak Hung to arrange a meeting.'

'Make sure you do.'

As the meal progressed, Antoine became aware that he and his companion were attracting the attention of the other diners sat on the tables around them. Every time he looked up, he caught people looking at them and whispering to each other, without much effort at hiding their interest.

'Ignore them, Antoine. They haven't seen me in the company of a single man for years. I told you that they find my long widowhood abnormal, almost obscene. It will give them something to gossip about. I am rather enjoying their scandalised attention.'

After the meal, they walked the few steps across to the Municipal Théâtre and joined the crowd that was processing up its monumental staircase. The architect had clearly aimed to replicate the style of the theatres that could be found in

Paris and the metropole's largest provincial cities. Along with the sweeping staircase leading to its front, it had high-arched porticos, adorned with allegorical sculptures, all clad in white marble.

Antoine took his seat alongside Marguerite in her box. It was a small, intimate space, with room for two people and a good view of the stage. Marguerite settled in and then started to tell Antoine about the occupants of the other boxes.

'Over there,' she said, pointing with her opera glasses, 'is the governor general's box.'

Antoine looked over to see a group of dignitaries, some dressed in formal evening wear, others in military uniforms, their chests freighted with ribbons and medals marking their service.

Marguerite snorted with barely concealed derision. 'Look at them. Like a bunch of strutting peacocks. The governor general's post is a sinecure. Whichever party is in control in Paris sends over one of its placemen to take up residence in the palace in Saigon. They spend two years here scrapping everything their predecessors have done and then promptly leave, usually having increased the taxes we have to pay. No wonder the country never improves and why we colons absolutely despise them. God knows what the natives think of them.'

In the box next to the governor general's, Antoine spotted another familiar face, that of Monsieur de la Lacaze, the director of the Banque de l'Indochine. To his surprise, Lacaze waved across to him. Antoine acknowledged this with a short wave of his own.

'You are well known among the high and mighty, aren't you?' Marguerite smiled at him.

'It's just because I represent the Rodins. That's who he is really waving at.'

The lights started to dim in the auditorium. The hubbub of chatter in the audience fell silent. Then the large red velvet stage curtain parted to reveal what looked like a court in Ancient China, with large paper lanterns hanging from pagodas covered in dragon motifs. The audience greeted the set with enthusiastic applause.

As the opera was sung in Italian, Antoine had no idea what the story was about. He decided that the best way to endure this experience was to close his eyes and just let the music wash over him. After about ten minutes, he felt Marguerite's hand search his out in the dark. He took it in his own and gently squeezed. He found himself aroused by this slight physical contact.

The performance was barely half an hour in, before Marguerite leant across to him and whispered into his ear, 'Don't make a scene, but I would like to leave.' She then stood up quietly and left the box, with Antoine close behind her. Marguerite said nothing further as she headed down the stairs and out into the warm balmy air in the Place du Théâtre. She again took his hand and started to walk quickly down Rue Mac-Mahon, until they came to a black iron gate leading up to a large townhouse, set back in its own gardens.

Marguerite pushed the gate open, ushered Antoine in and led him through the front door. She removed the light shawl she had on over her shoulders and tossed it onto a chair. She started to ascend the stairs that led from the hall up to the bedrooms on the second floor. Antoine followed.

The next morning, Antoine was woken by the sunlight filtering through the shutters and playing across his face.

He opened his eyes slowly to find that he was lying on a large double bed, shrouded in a mosquito net, that rippled in time to the movement of the ceiling fan. He felt a warm, soft heat pressed up alongside him.

'I thought you were never going to wake.'

He looked up to see Marguerite peering down at him, with a grin playing across her lips. The hair that she usually wore up cascaded around her shoulders, shielding her eyes.

'Well, to be honest, I am not used to these comforts.'

Marguerite slid down until she was lying beside him and started to gently stroke his hair.

'I never thought I would do that again, not after Charles's death.'

'Do you regret it, then?'

There was a pause.

'No, not at all. I do realise, though, that I know precious little about you. I think that you are kind and honourable. You are very different from the other male colons out here, who are mostly arrogant, drunken bullies. So, it is a low bar.' She laughed. 'Truly, though. Who are you, Antoine Martinet? I know you fought in the war. You work for the Rodins, whose reputation as hard taskmasters and ruthless plantation owners is well known. You disappear for months on end, on hush-hush missions. You're tangled up with that bastard Bernard. And now, you have slept with me. That's all I know.'

'There's not a lot more to know. Like most men of my generation, I volunteered to fight in the war for patriotic reasons. I got invalided out and had to find a job. I landed on my feet when the Rodins employed me in their factory in Clermont. They seem to have taken a shine to me because they promoted me and then sent me out here. Because of my military service, I am part of the reserve, which is why the likes of Bernard still have their claws in me.'

Marguerite pulled the sheet down from his chest. Her hand ran down his stomach. Her fingers gently played over the ridges of the scar tissue from the wounds he had received in the war.

'How did you get these?'

'Anyone who fought in the trenches in the war was wounded. They are nothing special, I assure you.'

'Antoine. I need to be able to trust you. I think you are a good man, but I really don't know you. So, you must be able to talk to me.'

'I know. I will.'

Marguerite pulled the rest of the sheet down until it fell off the bottom of the bed. She swung her leg over Antoine's thighs.

CHAPTER 14

ANTOINE AND MARGUERITE spent the week together in each other's company. She took him to the Cercle Sportif Saigonnais, the city's exclusive club for the French colonial elite. There she tried to get Antoine to play tennis with her, kitting him out in long white shorts and a short-sleeve sweater. Antoine felt ridiculous but exultant at the same time, as he swiped at and missed the balls served by his much more skilful partner. They wandered aimlessly through the botanical gardens, giggling at the antics of the snub-nosed monkeys as they pelted visitors with pieces of fruit and speculating on whether the slow loris would ever stir from its slumbers. Hours passed as they sat on the terraces of cafés, with Marguerite providing a running commentary on the peccadillos of the constant stream of passers-by. They, in turn, were subject to surreptitious glances from other café goers, scandalised at this social mismatch between the plantation owner and the hired hand.

Every afternoon, they would retire to the bedroom in Marguerite's townhouse on Rue Mac-Mahon and make love. For Marguerite, Antoine was only the second man she had ever slept with. His body was very different to her husband's. Charles had been slight of build, whereas Antoine had a larger frame and was more muscular. She felt herself enveloped by him, in a way that she had never been by her husband. For Antoine, Marguerite was the first woman whom he had spent long enough with to have time to explore her body and understand her desires.

In between bouts of love making, Marguerite tried to patch together scraps of Antoine's past. He told her about his childhood in the Cantal. His reverence for his father, who had lost an arm at the Battle of Sedan in the Franco-Prussian War. How his father had then struggled to run his small farm and raise his family as an invalid. This had forged Antoine's own patriotism and his hatred for the Germans. He had been a willing volunteer in 1914. Like most veterans Marguerite had met in the colony, Antoine avoided telling her much about his time in the trenches. He did talk, though, about the impact of losing his younger brother in the fighting and how he had felt responsible for not protecting him. He hinted at how he blamed the communist-inspired mutineers for being the cause of his brother's death. He ended by telling her that he felt he could make a go of his life in the colony by becoming an independent plantation owner in his own right and building up a business.

'Does that mean we might have a future together?' she asked, as she lay with her head nestled into his chest. He continued to stroke her hair.

'I hope so.'

At the end of the week, at Marguerite's prompting, he arranged to go and see Pak Hung about a loan for some land.

Pak Hung had sent word back that he would meet Antoine in his office in Cholon, the Chinese-run port that was the real commercial hub of Saigon. On the hottest afternoon of the week, when the air was oppressively humid, Antoine took a water taxi up the Arroyo Canal that linked Saigon to Cholon. The waterway was choked with sampans and junks, carrying the processed rice crop on its way to markets across South East Asia. When he arrived, he hailed a rickshaw driver to take him to Pak Hung's office.

The rickshaw driver dropped him outside an unprepossessing set of buildings that did not reflect Pak Hung's status as the head of one of the colony's great Chinese trading houses. The black paint that covered the wooden-framed building was starting to peel. There was a narrow veranda running along its frontage, with various doors leading inside. From one of them, Antoine could hear the clack of mahjong tiles being rammed together and the shouts of the players. From another, there came a sweet smell that reminded him of burnt syrup. Outside each door there were two young men propped against the walls eyeing him as he approached.

'I am Monsieur Martinet. I have an appointment with Yip Pak Hung.'

One of the young men peeled himself from the wall and gestured to Antoine to follow him. They went through a door at the end of the veranda that took them into a cramped office sparsely equipped with a desk and two chairs. The desk had a large abacus in its centre, surrounded by piles of paper that threatened to topple over. Sitting behind the desk was Pak Hung, wreathed in smoke from the cigarette that seemed to be permanently clamped into the side of his mouth.

'Welcome, Monsieur Martinet, to Cholon.' Antoine caught a glimpse of gold teeth as Pak Hung smiled.

'Now, before we get down to business, let me show you around my little emporium. Follow me, please.'

They walked back across the veranda, escorted by two of the young men, who stayed a few steps behind them.

'These are my boys. They run my errands. Collect my debts. I need them for protection sometimes as I have many enemies.' Pak Hung chuckled amiably. Antoine noticed that the young men had distinctive dragon tattoos on their arms and bare chests. They were armed with small revolvers, tucked into the backs of their trousers, and short knives worn in sheaths on their belts. Antoine assumed that these were the Triads that Bonnet had told him about.

They turned into the room from where the sound of mahjong was being played. It was difficult to see much as the air was thick with tobacco smoke. The room stretched back to a small bar at the back, from which it looked like tea, not alcohol, was being served by two diminutive waitresses. They scurried between the tables, filling up the players' cups. The sound of mahjong tiles being slammed onto the table was mixed with the raucous shouting of the players, all of whom were gesticulating wildly at each other.

'Favourite Chinese pastime.'

'Mahjong, you mean,' queried Antoine.

'No. Gambling.'

Antoine peered at the tables through the smoke. Now he could see bunches of piastres piled beside each player's elbows.

'They play for high stakes in here. I take a cut, of course. A reasonable cut. Follow me.'

They swept out of the room and then went through the next door. They were met with the sweet smell that Antoine had noticed when he first arrived. Again, it was difficult to see the interior as the air was filled with smoke. But unlike the mahjong room, in here there was no noise. As Antoine's eyes adjusted to the lack of light in the room, he could pick out comatose shapes lying on divans. Next to each divan was a cradle holding a long pipe. Some of the shapes would periodically stir themselves, reach down and take a lungful of smoke from the pipe next to them before falling back onto the divan.

'I think you westerners call this an opium den. I just call it business. Again, very good business. You can even see that some of your countrymen pay us a visit.' Pak Hung pointed towards a nearby divan, where a linen-suited middle-aged man was lying prone, oblivious to their attention. 'You would be surprised how many colons are attached to the pipe. One of them told me it was the only thing that kept him here. If you ask my opinion, it will be this,' he pointed to the crumpled shape of the man, 'that will bring your empire crashing down, not some revolutionary waving a pamphlet in the air. Come, let's go and discuss your loan.'

Pak Hung took Antoine back into his office.

'Tea?'

'No thank you.' Antoine was shaken by what he had seen. He wanted to get away as soon as he could. The Frenchman in the opium den had looked completely defeated and forlorn.

'As I recall, you want a loan to purchase five hundred hectares, isn't that right?'

'Yes, five hundred hectares next to the Rodins' estate in

Long Thành province. Having worked the land up there for some time now, I know it is fertile and will turn a good profit.'

'So, based on our previous discussions, it will be a loan of half a million piastres over twenty years. But, as it is you and not the Rodins, I can let you have it at 5% interest, 1% less than we agreed for them. I like to support small entrepreneurs. The Rodins have broader backs than you.' Pak Hung's gold teeth flashed as he smiled. 'There is one other difference,' he went on, 'this loan will be with me, not the bank. Is that understood?'

'Why?'

'Let's just say, I am taking a personal interest in you. I will send through the papers for you to sign.'

'Many thanks.' Antoine got up to go.

'Just one more thing. I hear that you have been up north and arrested a well-known Communist.'

'How do you know that?'

'I have my sources. Members of your Sûreté are frail human beings, like the rest of us. They have their vices. Remember, alongside gambling and opium, I also run some high-grade prostitutes. Women, girls, boys, whatever takes your fancy. So, I get information from my clients. Can I tempt you with anything, beyond a loan?'

Antoine stared back hard at him.

'No. I thought not. You have your high-class French widow to keep you company, don't you?'

Antoine remained silent.

'You should know that the Communists will come after you.' He held up his hand to stop Antoine from speaking. 'Yes, I have my sources with them, too. As I said, I have a personal interest in you, so I want to protect my investment. One final thing before you go. I would like you to be my personal guest at the procession of the dragons, which is coming up shortly in Cholon. It is when we honour our religious deities at our pagoda. Will you come?'

Antoine did not feel that it was an invitation he could refuse. He nodded his acceptance and left.

CHAPTER 15
Long Thành, February 1929

AS SOON AS Antoine had secured the concession for the additional hectares at Long Thành, Pak Hung released the loan for the purchase. Antoine enlisted Jouvin to oversee the clearing of the land and to plant the trees, using some of the well-developed stock from the existing plantation to give them a head start. Antoine had agreed to pay Jouvin an additional salary to the one he received from the Rodins to take on the day-to-day management of his plantation. He had had to overcome Jouvin's initial resistance to hiring free labour and providing the workforce with some basic amenities, such as decent washing facilities and a small school. In the end Jouvin acknowledged that it was Antoine's money to do with as he saw fit. Antoine was determined to run his own plantation in his own way. In this he had been heavily influenced by Marguerite's approach to plantation management and her more enlightened treatment of her workforce.

Since their week in Saigon, Antoine and Marguerite spent all their available spare time together. Antoine stayed most weekends at Marguerite's plantation. She visited his new venture to advise him on the more scientific and technical aspects of producing rubber and suggested that he should diversify into other crops like coffee. They paid regular visits to her townhouse on Rue Mac-Mahon in Saigon. Marguerite even invited some of her acquaintances for dinner to meet him. It was her way of making a statement that her relationship with Antoine was public and needed to be acknowledged as such by Saigon society.

For the first time since the start of the war, Antoine felt that his life was falling into place. Only a few things prevented him from being fully at ease. He knew that his contentment could be upended by any further interventions from Bernard and whoever was pulling his strings in the Sûreté. It seemed unreasonable that they could hold him to ransom with what he had done in the war for much longer. Surely, he had paid his debt to them in the mission he had undertaken in the north of the country. He resolved that the next time they came calling, he would simply refuse and take the consequences. Then there was the prospect of an impending visit from the Rodin brothers. They wanted to cast an eye over their huge investment and see how it was performing. Or more accurately, how well he and Jouvin were managing their investment. The problem was, Antoine no longer agreed with the way that they wanted the plantation run, with its use of indentured labour and lack of basic facilities for the workforce. The human toll was obvious, with a high percentage of workers falling sick and, in some cases, dying from overwork and the lack of an adequate diet. He planned to propose that they should improve the welfare of the workforce if they wanted to get the most out of them. He doubted that they would be very receptive. He knew he could well jeopardise his job.

CHAPTER 16

Grand Hôtel de la Rotonde, Saigon, March 1929

IT HAD BEEN four years since Antoine had last seen the Rodin brothers. They looked as physically vigorous and alert as ever. They had asked Antoine to meet with them in their hotel suite after they had spent the day inspecting the plantation. They had brought with them an accountant, who hovered behind them as they settled beside each other on the sofa.

'Please, Antoine, take a seat.' Édouard Rodin gestured at the chair positioned very formally in front of them.

'Now, first things first. We are very pleased with the results that you have achieved at the plantation in such a short time. Monsieur Gauthier here,' Rodin waved his hand behind him, 'says that the profits are healthy and that you have kept the accounts in an orderly fashion. From what we could see on the inspection, and we are not specialists in this field, you seem to have got the hang of how to grow and harvest rubber. So, all of that is excellent. The market for rubber seems to be holding up, although our friends on the bourse have hinted that the price might begin to slacken soon, so we are going to put on hold any plans for expansion for now.'

'Yes, as my brother has said, what you have done up to now has been excellent,' André Rodin's tone was harder than his brother's, 'but we have picked up disquieting information from some of our sources here in Saigon that you have started to flirt with, how shall we say, socialistic ideas.'

'How do you mean, sir?'

'Through your association with that Madame de la Souchère, who seems to run her plantation as a charity. Schools, health clinics, washing facilities. We hear that you have adopted these ideas for your own little venture. We have no objection to you branching out on your own, so long as our business remains your priority. But we will not have these communist practices anywhere near our plantation. Understand!'

'Of course I understand, sir. But if you will bear with me for a bit. A free labour force that is treated well and has access to good facilities will be more loyal and work harder for you. With the result that productivity, and hence profits, will grow. It is worth considering on business grounds alone.'

André snorted. 'No! No! We have an endless supply of indentured labour available to us. They are completely expendable. We do not need to treat them like the workers we have back in France, although God knows if I could, I would. The natives here do not know any better, and that is the way I, we, want to keep it.'

Édouard took over from his brother, 'So, Antoine, we have an understanding, don't we? No change to the way we hire and treat the workers on our plantation.'

'If you say so, sir, although I will introduce them on my own land.'

'As we said, that's your business. There is one more thing that we need to talk to you about before you go. We are very grateful for what you did for us at the factory back in Clermont. Your vigilance ensured that we kept the militants out. We understand, again from our sources here in Saigon and back in France, that you have a role with the Sûreté. Is that right?'

'To be clear, I am a military reservist who was seconded to the Sûreté to carry out a mission for them. I don't consider myself to be one of them.'

'These are formalities. You clearly have the aptitudes and skills for the role.'

'Why are you raising this with me? It has nothing to do with my work for you.'

'No. You are right,' André took over from his brother, 'but you should know that back in France, the country is becoming more polarised. The Republicans and the leftists are leading the country towards chaos. Several of us industrialists have started to get together to fund and support organisations who can begin to reimpose order. Have you heard of the Croix-de-Feu or the Camelots du Roi?'

Antoine shook his head.

'Well, these are new organisations, mainly made up of veterans like yourself, who are taking the fight to the communist rabble on the streets. They have a national presence, but they desperately need leadership if they are going to be effective. We think that you have a part to play there. We would pay you well if you were prepared to take on such a role for us.'

Antoine did not hesitate. 'No. I couldn't do that. I am settled here now. I am beginning to carve out a life for myself, for which I am very grateful to you for providing me with that opportunity. My future is here.'

The brothers looked at each other. André was about to say something, but his brother placed his hand on his arm to stop him.

'We totally understand, Antoine. Just remember, though, if anything should happen here, that offer remains open to you.'

'Thank you, sir.'

'Well, that's all for now. We bid you goodnight, Antoine.'

Antoine left the hotel feeling dejected by the Rodins' refusal to consider changes to the way they wanted the plantation run. He also believed that there had been an underlying threat in the reference to his role in the Sûreté. They had let him know they had contacts within the organisation. That offer of a role with these new paramilitary-type organisations, did that come from them, or was that Bernard talking?

He walked the few hundred metres from the hotel to Rue Mac-Mahon. When he entered Marguerite's house he was surprised not to be greeted by one of the servants, who usually offered to take his coat and get him a drink. He stood in the hall, listening. After a few seconds, he could detect a soft murmur of voices in the smaller of the two reception rooms off the downstairs hall. He approached the door and knocked. He could hear the rustling of skirts from the other side. Marguerite opened the door a crack and slid out into the hall. She placed her hand on his chest, fingers splayed.

'Antoine, I don't want you to be surprised or angry about who is here. He is a guest in my house. Before we go in, you must swear that you will not tell anyone that he is here.'

'Who, for God's sake?'

'Den Hieu.'

Antoine pushed Marguerite to one side and strode into the room.

'What are you doing here? I left you at Poulo Condor. Have you escaped?'

Den Hieu rose slowly and stiffly from the sofa. His period of imprisonment was imprinted on his features. His face was gaunt, with dark patches below both eyes. One of his arms hung loosely down his side. He had difficulty standing straight as his shoulders hunched over.

'No, nothing as dramatic as that. I was released as part of a general amnesty decreed by your new socialist governor general.' Antoine struggled to hear what Den Hieu was saying as his voice had been reduced to a whisper.

'Does Bernard know that you are out?'

'I would imagine so, although I don't think he will know I am here. Unless you tell him.'

Marguerite moved in between them.

'He won't do that, will you, Antoine? You have my word on that.'

'If he has been released by the governor general, then there is no need for me to say anything.'

'Good. That's settled then.'

'I might ask, though, why he is here. He is a known communist agitator.'

'Stop it, Antoine. I have known Den Hieu for many years. When Charles and I first arrived in Saigon, the Hieu family were very kind to us. His father taught me about Confucian culture, while I taught him French in return. Our families have stayed in touch since then. When Den knocked on the door this evening, it was the least I could do to provide him with some shelter until he recovers from the appalling treatment he received in that penal colony. What happens there makes me ashamed to be a French citizen.'

Antoine heard the rebuke but did not respond.

'Well, you can't stay here long. You will cause trouble for Marguerite if you do.'

'Antoine, I will decide when he will leave. This is my house.'

'Please, don't argue over me. I will not stay long. I already have plans to travel back up to the north of the country. I will be gone in the next few days.'

Marguerite approached Den Hieu. She took his injured arm gently in her hands.

'You can stay as long as you like. Now, get some rest. I am going up to bed. Are you coming, Antoine?'

'Yes, I will follow shortly. I just need a few minutes with Den Hieu.'

Marguerite shot him a warning look before leaving the room.

'So, how did you get those injuries?'

Den Hieu gave a hollow laugh. 'You know how. The guards there are sadists. They delight in inflicting pain at the slightest excuse. As I recall, they broke my arm when I refused to salute one of them.'

'Are you going back north to start organising again?'

'I'm not going to tell you that. But let's just say that my recent experience at Poulo Condor has only redoubled my hatred for the colonial regime that you are a part of. You may be intimate with someone that I and my family love and respect, but that doesn't absolve you in my eyes of your role as an oppressor. What I said to you when we last met, still holds.'

'And that was?'

'That you are a marked man.'

CHAPTER 17

Cholon, Saigon, May 1929

THE HEAD OF the dragon twisted furiously as it processed down the street. A group of men kept its body upright and in constant motion by manipulating the bamboo poles that were attached to various parts of the dragon's body. Inside its head, the smallest and most athletic of the group was writhing about to create its undulating movements. There was a cacophony of noise as children walking in front of the dragon set up a rhythmic drumbeat, accompanied by clashing cymbals. Each dragon was escorted by a white horse ridden by a young woman carrying a large parasol. The horses' manes were draped in pink and white lotus blossoms. In front of each horse, a young man carried a large banner, embroidered with the characters and slogans from each religious congregation. Firecrackers were thrown under the feet of the advancing procession, making the dragons leap even higher in the air.

The procession wound its way through the streets of the port city, visiting each of the pagodas that was represented by one of the dragons and its accompanying floats of children and worshippers. They were all dressed in gaudy silk costumes featuring dragon and serpent designs. The children's faces were all caked in a heavy white powder that made them look like wax effigies. Pak Hung touched Antoine's arm and pointed proudly to one of the dragons as it passed in front of them. It was the largest in the procession, with a troupe of at least twenty men working the dragon's movements. They had even contrived to make flames and smoke pour out of its snout, eliciting huge cheers from the crowd.

'I make sure that our pagoda's dragon is the biggest. We always win the prize awarded to the best dragon in the procession by the Mayor of Cholon.'

Antoine gazed across at Pak Hung. He was almost childlike in his enthusiasm. For the occasion, he had discarded his normal grubby black tunic and trousers and was wearing a bright-red silk trouser suit, topped off with a finely embroidered black cap.

They were standing next to the Pagode des Sept Congrégations, the end point of the procession. The tables spread across the road in front of the pagoda's gates were piled high with cakes and sweets. As each dragon reached the end of the procession, its crew of young men and children gathered around their designated table to devour the food.

'That's the children looked after. Come with me. Now is the time for some grown-up entertainment.'

Antoine followed Pak Hung down Rue de Canton, whose two-storey cafés and bars were starting to fill up with the revellers from the day. As they walked down the street, Pak Hung was constantly stopped by others who wanted to have a quiet word with him. Antoine was aware that a few steps behind them there were a couple of the young men whom he had first seen when he had visited Pak Hung's office. This was the protection that he had talked about.

Eventually, they entered a Chinese restaurant towards the end of the street. It had a set of paper lanterns strung across the entrance that were lit from behind by some coloured bulbs. They went upstairs and entered a banqueting room that was full of people spread around a series of circular tables. As soon as Pak Hung entered the room, the hubbub of conversation stopped immediately. Everyone rose from their chairs, turned towards Pak Hung and bowed. He bowed in return. Immediately, the interrupted conversations resumed, with an increased intensity.

They were shown to a table in the centre of the room, which was already fully occupied except for the two seats reserved for Pak Hung and Antoine.

'You are my guest of honour. I want to show you some real Chinese hospitality.'

'I am truly grateful and suitably honoured.'

Antoine looked round the table at the other occupants. They were a mix of elderly men and women, middle-aged couples, teenagers and young children, all dressed in silk finery.

Pak Hung swung his arm in a circular gesture. 'This is my extended family. Or, at least, my official family.' He chuckled. 'I have others.' Antoine knew that among French colons Pak Hung was known as 'ten-mistress Hung'.

What followed was a lavish banquet that stretched deep into the night. The dishes of soup, char siu, roast goose, shrimp dumplings, sticky rice were all cooked in sauces from the Guangdong province of China where Pak Hung's family was based. These were accompanied by alternating glasses of white and yellow rice wine. Antoine grimaced at his first taste of these wines, but as Pak Hung continually refilled his glass, they seemed to become more palatable.

Once the dishes were cleared, most of the women and children got up and left, leaving only the older and middle-aged men at each table. The room started to fill with smoke as the first of many cigarettes were lit. There was the sound of mahjong tiles being spread across each table. Before long the level of noise in the room rose as the players started to shout at each other as they placed their bets and slammed down their tiles. Antoine noticed that each group was joined by a couple of young women wearing very tight silk dresses, with slits up their sides that revealed the tops of their slender thighs as they walked from table to table.

'You are welcome to sample one of these,' Pak Hung gestured at the young women in the room. 'It is all part of the evening's entertainment.'

'I don't want to seem ungrateful, but I have no need, thank you.'

Pak Hung raised his eyebrows in a sceptical frown. 'So, it is true what they say about you and the grand Frenchwoman, the plantation owner.'

'Yes, it is true.'

They had moved on from the wine and were now drinking whisky. Antoine felt his head was becoming unmoored from his body.

'I am starting to hear not very good things about the price of rubber in the world markets. Is that the case?'

Antoine tried to concentrate. This sudden switch to business matters had caught him off guard.

'Yes, the price has softened a bit. But we can still sell at a level that is profitable. Traders have not stopped taking our produce. Demand is steady.'

'That's good to hear. I am sure there is nothing to worry about.'

Antoine decided that now was an opportune time to leave.

'I want to thank you for all your hospitality today. The procession was an event I would not have seen without your invitation. The meal was delicious.'

'Do you know how you are going to get home?'

'Yes, I'm taking the tram from Cholon into the centre of Saigon. I have a place to stay. So, goodnight, and thank you again.'

Pak Hung nodded his farewells and returned to his whisky drinking.

Antoine knew that he was drunk, the type of drunkenness when he had the illusion of being in control but clearly was not. He weaved down the stairs and onto the pavement. He pointed himself in the direction of the tram station and set off down the street. After about five hundred metres, he started to press himself against the wall, using it to keep him upright as he shuffled along. He was faintly aware that a saloon car had driven up beside him. It was idling along at a walking pace, matching his faltering strides. Suddenly, the back doors of the car were flung open. Two men dressed all in black leapt out and ran across the pavement towards him. Antoine turned slowly towards them, but before he could take evasive action, they had grabbed both his arms, pinning them behind his back. One of them hauled a hessian bag over his head, so he couldn't see. He gasped for breath. They dragged him across the pavement to the car and dumped him in the footwell behind the driver's seat. Before the door had even shut, the driver accelerated away, tires squealing and black smoke pouring from the exhaust. One of the men put his feet on Antoine's back and pressed him down hard.

After about ten minutes, the car slowed and then stopped. The doors opened. Antoine was dragged out and dumped on the ground. Someone got hold of his arms that were now tied behind his back. Antoine sucked in the night air through the sacking. He could hear the slapping of water against a quay and hear rigging stirring in the breeze. One of the men frogmarched him up a short gangplank. He stumbled when he reached the top, where he was unceremoniously thrown on the floor. The sound of the feet around him suggested that there were three or four men. They were speaking fast and in urgent whispers to each other. Antoine could not understand a word. He heard a door opening. Then he was hoisted up from behind and dragged to the top of some stairs. A man grabbed his feet from below and he was lowered into the cargo hold. He was shoved onto what felt like a large sack of rice. The door to the hold was slammed shut, and all the residual light that Antoine could see through the hood vanished. He put out his hands to feel his way round. There was very little space to move in as the hold was full of sacks and crates. He found the ladder up to the hatch, pushed up against it, but it was firmly locked.

After ten minutes he felt the boat judder into life as the engines were turned on. He heard the gangplank being hauled up and stowed on board. At that moment, two shots rang out, followed by the sound of feet running along the deck over his head. There was a loud grunt. Then the splash of water as first one, and then a second, heavy object fell into the water. After that, total silence, until the hatch to the cargo hold was wrenched open. Light and air streamed in.

'Are you in there?'

Antoine shuffled across to the steps and started to climb upwards. A hand reached out, grabbed his wrist and hauled him up. He felt the hood being untied and lifted off. Antoine blinked furiously, then looked around. In front of him were two of Pak Hung's Triads, looking grim-faced. Behind them were the bodies of two of his captors, one with a bloody hole on his forehead. He assumed the other two had been dumped overboard.

Without a word, the two Triads turned and led Antoine to a car parked on the quay. One of them opened the side door and gestured for Antoine to get in. As he slid onto the seat, he could see the unmistakeable silhouette of Paul Bernard sitting there.

'They made a mistake there, lifting you outside Pak Hung's. They may all go to university in Paris, but they aren't very intelligent these Communists.'

'Are you sure it was them?'

'Who else would it be? You arrested and imprisoned one of their rising stars. They weren't going to forget that.'

'You deliberately sent me on that mission, didn't you? Now you think I am permanently bound to you because I am a target of theirs, so I might as well sign up with you. Well, you can forget it.'

'It's not as easy as that. You cannot just opt out. This is a fight to the death between different civilizations, different belief systems. You must choose a side. Just remember communism is an international movement now. You've made enemies of them here. They will follow you wherever you go.'

'Just take me home.'

'Rue Mac-Mahon?' sneered Bernard as he signalled to the driver to set off.

CHAPTER 18

The Paris Bourse, October 1929

THE PRICE PAID for raw rubber on the bourse has declined by 58% between January 1929 and October 1929.

Traders paid seventy-three cents per pound of rubber in 1928. In 1929, they paid forty-eight cents per pound.

CHAPTER 19

Long Thành, January 1930

ANTOINE STARED GLUMLY at the barrels of liquid latex as they lay at the gate waiting for collection. The stockpile had been growing for the past two months. No one had been to collect them for shipment from the ports as there was no demand in world markets. Traders were offering prices that no longer met the costs of production, let alone afforded a profit. There was talk among planters of a world depression that could last for years.

'Boss! Boss!' Jouvin was running towards him and shouting at the same time. For such a normally phlegmatic man, he looked worried. 'You better come and see this. The workers have gone on strike. They have refused to come out of the compound for work.'

Antoine followed Jouvin down to the main compound, where the indentured labourers were housed in basic barrack-like buildings. This was the only accommodation that the Rodins had sanctioned for them. As they entered the compound, Antoine looked around at the squalid conditions that the workers were expected to live in. They had to cook their meals outside. Water for washing and cleaning had to be collected from a small river over a kilometre away. The only latrines available were those the workers had dug themselves. When the monsoon rains came, they often overflowed, flooding the site with human waste.

Antoine approached a group of men who were sitting on their haunches in a circle outside the main barrack block. He identified one of them as the person that he and Jouvin usually communicated with when they needed to give orders about what work was required. A combination of pidgin French and hand gestures usually sufficed to get the message across.

'Why no work today?'

'Cao Dai say no work.'

'Who?'

'Cao Dai!'

At this all the men in the group put their hands together and bowed. They looked as though they were praying.

'No understand. Who is Cao Dai? Why no work today?' Antoine could feel his patience draining away.

The man gestured to Antoine to follow him into the barrack block. They mounted the few steps and went inside. There were rows of men lying on rattan mats on the floor. Most of them were dozing. The man pointed to something hanging from the roof at the back of the block. Antoine went up to it to get a closer look. It was a large silk wall hanging strung from a joist in the roof. In the middle of the hanging was a black triangle with what looked like an eye staring out from it. The man put his hands together and bowed down before it.

'Cao Dai.'

Antoine stood there for a few seconds staring up at the hanging, none the wiser as to why the workforce had downed tools. Despite the poor conditions they had laboured under since the plantation had started, they had never had any problems getting them to work. They had always been meek and compliant. Antoine had assumed that this was because they were indentured to Pak Hung and were fearful of the consequences if they stepped out of line. He turned to leave but had an unnerving sensation as he walked towards the door of the barrack block that he was being watched by the disembodied eye in the ceiling.

He gestured to Jouvin to follow him and left the compound.

'You're not going to let them get away with that, are you?' Antoine could hear the exasperation in Jouvin's voice. 'I could give a couple of them a good beating. That might get them going. Or we could do what we did in the war. Take the ringleader and execute him in front of the rest of them. It worked in the army, so I don't see why it wouldn't do here.'

'No. We are up against something stronger than a couple of bad apples stirring up the rest. They seem to be following some spiritual leader or belief system that is instructing them not to work. I don't know, but I am going to find out, and then we might be able to deal with it.'

That evening, Antoine drove down into Saigon. He parked up on Rue Catinat and went looking for Vincent Bonnet in his usual haunt, the Café de la Musique. He found him, as he thought he would, at a table on the terrace, nursing a bottle of red wine.

'Can I join you, Vincent?'

‘Ah, Antoine! Good to see you again. Of course, of course, pull up a chair.’

Vincent called the waiter over to order more wine and another glass.

‘I see that you have been very busy since we last met. You and the wonderful Madame de la Souchère. You lucky dog.’ Vincent chuckled as he grabbed hold of and shook Antoine’s thigh. ‘Quite the talk of the town you two. Even provided me with some good copy in my gossip column, although, of course, I was very discreet. How’s that going then? Still an item?’

‘Yes, Vincent, we are still together.’

‘How’s the business? Not looking too good, I guess, with the depression.’

‘No, it is tough right now. In fact, it was business that I wanted to talk to you about. I have got some labour troubles on the plantation. The workforce has basically gone on strike. When I met with them this morning, I couldn’t get much sense out of them, except they seem to be motivated by something, or someone, called Cao Dai. Does that mean anything to you?’

‘Ah Cao Dai. Yes, I have been hearing more and more about this recently. Basically, it is a new spiritual movement that is sweeping across Cochinchina. Started, interestingly, by a district administrator in the province, one of the locals. Think he is called Ngo Van Chieu. Anyway, he had a vision of a divine eye that told him that there was going to be a third time of redemption, or some such claptrap. You can see this divine eye symbol springing up all over the place, on street side altars, banners, in shops. Spreading like wildfire.’

‘But what does it stand for?’

'Not too sure, to be honest. But it is millennial. Always bad news. Means that its followers have lost all reason. They think that there is going to be an apocalypse shortly, followed by their redemption. The rest of us, non-believers, perish.'

'Why would it lead my workers to go on strike, though?'

'Again, not too sure. Maybe you will have to go back to them and find out what it is that their deity wants. If you pose the question that way, they might be able to tell you. It might be as simple as letting them practise their religion on the plantation or giving them time for ceremonies. Worth a try.'

'Thanks, Vincent, I really appreciate your advice, as always.'

Antoine decided to go back to the plantation that night, so he could meet with the workers first thing in the morning and start the dialogue. As he crested the hill that overlooked the valley where the plantation was located, he could see a huge ball of flames and a pillar of black smoke reaching into the sky below him. He pushed the accelerator to the floor and careered down the track and into the main yard of the plantation.

He followed the groups of men carrying buckets of water running towards the workers' compound. As he approached, he could feel the intense heat and the stinging embers falling on his bare arms and legs. He took off his neckerchief, doused it in a nearby bucket of water and tied it round his mouth and nose to provide some protection against the suffocating smoke. The men had started to form a chain gang, down which they passed the buckets of water. But their actions were futile. The fire raced through the bamboo buildings, consuming everything in its path.

Antoine looked around to see if he could see Jouvin. He was standing at the front of the chain gang furiously heaving each bucket of water as it was passed to him onto the fire. Antoine ran up to him, grabbed him by the collar and dragged him away. He held him down on the floor and screamed into his face.

'Did you do this, you bastard! I told you I would sort it out in my way.'

Jouvin lay submissively on the ground below him. His face was black from the smoke and streaked in sweat. Antoine could feel that his arms were trembling through his exertions in trying to put out the fire.

'No, I didn't do it. After someone raised the alarm, I ran down here as quickly as I could. I was passed by three or four men, dressed in black with masks over their faces, running in the opposite direction. I then heard a car or truck racing out of the yard. They set the place alight, not me.'

Antoine let go of Jouvin's collar. He pulled him from the ground.

Antoine knew then that it had been either the Communists or the Triads who had burnt down the compound. It didn't matter which. In either case, they aimed to send him a message.

The next morning, Antoine and Jouvin inspected the damage. The compound buildings had been destroyed. Nothing remained apart from a smoking pile of black ashes. Among the debris, he could pick out the charred remains of at least five men, who had not been able to flee the buildings in time. They were so badly burnt that it was not possible to identify them. Spread out on the ground to one side was the Cao Dai wall hanging. The eye in its middle stared unblinkingly skywards.

Antoine heard a truck pull up behind him. He turned

to see a grim-faced Marguerite coming towards him. She pushed past him and stood looking down at the blackened remains of the compound buildings. He could see her shoulders start to heave and hear the gulps of air as she fought back the tears. He stepped up behind her and placed his hands gently on her back. She froze and then shook him off. She turned and, without looking at him, ran back to the truck.

'Marguerite!'

He continued to shout her name until the back of the truck had disappeared down the track.

CHAPTER 20

Long Thành, February 1930

ANTOINE LET A week go by before he decided to visit Marguerite. He had heard nothing from her. He hoped that her anger would have subsided. He needed to be able to explain to her that the way the workers were treated on the plantation was down to the Rodins and not him. He thought she knew that as they had talked about it many times. On his own small plantation, he followed her policy of employing free labour and providing decent facilities. Not that there was any work for anyone now, labourers, overseers or plantation managers, as the depression had brought all production to a halt, with no sign of it restarting.

As he drove up to the gates of the Plantations du Tan Loc, he was struck by the silence and stillness that met him. There was none of the usual hustle and bustle of a busy estate. As he got closer to the gates, he could see a large poster with lettering in bold red capitals plastered across them.

REPRIS DE POSSESSION.

Antoine got out of the truck to take a closer look at the information on the poster. It was a repossession order for the whole of the Plantations du Tan Loc, signed by René Thion de la Lacaze, director of the Banque de l'Indochine. No one could enter the property unless they were an employee or representative of the bank.

Antoine stared through the gates down the track that led up to Marguerite's house. There was no sign of any movement, apart from the rustling of the leaves on the serried ranks of rubber trees.

Antoine climbed back into the truck. He knew that Marguerite had taken on additional loans when times were good. He did not realise that she had been so overextended as to risk the whole plantation and everything that went with it. He swung the truck round and immediately set off for Saigon to see if he could find her there.

His heart sank as he drove down Rue Mac-Mahon and saw the same poster pasted onto the gate leading up to Marguerite's townhouse. The bank had repossessed everything that she owned.

He set off on foot to find Vincent Bonnet in his office at *Le Journal de Saigon*. He pushed open the door. Vincent looked up from his typewriter.

'Ah, Antoine, I thought you might pay me a visit.'

'So, do you know where Marguerite has gone? All her properties have been seized by the bank and there is no sign of her or anyone else at them.'

Vincent pushed a copy of the paper across to Antoine, opened at the page where his latest gossip column was printed. The headline read 'Leading Planter Flees Colony for Homeland'.

One of Saigon's most prominent plantation owners has fled the colony within a week of her properties being repossessed by the Bank of Indochina. Madame de la Souchère, a leading light in the local Chamber of Agriculture and a founder member of the Cercle Sportif Saigonnais, was seen boarding a ship for Marseille on Tuesday this week. She was accompanied by two of her most loyal servants. Sources from the shipping company state that she had not booked a return ticket and had requested an excess baggage allowance. Her townhouse on Rue Mac-Mahon has a repossession order from the bank on its front gate. When approached, a spokesman from the bank refused to comment, stating that they do not discuss the affairs of their clients. A leading local plantation owner, speaking anonymously, said that the bank had treated Madame de la Souchère very harshly. Everyone knows that we are in the middle of a world recession and that all rubber plantations are struggling. He did not understand why the bank had picked on her, unless they were using her as an example for others.

'Do you know anything more than what's printed here?'

'No, not really. She left in such a hurry that no one seems to know much more than what's in there. Can you enlighten me?'

Although Antoine liked Vincent a lot, he was not about to reveal his private affairs or thoughts to a gossip columnist.

'Not much. She had borrowed a lot to improve the facilities on the plantation. I didn't realise that she wasn't able to repay the loan. I'm in the same position myself now.

I will have to hand my small plantation back to Pak Hung. There is no way I can meet his payments.'

'I'm sorry, Antoine. On both counts. I know you had grown very close to Marguerite.'

Vincent paused.

'What are you going to do now?'

'Return to France. Maybe look for Marguerite. Work for the Rodins again, even though I despise them.'

Vincent got up from his desk. He gave Antoine a brief hug. They shook hands. They knew that this would be their last meeting.

CHAPTER 21

Hotel des Postes, Saigon, February 1930

TELEGRAM. FROM ANTOINE Martinet to Édouard Rodin.

> RETURNING TO TAKE UP OFFER OF WORK STOP LEAVING JOUVIN IN CHARGE STOP EXPECT TO ARRIVE END OF APRIL STOP

Hotel des Postes, Saigon, February 1930, later the same week

Telegram from Paul Bernard to Daniel Gallopin.

> MARTINET RETURNING TO CLERMONT STOP MAKE CONTACT IMMEDIATELY STOP DEPLOY UNDERCOVER STOP STILL OURS STOP

PART 2

France

CHAPTER 22
Clermont-Ferrand, September 1931

THE FACTORY SIREN at the large Rodin works in Clermont wailed to signal the end of the day shift. Hundreds of workers poured out of the workshops and quickly left the factory on foot and on bicycles. A few men stayed behind and started to collect in the main yard. Most had changed out of their work overalls into dark suits. Some of the younger men in the group wore light-blue shirts, dark-blue trousers and black berets. All of them were carrying thick walking sticks or wooden cudgels.

Antoine came out of the main office from where he had watched the men assembling. He, like them, was dressed smartly in a black suit. On his chest he had pinned the medals he had been awarded in the war. When he arrived in the middle of the yard, he barked out an order.

'Men, fall in.'

Within a few seconds, the men had formed two ranks of ten.

'Attention.'

The men brought their heels together and thrust back their shoulders, all looking straight ahead towards Antoine.

'All right, men. You know what today is. It is the day that we commemorate our comrades who fell at the First Battle of the Marne. A few of you were there. But all of you understand the sacrifices made on that day to protect our capital from the invading Boche. That was our enemy then and may be our enemy in the future. But for now, we face a new invasion. Bolshevism! So, as part of our commemorations this year, we are going to pay our communist friends in the town, some of whom work in this factory, a little visit.'

This was greeted with murmurs of approval.

'We are going on a raid into Champretel. The Communists are holding a meeting in one of the halls on the main avenue. Our aim is to disrupt it and intimidate anyone thinking of joining up with them. Those of you who have been on one of these before know the rules. We crack a few heads. We bust a few noses. We do not do any permanent harm to anyone, so no excessive violence. Understand?'

There were murmurs and nods of agreement from the men.

'After that we will pay a visit to the Communist Party office. Put it out of commission. Then return here. Now, get ready for inspection.'

Antoine proceeded to walk down the two lines of men. He recognised most of them. They were veterans from the last war whom the Rodins had employed at the factory. Most of them had been awarded the Croix de Guerre for their bravery. They still exuded military discipline in the way they dressed and conducted themselves. They were all fervently anti-communist. There were a few younger men, who had not served in the war. They had joined the Croix-de-Feu's recently formed paramilitary wing. Antoine congratulated them on the smartness of their uniforms. He could sense that some of them were nervous before their first experience of street fighting, so he gave them some words of encouragement.

While Antoine was speaking, a couple of open-top trucks had driven into the yard. These had had their factory markings covered over to disguise who had donated them for the raid. Antoine did not understand why, because everyone in the town knew that the Rodins sponsored this activity. It would allow the gendarmes to turn a blind eye. Not that they would intervene as they had already been forewarned of the raid through the usual channels.

'Okay, men. Mount up and let's go.'

Antoine climbed into the cabin of the lead truck alongside the driver, whom he recognised from their previous sorties.

'Pierre, isn't it? You know where you are going, yes?' Pierre nodded. 'Take us to the meeting hall first. Stay outside until we have done what we need to do. Then we will go on to their office. It's only a few hundred metres further along the avenue. Again, wait outside, pick us up and bring us back. OK?' Pierre nodded again.

They set off. The two trucks trundled through the old city, across the cobbled streets. People walking on the pavements cast them a quick glance, then looked away. Everyone knew who they were and what they were about to do. No one was going to raise the alarm.

After ten minutes, they entered the Champretel district as the gas street lights were coming on in the darkening early autumn evening sky. Behind the main avenue where the shops and cafés were located, there were rows of terrace houses and barrack-like apartment blocks that had been thrown up by private speculators and the municipal authorities to house the migrants flooding into the town for work. Some of these came from the surrounding countryside, just as Antoine had done when he left his father's farmstead in Cantal after the war. Most of them were Italians, who had crossed the Alps in their thousands. They had brought with them the extreme politics of their homeland, both left and right.

Antoine could see the meeting hall a few hundred metres down the avenue. It looked as though the rally was about to start as a few stragglers were hurrying into the door. There were two burly men standing outside acting as security and lookouts.

'Put your foot down, Pierre. They've already seen us. We need to get in there fast to catch them off guard.'

Pierre gunned the engine and accelerated across the road so that the back of the truck was sideways on to the door of the hall. Antoine banged his fist onto the back of the truck's cabin as they approached the pavement. The men were already jumping out of the back of the truck before it had come to a stop.

Antoine leapt out and barrelled into the first of the two men on the door who had rushed out to challenge them. Without a word, Antoine pinned him to the floor and swung the cudgel he had taken out of his coat pocket into the side of his head. The man let out a groan before he passed out. Within seconds, the two truckloads of men had piled into the hall. They raced down the aisle towards the stage, where there were a couple of speakers sitting behind a table draped with a red and yellow hammer and sickle flag. The audience of men and women started to scream and shout. Most of them tipped over their chairs and scrambled for the doorway. A few of the men started to grapple with the intruders. Some of them picked up chairs to throw at their attackers but most of them resorted to their fists. They were no match for Antoine's disciplined troops, who made short work of them with their flailing clubs. Antoine marched up to the stage, seized the flag and ripped it off the table. He grabbed the collar of the nearest speaker and threw him off the back of the stage, quickly followed by the table, which landed on top of him.

It was all over in a few minutes. Men were lying unconscious in crumpled heaps over the overturned chairs. The hall had been completely emptied of its audience.

Antoine signalled to his men to follow him. They ran outside, remounted the trucks and drove down the avenue. They arrived at the Communist Party office to find that a few of the party activists had left the meeting to warn those inside that Antoine and his men were on their way. They had managed to barricade the inside of the office door with desks and filing cabinets. Antoine ordered his men to dismount. He then instructed Pierre to ram the front of the office with the truck. Pierre reversed the truck to the other side of the avenue. He revved the engine and then drove it fast across the road, mounted the pavement and aimed the truck's bonnet at the office door. There was the sound of splintering wood and exploding glass. The tables and filing cabinets behind the door toppled over backwards. Antoine's men pushed the doorway open and charged in. All of those inside had fled out of the office's back door and down the alley that ran behind the building. They scattered among the terrace houses and apartment blocks. Antoine told the men not to follow them, as it could be a trap.

Antoine hauled a barrel of kerosene from the front of the second truck. He unscrewed the lid and poured the contents all over the floor and what remained of the office furniture. He told the men to get in the trucks, and for the drivers to reverse away from the front of the building. Antoine lit a match and threw it into the office as he retreated. There was an immediate whoosh of flame. Within seconds the first floor of the office was alight. It did not take long for the flames to snake up the stairs to the second floor. As they drove away, they could see black smoke billowing out of the windows of the offices on both floors.

The trucks raced back to the factory yard. The men were exultant, cheering and singing as they lurched from side to side in the back of the vehicles. As soon as they arrived, they leapt off and changed back into the clothes they had worn into work. Antoine briefly called them to order again. There were a few bloody noses but no serious injuries. It had been a perfect operation.

'All right, men. You have done very well today. Let's dedicate that action to our brave comrades who did not survive the Marne. Salute, brothers. Dismiss!'

The men gave out a huge cheer before leaving the yard to resume their normal lives.

Antoine looked up behind him at the windows of the company's boardroom. Staring down at him were André and Édouard Rodin.

CHAPTER 23

Café Dominique, Paris, October 1932

ANTOINE WAS SURPRISED that the summons had taken so long. He had expected to be contacted as soon as he had disembarked in Marseille and taken up employment again with the Rodins. Instead, they had waited for over a year before he got a message that they wanted to meet. Antoine knew they would have their reasons for the delay. They just would not explain it to him.

He had taken a night train from Clermont, arriving at the Gare de Lyon just as the city was bustling into life for the day ahead. He took the metro, getting off at Invalides, as instructed. Looking around him, he could see that he was in the centre of the district from where the country was ruled. He passed by a succession of imposing government buildings, with their white marble slabs and faux Roman columns, designed to provoke awe in people like him, up from the provinces.

It was not to one of these buildings that Gallopin had directed him. Instead, they were to meet in Café Dominique, on Rue du Bac. It was run by a Prince Vyazemsky, an impoverished White Russian general, who had fled to Paris in the 1920s after the civil war.

Antoine pushed open the café door, pulling aside the bead curtain to let himself in. Gallopin was sitting in the far corner, facing him. The last time Antoine had seen him had been thirteen years ago. Antoine, as an infantry corporal, had been ordered by his regimental commander to provide Gallopin with the names of the army mutineers. Antoine was further ordered to command the firing squad that executed them. This had been the moment when the Sûreté had, as far as it was concerned, recruited him. They had tightened their grip in Indochina by enlisting him in a mission to hunt down members of the Communist Party.

Antoine gave a short appraising glance towards Gallopin. He noticed that his long, swept-back hair was turning grey at the sideburns. He was thickening around the waist, presumably from all the desk work he had to do. He wore the same outfit now as he had worn all those years ago, with his unbuttoned white satin shirt partially concealing the Star of David on his hairless chest.

Gallopin got up and offered his hand. Antoine ignored it and sat down.

'Antoine, you look very well. Must be all that tropical sunshine and colonial lifestyle.'

'You can quit the small talk, Gallopin. You haven't made me come all the way up here just to swap pleasantries.'

'True. Down to business, then. So, I understand that the Rodins asked you back to do some work for them. Can you tell me what that entails?'

'I don't know why I am telling you this as you already know, as the Rodins seem to work hand in glove with the security service. Or at least, they have the local gendarmerie in their pockets.'

'You are wrong, Antoine. We don't know what the Rodins are up to. We have our suspicions, but we are not completely sure. To be honest, we don't really trust them. They, along with some other big industrialists and bankers, seem to be funding the right-wing leagues, like the Croix-de-Feu and the Camelots du Roi, but for what purpose is not clear. It could be just to protect their narrow business interests by intimidating the trade unions and Communists. Or, and this is our concern, they may be aiming to overthrow the Republic and set up some authoritarian regime. It could be royalist, or it could be along the lines of what Mussolini has established in Italy. We really don't know.'

Antoine said nothing. He needed to know where this conversation was leading before committing himself to anything.

'So, Antoine, what do you actually do for them?'

'They asked me back from Indochina to take up again the role that I had with them before they sent me over there to manage their plantation. Essentially, I oversee their security at the factory in Clermont. However, this time they have given me the broader brief of organising the Croix-de-Feu in the east and south of France. They fund the organisation and want me to turn it into something more disciplined and effective. As far as I can see, they want it to counter left-wing organisations, particularly the Communists, who try and recruit their workers as members.'

'And when you say they want it to be more disciplined and effective, does that mean that they are creating a paramilitary body? Are they arming them?'

'No. I instil a military-like discipline. We have adopted uniforms to give them an identity. We are organising them into regiments and battalions in towns and cities. The only weapons they have are their fists and the odd knuckleduster and cudgel to bloody some noses. They have no arms.'

'Antoine, what loyalty do you have to the Rodins?'

Antoine knew that this was the tipping point of the conversation, the moment when he would have to go one way or the other.

'Not a lot. They gave me an opportunity when they sent me to Indochina. But the way they wanted things run there on their plantations, and the people they were in league with, disgusted me.'

'Such as?'

'The banks, the money lenders, the Chinese compradors they got to source their labour. They were predatory and vicious, and I colluded with them, much to my personal cost.'

'You mean, Madame de la Souchère?'

Antoine shot him a sharp glance.

'How do you know about her?'

Gallopin hesitated.

'Of course, Bernard would have told you.'

'Well, we are paid to find out what is going on.'

'Do you know where she is?'

'No. Once she left Indochina, she ceased to be of interest to us. But, if you continue to help us, I could find out if she came back to France and where she is.'

'What do I have to do in return?'

'Basically, just report back to me what the Rodins are up to. We are not interested in the anti-communist stuff. That's to be expected. Who wants to be ruled by the Bolsheviks? No, we just want to know whether they are looking to undermine the Third Republic.'

'So, I work undercover for you, while carrying on organising the right-wing leagues for them?'

'Yes.'

Antoine looked across warily at Gallopin. He gave a brief nod of the head to acknowledge his consent to the proposal.

Antoine got up to leave. As he did so, he leant in close to Gallopin. 'I want to know where she is. Tell me as soon as you find out.'

CHAPTER 24

Clermont-Ferrand, January 1933

ANTOINE KNOCKED ON the door of the boardroom at the Rodin works. He recalled when he had first visited the room and how that had led him to Indochina. It seemed like a world away, both in time and place.

'Enter.'

Antoine opened the door to find Édouard and André Rodin sitting at the top of a large mahogany table.

'Come in, Antoine. Take a seat. Maybe some wine, or something stronger?'

Antoine noticed that neither of them had a drink in front of them.

'No, thank you.'

'It's some time since we have had a chance to have a chat with you. We thought it was an opportune time to review how our boys are getting on and to make some plans on how best we can use them in the future.' This was Édouard. Antoine was used to the way the brothers worked by now. Édouard was the emollient one. André provided the steel.

'How are we doing with our communist friends?'

'Well, as you know, we have escaped the strikes that have broken out across the rest of the country. We regularly pay them a visit in town to keep them quiet.'

'Excellent. And how are they shaping up as a more organised outfit?'

'The Croix-de-Feu in Clermont and the wider region, stretching across to Lyon and down to Montpellier, is now formed into regiments and battalions. We have a youth section, which is recruiting well. Across the region, we have replicated what we have done here in Clermont in taking on the communist and socialist leagues and trade unions. I think we can say that we control the street in most places.'

'Good, good. I am assuming that although they are organised along military lines, they do not have any weapons?'

'Correct. That would mark a major escalation. It would most probably result in us losing the support of the gendarmerie and bring us to the attention of the Sûreté.'

'Perhaps we should not be so concerned about that.' André had entered the conversation. 'The Third Republic is starting to fall apart. We have this Stavisky affair in Bayonne brewing up. A Jew selling worthless bonds to innocent French citizens. You mark my word, that is going to go badly for the government. We have Jews flooding in from Germany and Italy, all of them Bolsheviks. No, we need to stop being so provincial and get a grip nationally.'

'What do you mean, sir?'

'What I mean, Antoine, is that we need to start collaborating with the other leagues across the country. The Jeunesses Patriotes, Action Française, Camelots du Roi. They may have some petty differences between them, but essentially, they all want to stop the Bolsheviks, the Jews, the Freemasons. We are drawing on the same pool of patriots. So, we need to co-ordinate our actions. Now that there is a military man in charge of the Croix-de-Feu, we should be able to make progress in that direction. What's his name, Antoine?'

'Colonel François de la Roque.'

'Know anything about him?'

'Yes. He fought in Morocco in the Rif wars and at the Somme. After the war he remained in the army and seems to have had a role in its security service, the Deuxième Bureau. Left a few years ago before taking on the leadership role of the Croix-de-Feu. In the short time he has been in charge he has reorganised it along more military lines. He has even set up a vanguard group of activists, *les dispos*, who are available and ready for action at any time. I haven't met him yet personally.'

'Well, maybe you could arrange to do that. We also want you to contact the leaders of the other organisations and suggest a meeting where we can look at joint action. But not just cracking more communist heads. No, we need to crank it up a level. We need to target the source of our ills. The Third Republic itself.'

'That's a big step, sir.'

'We know. But we, and our associates, have deep pockets. We can back this.'

'Just so I am clear, you are suggesting that we arm the leagues. With a view to what?'

'Changing the regime.'

Antoine let those words hang in the air.

'Will you do it, Antoine?'

'I will arrange to meet with them.'

'That's all we ask, Antoine.' Édouard had rejoined the conversation. 'Do you miss Saigon?'

Antoine nodded.

'Well, you will be glad to know that Jouvin reports that the plantations are doing well. We are coming out of the depression, so prices are improving. Pak Hung let us buy out the loan you had taken out on that small plot next to ours. We bought up Madame de la Souchère's estate at Long Thành from the Banque de l'Indochine. We got them at a good price, given that they were distressed assets. Good business all round, don't you think?'

CHAPTER 25
Nice, April 1933

ANTOINE HAD ARRANGED to see Joseph Darnot first in the round of visits that the Rodins had asked him to organise. He was one of the most influential regional leaders of the Croix-de-Feu, overseeing Provence, the neighbouring area to Antoine's. He knew that Darnot was a much-decorated war hero. He also knew, by reputation, that he was an advocate of direct action.

Darnot had invited Antoine to meet him at the headquarters of his growing haulage business on the edge of Nice. When Antoine drove into the main yard, he picked out Darnot immediately. He was a powerfully built man, with a pencil-thin black moustache, yelling at his drivers to get moving. Antoine got out of his car and approached him.

'Monsieur Darnot? I am Antoine Martinet.'

'Ah yes, I have been expecting you. We'll go to my office.' For a man who exuded masculinity from every pore, Antoine was surprised by his high-pitched voice.

'You've got to keep on top of these lazy bastards. I have to rely on too many Italian migrants for my liking. Least excuse they get, they skive off.'

He led Antoine into a small office at the side of the yard. There was hardly room for the two of them to squeeze on either side of a desk that was submerged in invoices and order papers.

'Can I offer you a coffee, a pastis?'

'No, I am fine.'

'So, tell me a little bit about yourself. I've heard that you are a veteran like me.'

'Yes. The Marne, Argonne, Champagne, Verdun. Infantry. 97th Regiment.'

'You are being too modest. I have heard that you were a hero at Verdun in that assault on Fort Douaumont.'

'Yes, well, we all did our bit.'

'So, in your message, you said that you wanted to sound me out about something. What, exactly?'

'My employers, the Rodins, are looking to, how can I put this, expand our operations.'

'Expand? How?'

'They, and some other wealthy backers, want us to move beyond street fighting with the reds. They think we should be posing a challenge to the authority of the state. For that, we would need to be more militarised, and we would need access to weapons. They believe that now that we have a military man in charge, the colonel, that we are best placed to lead on this, working with the other leagues, like the Camelots du Roi.'

Darnot snorted. 'Military man in charge, my arse. Colonel de la Roque is no Mussolini. He's like all the other army high-ups. In it for his own gains. I don't trust any of them, not after what they did to me.'

'What do you mean?'

'I'm not bragging, but my army career was as illustrious as yours, if not more so. I too carried out special combat missions at Verdun and then fought right through to the Armistice. When the war ended, I wanted to stay on in the army. I requested a commission. Did they give me one? Did they hell! I worked my way up through the ranks. I'm not one of those St Cyr types, spoon-fed through officer training. No, they are all snobs, protecting their own privileges.'

Darnot's high-pitched voice had risen into a piercing rant. After a while, he calmed down.

'Apologies. But aristos like de la Roque make me sick, even if, technically, he is my commanding officer in the Croix. Come with me.' Darnot stood up, marched out of the office and strode across the yard towards one of the outbuildings. Antoine nearly had to run to keep up. Darnot unclipped a set of keys from his belt and used one of them to open a large padlock on the doors of the building. He beckoned Antoine in, switched on a dim overhead light and then locked the door behind them.

There was a flatbed truck parked at the back of the building. It did not have the Darnot haulage livery on its door or side, unlike the rest of the vehicles that Antoine had spotted in the main yard. Darnot unhitched the tailgate, reached in and pulled a tarpaulin off the rows of boxes packed closely together on the truck's floor.

'I am already a step ahead of the higher-ups.' He lifted the lid on the box nearest to him. Inside were a row of Mannlicher-Carcano bolt-action rifles. In the next box, tightly packed together, were Besozzi fragmentation grenades.

'OK, so not the best, I admit. But, given that my trucks frequently cross the Italian border, the easiest source of weaponry is from there. Most of it is standard First World War issue that is now surplus to requirements. With Mussolini in charge, the Italian police and border officials turn a blind eye to gun running. It is in their interests to support the likes of us. They think at best we can be an ally, at worst cause chaos.'

'Have you tried any of it out?'

'No. That's the next step. I plan over the summer to take the boys up into the Alps and do some live weapon training. Hopefully, by then, I might have expanded the armoury a bit and got some machine guns in.'

Darnot shut the boxes and threw the tarpaulin back over the top of them. They returned to the office.

'So, in answer to your question. Yes, I am already preparing to take up armed resistance if needed. Of course, it will be handy should the Communists ever try a full-blown revolution. But I have brought in this stuff with the longer-term view of overthrowing the Third Republic and replacing it with something more to our liking.'

A silence descended between them.

'And where do you stand, Antoine?'

'I'm just the go-between at the moment, sounding out people to see if they have an appetite for more radical action.'

'OK. Well, I can tell you that you need to go and meet the Paris lot. Deblonde, Fignon and Jeantot. They are all in Action Française and the Croix. They head up the divisions in the capital. They are also waking up to the fact that de la Roque is a traditional conservative and not a radical leader of men. They do have an appetite for direct action.'

Antoine stood to leave.

'Thank you, Joseph, for these contacts and for showing

me the hardware. I will be back in touch once our plans have taken more shape.'

'You had better. I am getting impatient. And, Antoine?'

'Yes?'

'You are one of the few people who now know about this arms stash. Let's keep it that way, shall we.'

'Of course.'

'Otherwise…' Darnot drew a finger across his throat.

CHAPTER 26
Rue de Milan, Paris, June 1933

WHEN ANTOINE HAD first become involved with the Croix-de-Feu, it was based in the offices of *Le Figaro*, the newspaper. This was through the sponsorship of the perfumier, Francois Coty. When Colonel de la Roque became its leader, he moved the Croix's headquarters to a rather austere building on Rue de Milan. Antoine presumed this was to demonstrate the independence of the movement from its rich backers. As far as Antoine knew, this was for public consumption only, as the Rodins and other large employers still funded the organisation.

Antoine had arranged a meeting with the colonel, ostensibly to give a progress report on his region's activities. In reality, he wanted to find out how much he knew about the plans being discussed by the Rodins and their associates and, if he did know anything, where he stood on them.

'Antoine. It is good to see you. I think this is the first time we have met.' The colonel stood up and shook Antoine's hand. He was an urbane man, dressed in a charcoal-grey double-breasted suit, with slicked-back black hair cut close to his scalp. His back was ramrod straight as befitted an ex-senior military man. He wore a large pin in his breast pocket, displaying a skull resting on two crossed swords, the emblem of the organisation.

'So, how is it going down in Clermont and Lyon?'

'Membership is growing, particularly among the young. We hold regular marches. The sales of the newspaper are going well. We are on top of the Communists and the trade unions.'

'That is good to hear.'

'My employers, the Rodins, who, as you know, are generous benefactors, wanted me to ask you what plans you have for further developing the organisation. They feel that the times we are currently living in, what with the growing Stavisky scandal and the corruption of the left-wing government, demand that we do more than we are currently.'

The colonel leant forward on his desk and stared intently at Antoine.

'Well, I am not sure what they mean by doing more. What I intend to do is to engage politically, while maintaining our pressure on the street. We can win a place in the Third Republic by promoting a new philosophy. We must put the social interest first, by bringing the different sides of industry together to remove conflict, reform parliamentary procedures so that they are no longer corrupt, give workers a minimum wage and enfranchise women. Women, after all, are the true conservatives and will vote for us. Finally, we must get rid of the Jews or reduce their influence in society.'

'So, you are still supportive of the Third Republic?'

'Yes. But only if we can clean up the corruption.'

'And you want the Croix to remain unarmed?'

'Of course! The only people who should bear arms are the gendarmerie and the army.'

'Thank you for clarifying your thinking. I shall report back to the Rodins. I am sure they will welcome this update.'

'Please pass on my thanks for their continued support.'

CHAPTER 27

Rue Nicolo, Passy, Paris, June 1933

THE LEADERSHIP OF the Croix-de-Feu lived in the exclusive 16th arrondissement, one of the wealthiest neighbourhoods in Paris. Antoine found himself in the early evening outside a building constructed in the Art Deco style on Rue Nicolo. He rang the bell. A concierge in a stiff short white jacket opened the door.

'Monsieur Antoine Martinet to see Monsieur Eugène Deblonde.'

'Follow me please, Monsieur Martinet.'

They crossed a white marble floor in the hall and went up a curving staircase with handrails made from tightly wrought black ironwork. Overhead swung a chandelier giving off a soft yellow light from its candle-like bulbs.

The concierge opened the double doors, which led into a sitting room that took up the whole frontage of the house. Spread around the room, some sitting, some standing against the mantlepiece, was a group of men. The air was blue with tobacco smoke.

The concierge announced his name. One of the men

rose from an armchair and approached Antoine, with his hand outstretched.

'Antoine. Welcome. I am Eugène.'

Eugène Deblonde was a short, stocky man. His receding dark hair was offset by a pair of bushy eyebrows and a black moustache, which looked as though it had been enhanced by hair dye. Despite his stature, his every movement projected dynamism and physical energy.

'Let me introduce you to everybody. This is my brother Henri.'

Like his brother, Henri was short and stocky. However, he lacked his brother's vitality. His skin was pallid. His handshake, damp and limp.

'Here we have Gabriel Jeantot.' A tall, languid man stood up and nodded his head in acknowledgement. He peered down at Antoine through a pair of wire-framed glasses that gave him a professorial air.

'And finally, Jean Fignon.' Jean raised a hand and waved across the room. All of the men were dressed with a casual elegance, apart from Jean. His jacket had worn thin at the elbows. He had a couple of days' stubble on his top lip and cheeks. From his eyes, two jet-black pupils stared intently at Antoine, as though he was eyeing up some prey.

'I'm pleased to meet you all.'

'Paul, get Monsieur Martinet here a drink. Sit, Antoine, sit.'

Antoine found a chair where he could survey the group all together.

'So, Antoine, how are things going down in the provinces?'

Antoine tried his best to ignore the Parisian condescension. 'Good, if you mean in terms of the growth of the organisation and dealing with the reds. I won't waste your time, though, with this banal stuff. What I am here to talk to you about is whether you are prepared to go further than cracking a few communist heads and take on the real enemy.'

'And that is?' asked Henri Deblonde.

'The Third Republic, of course.'

Antoine had got their attention now. He continued. 'I have been speaking to Joseph Darnot in the south. He said that you had lost patience with the current leadership of the Croix and wanted to take more radical action. Is that right?'

Eugène Deblonde stood up and started to stride round the room as he spoke.

'God, yes. We are sick of the timidity of the leadership. The colonel does nothing but prattle on about his *social d'abord*. Which even includes giving women the vote!' he scoffed. 'No, there is a sizeable group of us in Paris who want to take radical action. The Third Republic is corrupt to its core, held to ransom by the Bolsheviks and the Jews. It must be overthrown.'

'And how do you intend to do that?'

'We think that we must go underground for a period. We must build a paramilitary organisation with access to its own arms. We need to infiltrate the army and get them to lead a coup against the state, with our support on the streets.'

'Do you have the funds for that?'

'We have some serious backing from leading industrialists and bankers. Including, we think, the Rodins, your employers. They are biding their time. Watching how events unfold. Looking for us to prove ourselves.'

'How are you going to do that?'

'We believe that there is a showdown coming between the right on the streets and the establishment over this whole Stavisky affair. When that blows up, we think we will have an opportunity to seize power. If that fails, then we must prepare to go underground, work with the army, the security services, whoever, to bring the Third Republic down.'

'And replace it with what?'

'Something that resembles what Mussolini has achieved in Italy. An authoritarian regime.'

'You understand that I will report this back to the Rodins. They want to know how serious you are about this before committing more funds. I think I can convince them to back you.'

The whole group raised their glasses for a toast.

'Down with the Republic!' exclaimed Eugène.

'Down with the Republic!' the others echoed.

Antoine was on the point of leaving when Gabriel Jeantot put a hand on his arm. 'Antoine, the night is young. You must come out with me and Jean and sample some Parisian nightlife.'

Antoine hesitated. He needed to get a train back south in the morning. He started to decline. Before he could get to the end of his sentence, they thrust his arms into his jacket and bundled him out of the front door.

CHAPTER 28

La Boule Rouge, Rue de Lappe, Paris, June 1933

THE THREE MEN weaved their way from the 16th arrondissement towards the Latin Quarter, stopping off at the occasional bar for a drink. Gabriel and Jean appeared to have a huge capacity for alcohol, which Antoine struggled to match. In every bar they called into, the pair were met with shouts of greeting and offers of drinks. Towards the small hours of the morning they arrived at a seedy-looking street, Rue de Lappe. The street was narrow, with the roofs of the buildings on either side giving the impression that they were leaning over to meet in the middle. Even at this time in the early morning, there were plenty of people flitting between cafés, bars and dance rooms.

'Right, Antoine, time for some serious entertainment to finish the night off.'

Gabriel opened the door of an establishment called La Boule Rouge and pushed Antoine inside.

'This is one of our favourite bal musettes. We get to dance and meet with some lively girls. And if they are coming to this place, then you know that they are easy.'

Gabriel was shouting into Antoine's ear to cut through the wall of noise coming from the musicians playing to one side of the compact dance floor. This was packed with heaving bodies, colliding into each other as they tried to get into the swing of the music. Gabriel steered Antoine towards the bar tucked towards the back of the room.

Gabriel ordered a couple of beers for him and Antoine. Jean seemed to have detached himself from them. Antoine could see him talking very animatedly to a young woman. He was gripping one of her arms and pointing at someone on the dance floor.

'We come here a lot. Apart from the women, these are also good places to find out and pass on information. The police recruit some of the dancers to act as informers, so be careful what you say if you pick anyone up.'

Their conversation was disrupted by the noise of a disturbance breaking out on their left. Antoine looked over to see Jean leaning over the body of a man who was curled up in a ball on the floor. Jean was relentlessly punching the man's face in between kicking him in the stomach. Antoine and Gabriel rushed over and pulled Jean off the man.

'Hey, Jean, give it a rest.'

Jean wrestled free from their grip and swung round. His face was exultant, his dark eyes wide open and alert.

'That shit was talking to my girl, so he got what he deserved.'

Antoine went over to the man lying on the floor, who was not moving. He rolled him onto his back. His face had been beaten to a pulp. A couple of men detached themselves from the onlooking crowd that had gathered around to watch the entertainment. They lifted their friend and dragged him from the dance floor.

'I am going to take Jean home in case the police turn up. Keep in touch, Antoine. Things are going to get interesting from now on.' He gave Antoine a wide smile before steering a reluctant Jean towards the door.

Antoine turned to the bar to finish off his beer. He could still see the look on Jean's face. The last time he had seen that bloodlust was during hand-to-hand combat in the trenches.

'Will you buy me one of those?'

Antoine turned to find a dark-skinned young woman standing a few inches away from him. She had thick curly hair that was fashionably cut to fall just below her ears. Perched on top of her head was a small beret, slanted down to hide one of her eyes. She wore a white blouse with a ruffle down the front and a tight dark-green satin dress.

'Do you want something else, rather than a beer?'

'Yes, I'll have a P'tit Blanc. More refreshing.'

Antoine detected an accent but could not place it.

'You are not French.'

'No. I am from Spain. From just outside Sevilla in the south. I moved to Paris a few years ago. To find work. My name is Carmel.'

'Hello. I am Antoine.'

There the conversation ended. They both stared into their drinks.

'Would you like to dance, Antoine? They are playing a foxtrot.' She held out her hand to him.

Not sure why he agreed, he took her hand and followed her onto the dance floor. He placed his right hand on the small of her back and raised his left hand to take hers.

Immediately, he recalled the sensations that he used to have when dancing with Marguerite. The feel and warmth of her flesh moving softly under the fabric of her skirt as they stepped forward and back. He could smell the mix of perfume and sweat coming from the top of her blouse where there was one undone button. He could feel himself becoming aroused. She pushed her thighs more tightly against his. Her lips parted in a small smile.

The dance finished. Antoine held onto her for a few seconds after the music stopped.

'I must go. I have a train to catch in the morning.'

'I must go too. I will come with you.'

CHAPTER 29

Café Dominique, Paris, June 1933

ANTOINE HAD ARRANGED to brief Gallopin before he returned to Clermont on the train. His brain felt foggy with fatigue after the early morning spent with Carmel in the hotel. His body, on the other hand, still tingled with the sensations of her touch.

Gallopin eyed him with some amusement as he sat down at the table.

'Good night?'

Antoine did not reply. Instead, he ordered himself another cup of black coffee to try and revive himself.

'So, what are they up to?'

'They are starting to split. The radicals are growing impatient with the caution displayed by the leadership of the Croix-de-Feu, particularly Colonel de la Roque. They think he has traditional political ambitions. To set up a party. To run for elections. They want direct action to overthrow the Republic. Either with or without the army.'

'How large a faction are the radicals?'

'In numbers, small. But they hold influential positions

in regional leadership posts. Paris, the south. And they have financial backing from certain quarters of big business. Including the Rodins, who are pushing me to co-ordinate meetings to find out the level of appetite for direct action.'

'How well advanced are their plans?'

'At the first stages. They have started to build a stockpile of weapons, although it is small at the moment. They don't yet have, as far as I can see, an infrastructure that is not part of the existing far-right groups. They haven't made any inroads with the army.'

'So, not too threatening, then.'

'I think the radicals are prepared to play the long game. They will seize any opportunities to attack the state. If those don't arise, then they will go underground and build from there.'

'Opportunities?'

'Look, you are the security service, so you must have your own assessments of the situation. But they see the Stavisky scandal as building and building. That could provide them with a launch pad.'

'We think it will blow over.'

'Fine. But in their circles, they talk about it a lot.'

'Anything else?'

'Yes. And this is for you personally.' Antoine reached across the table and pointed at the Star of David pendant nestling against Gallopin's chest. 'They are increasingly seeing their crusade against Bolshevism as including the Jews. They are one and the same as far as they are concerned.'

Gallopin looked at Antoine for some time, considering his next remark.

'Jews like me are well integrated into French society. They won't get away with that cheap rhetorical trick.'

'If you say so. But have you forgotten how they used Dreyfus's Jewish origins?'

'No. But it is irrelevant for now. OK, we don't want you to do anything different for now. Just keep me abreast of what is going on. I need to know as soon as they cross the line from anti-Bolshevik bashing to sedition. I think that is all.'

'Not quite. Have you found out anything about Madame de la Souchère's whereabouts?'

'No. Not yet. But I can assure you that I have put out informal feelers among our network of agents to flush out any information. As soon as I get some, I will let you know.'

'You had better.'

CHAPTER 30

Le Flambeau, 9 January 1934

STAVISKY FOUND DEAD. POLICE CLAIM SUICIDE

Crooked businessman and Jew, Alexandre Stavisky, was found dead in a chalet in Chamonix yesterday morning.

Police claim that Stavisky had taken his own life in an attempt to evade justice. They have not allowed any independent doctors to examine the corpse to verify their claims.

Colonel de la Roque, leader of the Croix-de-Feu, put out a statement today.

'Without independent corroboration that Stavisky took his own life, it is the belief of my organisation, and many others, that this is an attempt by the police to cover up the misdeeds of their political masters. We accuse the thieves that make up the government of the left, particularly the thief in chief, Édouard Daladier, of having Stavisky MURDERED. This was to prevent him from revealing all when he came to trial.

'As leader of the largest veterans' organisation in France, and as an upholder of the virtues of the Third Republic,

I call on my members to join their comrades from other leagues at demonstrations outside the National Assembly. The demonstrations should have one rallying cry: DOWN WITH THE THIEVES.

'Long live France!'

CHAPTER 31

Le Figaro, 3 February 1934

CHIAPPE FORCED TO RESIGN BY DALADIER. RIGHT-WING LEADERS DEMAND MASS MOBILISATION OF LEAGUES

Popular Prefect of Police for Paris, Jean Chiappe, was forced to resign by Prime Minister Daladier today.

After weeks of street demonstrations by right-wing leagues in the streets of Paris following the alleged suicide of Alexandre Stavisky, Daladier has lost patience with Chiappe, who he claims is too lenient towards the rightists. Supporters of Chiappe say that he has been sacked because he is an anti-communist patriot.

Leaders of all the major right-wing leagues, including veterans' associations, are meeting today to decide what action they should take. This will include a mass demonstration outside the National Assembly, calling on the Radical Socialist government led by Daladier to resign.

CHAPTER 32

Rue Nicolo, Passy, Paris, 5 February 1934

ALL THE COMMANDERS of the Croix-de-Feu's regional divisions had been invited to attend the meeting on the evening before the mass demonstration. Antoine recognised the Deblonde brothers, Jeantot, Fignon and Darnot. Some people he did not know. From his calculations, about half of the divisions across the country were represented in the room.

Eugène Deblonde quelled the hubbub and called the meeting together.

'Thank you for attending. Your presence suggests that you are ready to heed the call for action. Tomorrow evening will witness the largest demonstration in French history against our rulers. Or should I say "so-called" rulers.'

This remark was met by guffaws and derisive whistles.

'Our own leaders, the colonel and his advisors, have instructed that we should lead our men on a peaceful demonstration to call for the resignation of the government. He believes that our sheer weight of numbers will persuade the government to stand down. I think, and I know that you agree with me, that that is utter rubbish.'

The men cheered. Some shouted out their contempt for Colonel de la Roque, calling him a coward.

'Tomorrow is a massive opportunity,' Deblonde paused, 'for us to overthrow the Third Republic and replace it with something more to our liking.'

Again, the men cheered and whistled, this time more loudly.

'While the other leagues, Action Française, Jeunesses Patriotes, Camelots du Roi, will converge on the Place de la Concorde, from the right bank of the Seine, we will take up position on the left bank, right behind the National Assembly. This makes it much easier for us, if we so choose, to storm and occupy the building.'

Silence had descended on the room, as the significance of this remark sank in.

Deblonde slowed down his delivery so everyone could fully understand his next statement.

'We can, through direct action, cause such chaos that the government will fall. There is not an alternative government waiting in the wings, so the country will be ungovernable. At that point, elements within the armed forces will seize power. They will look to replace the Third Republic with something more stable and more to our liking. Along the lines of what Mussolini has established in Italy. Our role is to be the handmaiden for that.'

The room remained silent.

'Do we know if the army is ready to step in?' It was Darnot who had broken the silence.

'We have contacts within the army. They are passing on

the word. I am hopeful that there will be enough of them to step in when called upon.'

Darnot persisted. 'Not all the divisions are represented here. How do you know if the others will follow us? We need force in numbers for this to succeed.'

'I think when they see how easy it will be to storm the Assembly, they will be behind us. Any more questions? No. Good. So, do I have your support for tomorrow?'

The men replied with a cheer. It was more muted than the one that had greeted the start of Deblonde's speech. Antoine looked around him at the faces of the other men in the room. Apart from Jeantot and Fignon, who were slapping each other's backs in premature celebration of tomorrow's victory, the others looked nervous and sceptical.

Antoine slid from the back of the room and let himself out into the freezing cold February air.

CHAPTER 33

Café Dominique, Paris, later that same night, 5 February 1934

'THEY ARE GOING to try and cause such chaos tomorrow night that the government will collapse and the army step in.'

Gallopin eyed Antoine quizzically. He appeared completely unruffled by this statement.

'And how are they going to achieve that?'

'By storming the National Assembly. Seizing the prime minister and Cabinet. Forcing them to resign. Their calculation is that no one else can form a government if they control the streets outside. Then the army steps in to end the chaos.'

'And this is the whole of the Croix-de-Feu, de la Roque included?'

'No, just a faction. Maybe half of the divisions. De la Roque has sent out instructions that the demonstration remain peaceful.'

'We can deal with this. We will have enough force in place to prevent it.'

'You know that I will have to be a part of it, if I am to maintain my credibility with them. I will have to lead my division into the National Assembly.'

'Yes, you do that. I need you on the inside. But, Antoine?'

'Yes?'

'Keep your head down.'

CHAPTER 34

Rue de Lappe, Paris, early hours of 6 February 1934

ANTOINE HAD ARRANGED to meet Carmel outside Des Barreaux Verte, a bal musette, where she worked part-time as a concierge. He could see her small figure, wrapped in a winter coat, huddled against the door as he approached. Her head was wreathed in plumes of condensed air as she exhaled in the freezing night-time temperature. He put his arm through hers, pulled her to him and gave her a long, lingering kiss. This was only the second time they had met. He needed to convince himself that this is what he wanted. As soon as their mouths met and he felt her tongue seek out his, he knew that they would spend another night together.

They walked fast towards the same hotel he had stayed at the last time he was in Paris. It was too cold to linger and speak. They went upstairs to his room. He had hardly closed the door before they were grappling with each other's clothes. Within seconds, he had pushed her down onto the bed and was inside her. It was not long before he climaxed and collapsed on top of her.

Antoine woke with a start. It was still dark outside. The realisation of what was going to happen later that day hit him. He slumped back onto the bed. He felt a hand reach out and take his under the sheets. He could make out Carmel's dark curls spread across the white of the pillow.

'Are you OK?'

'Yes, just a bad dream.'

'About what?'

'The war,' he lied.

'I felt your scars. Are they from then?' She traced a finger across his stomach.

'Yes.'

'Do you want to tell me about them?'

'No,' he said it more brusquely than he meant to.

He removed his hand from hers and used it to stroke back the hair from her forehead.

'Tell me a little bit about yourself instead.'

'Not a lot to tell. I came here a couple of years ago. Or rather, my parents sent me. My father is a landowner in Real de la Jara, just outside Sevilla. For several years, our estate has been targeted by the local anarchists and trade unionists. Our workers went on strike. Then they set fire to our local church. The priest was beaten up. The atmosphere in Spain is getting ugly. So, my parents packed me off to stay safe. I worry about them all the time.'

'Have you been back?'

'No. It is too dangerous. The reds control our pueblo. So, I stay away.'

'How do you make a living?'

'It's OK. I get by. There is a small Spanish community here, though you must be careful who you mix with, as some of them are political exiles. They might not take too kindly to my background. I work evenings as a concierge at the bal musettes where we met tonight.'

'Anything else?'

He could feel her body stiffen slightly.

'Such as?'

'I heard that some of you working at the bals are police informers or work for private investigators.'

'Well, I don't.' She giggled, taking his hand and placing it between her legs.

CHAPTER 35

Place de la Concorde, Paris, 6 February 1934

THEY COULD SEE the runner come weaving between the columns of men who were lined up in divisional formations behind the National Assembly building. He came to a shuddering halt in front of Colonel de la Roque's grey mare and the group of divisional commanders who were grouped around him.

'Take your time, Gaston, get your breath back.'

Gaston, who was no more than seventeen years old, was bent over, clutching his knees, gasping for air. He undid the buttons on his military overcoat to cool himself down, even though the air was starting to freeze as the dusk fell.

'Make your report, Gaston.'

Gaston straightened up and came to attention. His sweating face gleamed in the light given out by the braziers that had been set up to provide the men with warmth.

'Sir, the members of the Jeunesses Patriotes and the Camelots du Roi tried to storm the Concorde bridge over the river to get closer to the National Assembly. The police have erected barricades on the bridge. They have mounted horsemen behind them. A few men got through but were beaten back by the police. There have been many arrests and injuries. I don't think that they are going to be able to get through to join us on this side of the river.'

'Thank you, Gaston. Very clear report.'

From where they were standing, they could hear, but not see, the confrontation taking place on the bridge. The chants of 'down with the thieves, long live France' rose into the air. These were followed by the sound of men's boots clattering over cobbles as they rushed towards the barricades. There was a brief pause before they could hear the collision, with men shouting and groaning, as they pushed against each other, one group intent on breaking through, the other in stopping them. Suddenly, there was the distinctive popping sound of shots being fired that were all too familiar to the listening veterans.

'Christ, they're shooting them. The bastards!'

'Colonel, we need to act now. We must storm the building. The police are occupied on the bridge. We will have the numbers if we act now.' Eugène Deblonde was gripping the bridle of de la Roque's horse and shouting up at him.

'Don't be a bloody fool, Deblonde. Can't you hear that? They are shooting our men down.'

'Well, we can reply in kind.'

'What do you mean, Darnot?'

'I've brought up some rifles from the south, just in case.' Darnot pointed at the flatbed truck that was parked up behind them.

'No. Absolutely not. This is supposed to be a peaceful

demonstration. Our sheer weight of numbers is a clear sign to the government that they must respect our wishes.'

'So, what are we going to do? Just stay here, chanting?' sneered Deblonde.

'Right now, we are going to stand the men down and march out of the square with our heads held high. We have made our point. Give the order to your men.'

The other divisional commanders wheeled away and started to shout out the order to their men to fall into line and prepare to march off. Deblonde, Darnot, Jeantot, Fignon and Antoine stood where they were, refusing to move.

'I gave the order to disband. Follow it. If you don't, you will be expelled from the Croix, with immediate effect,' bellowed the colonel.

The five men turned their backs and walked off towards their own divisions. They waited until the other divisions had marched off, following the colonel riding stiff-backed on his horse, without giving a backward glance at those he was leaving behind.

The remaining men had been briefed about what to do. They took off their army greatcoats and laid them on the ground, removing the wooden cudgels and staves that they had been hiding inside them. Standard bearers with flags of each of the divisions came to the front and raised their banners high into the night sky. A small group from Darnot's division, armed with rifles, detached themselves from the main group. They moved off to the side to provide covering fire in case the police decided to use firearms against them.

Eugène Deblonde strode to the front of the assembled ranks. Silence descended over them.

'Men. Now is the time to take destiny into our own hands. In that building over there,' he pointed towards the National Assembly, 'are a bunch of crooks and thieves who run the Third Republic. We are going in there to throw them out and bring about a new order.'

A wave of 'down with the thieves, long live France!' rose from the ranks. Several men who had fashioned shields out of dustbin lids started to beat them with their cudgels, in time with the chanting. A cloud of steam rose from the men as they waited for the order to move off.

Deblonde raised his arm high in the air and then brought it down in one sudden movement. Antoine, who was now in the front of his division, gave the order to move forward. The columns of men, in serried ranks, started to march across the square towards the Assembly building, keeping a steady pace. When they got halfway across the square, Antoine picked out the sound of horses' hooves emerging from the general hubbub of noise generated by his men's marching boots. Emerging from either side of the Assembly building were two phalanxes of mounted policemen. They met in the middle, creating a solid line from one side of the square to the other.

Deblonde signalled to his divisional commanders to halt their men. The marchers and the mounted policemen were separated by no more than fifty metres. Horses skittered and snorted, twisting backwards and forwards as their riders brought them under control. Jets of hot urine hosed the cobbles under the horses' bellies.

Deblonde walked across the gap so he could address the policemen.

'Brothers. We are all men in uniform. We are all patriots, serving our country. We are here to remove the crooks and robbers holed up in that building. They are not friends of yours. Join us and we can bring down this rotten Third Republic!'

A police sergeant detached himself from the middle of the group. He trotted up slowly towards Deblonde. As he came alongside him, he stopped. He turned in his saddle and hawked onto the ground. A globule of spit glistened on the cobbles below. In one sudden movement, so fast that there was no warning, the policeman raised his baton and brought it crashing down onto Deblonde's head. There was a spurt of blood. Deblonde collapsed in a heap to the ground.

There was a stunned silence. Then, the men gave out a roar and ran towards the police lines. They smashed into them. Some of the horses reared up into the air, bringing their hooves crashing down on the advancing men's heads and shoulders. Others broke ranks and careered around, bowling men over and trampling them underfoot. More experienced veterans, who had faced calvary charges in the early days of the war, grabbed hold of the horses' reins and jerked their heads down. Others reached up and hauled the riders onto the ground and laid about them with their clubs.

Antoine raced up to Eugène's prone figure on the ground and dragged him backwards, away from the thrashing hooves and flailing batons. He could see that his nose was broken. He had a gash on the top of his skull. Blood covered his face. He signalled to two of his men to get hold of Eugène's arms and legs. They grabbed him and scuttled back to their lines to give him medical attention.

Antoine peered through the horses' legs to see whether any of his men had broken the lines of mounted policemen. Only a few had got through. They were sprinting up the steps of the Assembly towards its large wooden doors. As they did so, several shots rang out. Two of the men collapsed and rolled backwards down the steps, landing in a heap at the bottom. A group of armed policemen emerged from inside the Assembly and took up position in front of the doors. They aimed their rifles in the air and let off a volley that went over the heads of the remaining men who had managed to get through the line of horses. The men stopped, turned and ran back down the steps. Antoine waited to see whether Darnot and his unit were going to return fire, but there was no response. He was relieved. He knew that they were just as likely to hit their own men as the enemy when they were fighting at such close quarters.

Antoine got up from his knees. He could feel the pressure of his men being pushed backwards by the mounted police. He knew that the fight had gone out of them. They had been defeated. Men from both sides were lying on the floor, clutching their wounds and broken bones, moaning softly. There was a clattering sound, as the men threw down their cudgels. They retreated to the edge of the square. The police maintained a line across the centre of the square, barring any further access to the steps of the Assembly.

As Antoine was rallying the stragglers from his division and making sure that those that needed it received medical aid, he could hear shouting and cheering coming from the steps of the Assembly. He turned to see that the doors of the building had been thrown wide open. Light was streaming out of the entrance, lighting up the steps. Men were hugging each other and waving pieces of paper in the air.

'Daladier has resigned! The government has fallen! Long live the Republic. Long live France!'

CHAPTER 36

Rue Nicolo, Passy, Paris, 9 February 1934

EUGÈNE DEBLONDE RESTED on the sofa, his back propped up by a couple of pillows. The bruising around his broken nose and swollen eyes was starting to turn from black to a mustard yellow. Jagged black stitching was still clearly visible through his thinning hair.

'I see that the colonel is claiming that the "veterans' march", as he calls it, was directly responsible for the downfall of the leftist government and its replacement by a more amenable one of national unity. Absolute rubbish! Just because you've got people like Marshal Pétain in the government, doesn't mean it will be any better for us. It is still part of the corrupt Third Republic.'

'Calm down, Eugène. You'll burst your stitches if you're not careful.' Henri Deblonde handed a small brandy to his brother. 'It doesn't matter what the colonel thinks anymore. Remember, he's kicked us out of the organisation. We are on our own now. It's what we decide to do next that's important.'

‘Well, I have been giving some thought to that, of course.’ Eugène struggled up from the sofa and walked across to the mantlepiece, along which he could rest his arm and survey the small group of men in front of him. As well as his brother, he had asked Antoine, Fignon, Jeantot and Darnot to this meeting. They had demonstrated their loyalty and commitment by staying beside him at the Place de la Concorde.

‘Now is the time to go underground. To build a paramilitary organisation that can work with the army to prepare for a coup d’état. That way we get to finally deal with the Bolsheviks, Jews and Freemasons. Are you all behind that?’

‘Of course we are. It is just, how do we do all that? There are only six of us, for God’s sake!’ protested Darnot.

‘No. There are more than that. We have financial backing from the likes of the Rodins, Tattinger and Coty. They can rope in others once we prove our credibility. We have the men in our divisions. Some will remain with the colonel, but I bet a lot will follow us once we sell them our mission. We already have contacts abroad, in Italy and Spain, from where we can get weapons. You’ve proved that already, Darnot. Our biggest challenge will be getting the military on our side. Many of them loathe and fear the Communists. We just need to persuade enough of them that they pose a real threat to social order. The beginnings of the leftist popular front we see demonstrating on our streets now is something we can play on.’

‘All true. But how can we grow an organisation if we must operate underground?’ quizzed Jeantot.

‘Good point. I have given that some thought as well. We will have to operate like a secret society. Like the Ku Klux Klan in America, for instance.' Eugène pulled an encyclopaedia from the shelf of the nearest bookcase and opened it to a page with a large black-and-white photograph. It showed two Klansmen from south Tennessee dressed in their full regalia of white cowls and monk-like habits. Antoine found himself unnerved by the two black eye sockets staring out at him from the wizard-shaped hoods.

'I think we can copy plenty from organisations like this. Their members are nominated by others who have already joined who can vouch for them. They go through an initiation ceremony where they must swear allegiance to the cause on pain of death if they betray it or other members. They use terror tactics to intimidate their enemies. They operate on military-like lines. We can learn a lot from them.'

'You're not saying we must wear those stupid clothes, are you? Dress up like some medieval monks?' objected Fignon.

'No. But we could adapt some of them. I think the hood is a good idea. We should definitely use them during initiation ceremonies. And when we conduct terror attacks. In fact, I think it provides us with a name. La Cagoule. The Hood.'

The others murmured their appreciation at Eugène's suggestion.

'Good. I am glad that is agreed. Now, as well as the name, I also have a proposal about how we organise ourselves. I suggest that we operate like an army central staff. We have four different bureaux. The first for recruitment and discipline. The second for intelligence gathering and surveillance. The third for operations and training. And the fourth for logistics and gun running. I will lead the first one. Martinet the second. Jeantot the third, assisted by Fignon.

And Darnot the fourth. My brother will look after the finances. I think that plays to our strengths. Agreed?'

No one objected.

'We start from today. We will meet regularly to report progress and to co-ordinate plans. Your immediate tasks are to start recruiting members in each of your regions. We can form them into cells and build up to battalions, regiments and divisions, if we grow big enough. But you need to initiate each of your new members. I will devise a ceremony and wording for you to use. Then you need to start working on your own areas of responsibility for the wider organisation. Agreed? *Bonne chance!*'

CHAPTER 37

Café Dominique, Paris, later that same day, 9 February 1934

'ARE THEY SERIOUS? How likely is any of that to come off? The Ku Klux Klan, for God's sake!' Gallopin could not hide his disdain or disbelief after Antoine had told him about what had been agreed at the meeting.

'That's for you to work out, not me. More pressingly, if you want me to remain working for you, then I need some help.'

'What kind of help?'

'I need a contact within the army's intelligence service, their Deuxième Bureau. I've got to demonstrate to the others that I'm making inroads with the military. Building up a network of officers who are opposed to the Third Republic and might be prepared to do something about it.'

'I'll see what I can do. The military are suspicious of us. They guard their secrets carefully. The fact is, we already have our eyes on some officers who we think might lead a coup d'état. You would be surprised how high up some of them are. Anything else?'

'No.'

Gallopin stood to leave. As he did so, he slid a piece of paper across the table to Antoine.

'The address you were asking for.'

After Gallopin had closed the café door behind him, Antoine turned the piece of paper over.

Villa Tan Loc, Rue Maréchal, Biarritz.

CHAPTER 38

Clermont-Ferrand, September 1934

ANTOINE PEERED OUT of the eye sockets of his red velvet mask at the new recruits lined up before him. He was sweltering inside the red woollen gown draped over his shoulders that came down to his knees. He could feel the sweat pooling around his waist where the gown was tied tight with a belt of rope. The new recruits were also wearing red velvet masks that were handed to them as they entered the room to hide their identities from each other. This was all part of the elaborate ceremony that Eugène Deblonde had devised to give the Cagoule its aura as a secret society.

Since their meeting in February, Antoine had been building the numbers of members of the Cagoule in his region. He knew that the others had been doing the same in their own areas. Antoine had weeded out those who had wanted to remain loyal to the Croix-de-Feu from his existing divisions. He had then formed the remainder into a new set of battalions for the Cagoule. He had told them that they were being turned into a self-defence force to defend their country against an imminent communist takeover. He withheld the fact they were going to be the shock troops for a coup d'état.

The Rodins had been delighted to support the new organisation, diverting all the money that they had given to the Croix-de-Feu to the Cagoule. In the meeting that he had had with them after the February events, they had accused Colonel de la Roque of having a *froid queue*, a cold dick. With the money they provided, Antoine had been able to buy some weapons from Italy through Darnot. The Rodins had loaned their isolated country mansion in the Massif Central, so Antoine could train his men in live weapons drills. Now, they had handed over one of their large warehouses on the edge of the factory complex in Clermont so Antoine could conduct the initiation ceremony for the new recruits in total privacy.

Beyond the wording for the oath and the red masks, Deblonde had given little further guidance on how he wanted the ceremony to be conducted. Antoine reverted to his Catholic childhood and his visits to mass to create a spiritual atmosphere that might strike reverence and awe into the recruits for the cause they were signing up to. He had fashioned a font-like structure out of some discarded crates he had found in the warehouse. He covered it with a red silk sheet. Around the font he had placed a ring of candles that provided the only light in the room.

Antoine stood in front of the font. In his right hand he held a flag staff with the tricolour attached to it. The room was completely silent, apart from the sound of guttering candles.

Antoine's deputy, who was also dressed in a red mask and full-length gown, tapped the shoulder of the first in line of the new recruits and indicated that he should follow him to the font. When they arrived, the deputy peeled away to the side, leaving the recruit standing on one side of the font, looking across at Antoine on the other side.

'Raise your left hand. Place your right hand on the French flag. And say after me: I swear in the name of Almighty God.'

'I swear in the name of Almighty God.' The recruit's voice was muffled by his mask.

'Louder! Everyone must hear you swear the oath of allegiance.'

'I swear by Almighty God!' shouted the recruit.

'To swear fidelity, discipline and absolute secrecy to the Cagoule!'

'To swear fidelity, discipline and absolute secrecy to the Cagoule!'

Antoine paused. 'On pain of death.'

The recruit faltered. 'On pain of death.'

'Louder.'

'On pain of death!'

As soon as the recruit had finished his oath, Antoine's deputy took hold of his arm and led him to the side door of the warehouse. He unlocked it, pushed the recruit out into the night and then locked the door again. He returned to guide the next recruit up to the font. By the end of the night, they had initiated another twenty-five new members into the Cagoule.

CHAPTER 39

Café Dominique, Paris, October 1934

GALLOPIN HAD SENT through a message to Antoine that he had arranged a meeting with his contact in the army's Deuxième Bureau.

When Antoine opened the door and pushed aside the bead curtain, he could see Gallopin sitting at his customary table at the rear of the café. He was engrossed in a conversation with another man sitting opposite him, whose face was hidden from Antoine. Gallopin stood up to greet Antoine.

'Ah, Antoine, good to see you. Let me introduce you.'

By now Antoine had drawn level with the table. He found himself staring down into a face he had hoped he would never see again.

Paul Bernard stood up very slowly and held out his hand. Antoine ignored it. Even in a chilly Parisian autumn, Bernard was still wearing his crumpled and stained white tropical suit.

'No need for introductions. Monsieur Martinet and I know each other well of old, don't we, Antoine?'

'Ah yes, you said that you worked together in Indochina.'

Antoine had recovered himself after the initial shock of seeing Bernard again.

'Yes. I can't say that any of it was voluntary… or pleasant.'

'Now, now, Antoine. We were only doing our duty. Both of us.'

'What are you doing in France? You were a big fish in a small pond when I left Saigon. You'll be a bit out of your league here.'

'The army called me back. Thought they could use my nose for a communist to root out any subversives hiding in the ranks.'

Gallopin intervened. 'OK, let's get down to business. Antoine, I have explained to Paul that you are working for us and that we need to protect your cover. So, tell Paul what you need from him.'

'I've been tasked with making contacts with officers in the army who have authoritarian sympathies, enough that they might contemplate overthrowing the Republic. Apart from giving me credibility within my organisation, it could also make them break cover. So, when the time comes, they can be arrested.'

'These people are well known within the army. Many of them are high up or have recently retired but are still influential with those they have left behind. I can get you some introductions.'

'Well, I will leave you two alone, so you can catch up on your times in Indochina together.'

Antoine turned to stop Gallopin from leaving, but he was already halfway to the door.

After Gallopin had left, Bernard leered at Antoine. 'Still seeing that aristo communist?'

'What?'

'You know, Madame de la Souchère.'

'She wasn't a communist. She just treated her workers well.'

'She did more than that. She was a communist sympathiser. She protected the likes of your friend Den Hieu.'

'You're a liar!'

'No, I'm not. You didn't see it because you were besotted with her.'

'Fuck off, Bernard.'

'It was me, you know, who made sure that she couldn't stay in Indochina.'

'What do you mean?'

'It was me that went to the Banque de l'Indochine. I told de la Lacaze that he had to foreclose on her estate, even though she could have survived financially. I said that it was a matter of state security. That the bank had to act in the national interest and bankrupt her. They knew, at the end of the day, who they must keep sweet.'

Antoine said nothing. His hands were gripping the underside of the table, his blood draining from his knuckles.

'One last thing. I wasn't responsible for bankrupting you. That was just Pak Hung. Just doing business. Goodnight, Antoine, I will be in touch.'

CHAPTER 40
Biarritz, October 1934

ANTOINE DROVE ALONG the palm tree-lined avenue behind the Casino Municipal. Although it was early afternoon, there were only a few pedestrians out braving the winds that were barrelling in from the Atlantic and sweeping across the deserted Grande Plage. All the holidaymakers had left weeks ago, giving the town a desolate air.

Antoine drove up the hill until he turned right onto Rue Maréchal. All the houses were set back from the road, behind gates and high walls. From their upper storeys, they commanded a good view of the beach and the wider bay. Today, these were obscured by clouds that were darkening as the threatened rain came in from the ocean. Antoine parked the car outside the gate of Villa Tan Loc. He sat for a while thinking about what he would say to Marguerite. That was if she would even let him see her. It had been over four years since they had parted so acrimoniously, and she had disappeared overnight from Saigon. If nothing else, he wanted the opportunity to put the record straight.

He got out of the car and pulled the chain that hung from the door. He could hear a bell faintly tinkling inside the villa. After a minute, light footsteps approached the gate. A bolt was pulled across from inside and the gate opened a crack to reveal the face of the servant who had greeted Antoine on his very first visit to Marguerite's bungalow at Long Thành. He wore the same uniform of a stiff white jacket and black trousers as he had then, except he no longer had the initials of her plantation embroidered on his jacket. If he recognised Antoine, he did not show any sign of doing so.

'I am here to visit Madame de la Souchère. My name is Antoine Martinet. I am an old acquaintance from Indochina. Could you tell Madame that I apologise for my unannounced arrival, but I would very much like an opportunity to see her.'

The gate closed, leaving Antoine on the outside. The first drops of rain started to fall, so he got back into the car to wait.

Ten minutes passed with no sign of the gate opening. The rain started to drum on the roof of the car. Suddenly both gates swung open. The servant, now with a large umbrella, signalled to him to drive in. Once through the gates, Antoine could see that the villa was modest in size, with a small garden at the front. The servant indicated that Antoine should park his car against the garage door. He waited for Antoine to get out and escorted him to the front door, shielding them both from the rain with the umbrella.

When they were in the hall, the servant took Antoine's jacket.

'Madame says she will see you for five minutes.' He pointed to one of the doors leading off from the hall.

Antoine knocked. An unmistakable voice asked him to enter.

He opened the door and went in. Marguerite was standing a few feet in front of him. She made no move to greet him. Antoine stood still, unsure how to proceed. All the words he had rehearsed had deserted him as his intense feelings for her flooded back. She was the same beautiful woman he had fallen in love with back in Indochina.

'Marguerite, I apologise for just turning up like this out of the blue. But I thought if I pre-warned you, you might refuse to see me.'

She said nothing. She continued to stare at him intently. The only sign of emotion was a slight reddening of her cheeks.

'I wanted to give you my account of what happened at the plantation that night and tell you a few things that I've learnt since then.'

'Are you still mixed up with the Rodins and those filthy Sûreté people?' Marguerite blurted out.

'Yes. But there is a reason for that.'

'There can't be any good reason. They are hateful people. You are just like them.'

'No!' Antoine tried to keep his voice steady.

'Explain, then.'

'I acknowledge that when I first went to Indochina to work for the Rodins, I did what they asked me to do. I ran their plantation in the way they wanted it done. The indentured labour, the poor working conditions. But after I met you, I realised that there was another way. So, I followed your approach when I got my own plantation, small as it was.'

Marguerite had sat down. She did not offer Antoine a seat, so he remained standing. Her head was bowed.

'I still have nightmares, seeing the burnt bodies of those poor labourers that you set alight that night.'

'I promise you that was not me. It was either Triads, working for Pak Hung, or it was the Communists, out for revenge after I had imprisoned one of their leaders.'

Marguerite looked up at him. 'That was because you worked for that bastard Bernard.'

'I was still part of the army reserve so was conscripted to do that. It was not my choice.'

'We all have choices, Antoine.'

'We do. And I have made mine. When you left, I returned to France. I went back to work for the Rodins.'

'Why? They are murderers. Can't you see that?'

'Yes, I know that now. I came back to take revenge on them for what they have done to you and to me.'

'How do you mean?'

'As well as working for the Rodins, I am also working for the Sûreté.'

'That makes it even worse.'

'No. Please hear me out. The Sûreté have asked me to go undercover within the Rodins' factory because they know that the Rodins and their allies are plotting to overthrow the Third Republic. And they are right. The Rodins have financed a secret society who are preparing for a coup. My role is to give the Sûreté the information they need in time to stop them.'

'Go on.'

'I can't tell you much more than that. It wouldn't be safe for you if I did. I just want you to know that I have changed and that this is my way of trying to make reparations for what happened in Indochina.'

Marguerite remained silent.

'One final thing. You should know that Bernard was behind the Banque de l'Indochine foreclosing on your loans. As far as he is concerned, you are a communist. He even claims that you were supporting the growth of the movement in the province. Without him, they wouldn't have called in that loan. I intend to make him pay for it one day.'

'I always suspected that. I had enough capital to ride out the recession. I thought they did it because I was a woman.' Marguerite laughed. 'They hated the fact that I knew more about running a rubber plantation than them, all those crusty old male colons.'

Marguerite stood up, so they were now facing each other, with only a small space between them. Antoine could feel the warmth of her breath against his cheek. He resisted the urge to reach out and touch her.

'Antoine, I am grateful for you telling me this. But you need to know that I can no longer trust you. What you say may be true. Maybe none of this was your fault or your choice. But while you continue working for these people, the Rodins, Bernard, whatever your reasons for doing so, I cannot have anything to do with you. You know that I supported the Communists in Indochina from their earliest days, and I still do. I met and befriended Den Hieu on the voyage to Saigon when I also first met you. He was already a member of the Revolutionary Youth League before it became the Communist Party. I allowed him to recruit among my workforce and I supported him with funds. You met him when I gave him shelter in my house after his imprisonment. I am still in contact with him.'

Antoine looked into her eyes to see if there was any softness there to counter the harshness of these words, but there was nothing.

'So, please leave now.'

CHAPTER 41

Le Figaro, 3 July 1935

COMMUNISTS AND SOCIALISTS SIGN PACT TO DISARM VETERANS' LEAGUES

After years of being at each other's throats, the leaders of the Socialist and Communist Parties have signed a pact to work together.

They agreed on a joint political platform that includes measures such as a reduction of the working week, statutory holidays, a raising of the school leaving age and more rights for women. At the top of their proposed 'reforms' is the dissolution of what they call the Fascist Leagues, by which they mean the veterans' associations who took part in last year's demonstration outside the National Assembly.

Spokesmen from the right-wing leagues vowed to resist the popular front in parliament and on the streets.

CHAPTER 42

Rue Nicolo, Passy, Paris, December 1935

AFTER MONTHS OF putting out gentle feelers, Antoine had finally managed to get some high-level representatives from the army to agree to attend a meeting to explore whether they had any shared interests. As much as Antoine despised Bernard, he had honoured his word and provided Antoine with some useful contacts. One was the adjutant for Marshal Louis Franchet d'Espèray, Colonel George Croussard, and the other, Pierre Lacau, was the chief of staff of Marshal Philippe Pétain.

Antoine had agreed with Eugène Deblonde that only the two of them should meet with the marshals' spokesmen to keep the discussions as confidential as possible. It had been impressed on Antoine that they would deny all knowledge of the conversations if challenged in public. They made it clear that they were only attending the meeting to listen to what Deblonde had to say and to ask questions. No commitments would be made at this stage.

Croussard and Lacau arrived at the meeting at Eugène's

townhouse in unmarked cars. Both men wore formal suits rather than their customary military uniforms. Eugène tried to act as though he was hosting a social event by offering the two men drinks and trying to engage them in some light conversation. Croussard cut him short.

'Please excuse my bluntness, Monsieur Deblonde, but we are only here to collect information. We have not been authorised to make any decisions. So, without any further delay, we would like to get down to business.'

'Of course, of course.' Antoine could see that Eugène felt unnerved by Croussard's brusqueness. He did his best to hide it by promptly ushering the men to a table he had set up for the meeting in the middle of the room.

'Briefly explain to us the nature and size of your organisation.' It was clear that Croussard was going to lead the meeting, with Lacau there as an observer and notetaker.

'I will try and be as precise as I can. We are an underground organisation, operating as a secret society. We call ourselves the Cagoule.' Eugène looked across at Croussard to see how his opening remarks had been received. Croussard remained impassive.

'Continue, please.'

'We have a regional structure, with units, battalions and divisions. It is organised vertically, so members are only aware of the identity of those in their own units and the commanders of the level above them. Our membership is now around seven thousand, with three thousand of those in Paris. We have access to weapons. We are continually growing our stockpile through Italy, Spain and Switzerland.'

'Are your men trained in how to use these weapons?'

'We have a programme of training, so increasing numbers can use rifles, grenades, and we are currently training up machine gun units.'

'And you are training them with what purpose, exactly?'

'To assist the army when it decides that the time is right to overthrow the Third Republic.'

'You mean, a Bonapartist coup d'état.'

'If that is how you would like to describe it. We prefer more contemporary models of authoritarian leadership, such as Mussolini in Italy.'

Croussard paused in his questioning. His reactions gave nothing away about what he was thinking. He drummed his fingers on the tabletop as he formed his next question.

'So, what kind of timescale do you have in mind?'

'Well, that depends on you and perhaps on how current events unfold. We think a coup will only work if the army leads it. We are not going to do it on our own. We can create the pre-conditions through terrorist actions and provocations. Those should bring about enough instability for the public to cry out for a strong leader. We think that you represent the sort of men who can provide that leadership.'

Croussard fixed Eugène with a firm stare. He leant slightly forward, bracing himself with his hands flat on the table.

'Monsieur Deblonde, do not presume anything of anyone.'

'Of course, Colonel.'

'I would like to discuss matters with my colleague here in private. Could you leave us for a few minutes please.'

Eugène and Antoine rose from the table and went out into the corridor. As soon as they had closed the door, Eugène pulled a packet of Belga cigarettes out of his jacket pocket. After he had extracted one and lit it, he started to pace up and down the carpet, jabbing the cigarette towards Antoine to emphasise his points. Eugène hissed with exasperation.

'Did you hear the way he talked to me, that fucking high and mighty bastard. I've met his type before in the war. Promoted way above his ability. Brown-nosing his way to the top. Cushy office job well away from any fighting. Fuck him!'

'Calm down, Eugène, for Christ's sake. He's only doing his job.'

'Fuck him!'

'Let's see what they have to say next. You need to ask a few questions of your own before they go. We need to know what level of support they have in the army for what we are proposing, even if it is just an indication rather than a firm view. We also need to know whether they can help us make high-level contacts in Italy– in the army or the regime – because that is where we can get more arms from.'

'OK. But what I really want to do is punch that smug expression off his face.'

'That would really help.' Antoine laughed.

After a few minutes, the door into the sitting room opened. Lacau asked them to rejoin the meeting.

Croussard sat back against his seat, his back erect. Antoine noticed for the first time that he was missing the lobe of his left ear. He looked down at the colonel's left hand, which was resting limply on the top of the table. He realised that it was a prosthetic limb. Despite what Eugène thought, Croussard had seen frontline action.

'To be clear. Anything I say now does not represent a commitment to any further action. However, we have been very interested in what you have told us, Monsieur Deblonde. We will report it back to those we represent. I think that there are grounds to keep the channels of communication open between us. We, like you, are worried about the direction our country is taking. It looks like we are about to be governed by a popular front of socialists and communists. They will appease the Germans and the Russians. They will starve the armed forces of weapons, if they don't bankrupt the country first. So, yes, we in the army are keeping a watchful eye on events and biding our time. So, it is good to know that there are others in society who will back us if, and I do emphasise *if*, we decide to act.'

Croussard paused to let his remarks sink in.

Antoine caught Eugène's eye.

'Colonel, if I may, can I ask a couple of questions?'

'Of course, Monsieur Deblonde. I cannot promise to answer them, of course.' Croussard allowed himself a slight smile.

'Do you think there is support in the armed forces for the kind of radical solution that we are advocating?'

'I cannot say. However, we would not be here if those we represent did not, how shall I put it, think that this is a contingency that should be considered, and prepared for. Anything else?'

'Yes. We need some contacts within the Italian regime or military who might be prepared to supply us with more arms. Can you provide those to us?'

'We can. We see the Mussolini regime as a potential ally for us against the Germans, so we have been cultivating links. They, too, would like to see things change in France, as the current regime does not look kindly on them.'

'Many thanks.'

'I think that will be all, gentlemen. We shall be in contact.'

After they had left, Eugène asked Antoine to stay behind. He had calmed down since his previous outburst. He poured them both a couple of large cognacs.

'After a bit of a rocky start, I thought that went well. What about you?'

'Yes. We know that the highest-level of the army, at least, are worried enough to find out if they have allies in society who will support them if they decide to act. They are going to open some doors for us with the Italians. I would say, for a first meeting, that was positive.'

'I also think that they were giving us a green light to start taking some freelance actions of our own to help prepare the ground.'

'How do you mean?'

'Come on! You heard him. They are really worried about the prospect of a government full of Bolsheviks, Jews and Freemasons, laughingly called the popular front. I think we should target them.'

'How?'

'Through acts of terror, of course.'

CHAPTER 43

Rue de Reuilly, Paris, December 1935

WHEN ANTOINE CAME up to Paris, he often stayed with Carmel. She had a small, rented apartment in Rue de Reuilly in the 12th arrondissement. It was close to the Gare de Lyon, so was handy when he needed to catch the train back to Clermont. Most of the people living in the arrondissement were migrants like Carmel, either from the French countryside or from Italy, Spain or other parts of Europe. They were poor but had ambitions to improve their lot through hard work, not all of it legitimate.

Antoine did not reflect deeply on how he felt about Carmel. Whenever they were together, they had a good time. They went out dancing at the bals, spent hours at the cinema and enjoyed drinking and eating in the local bistros. After seeing Marguerite again in Biarritz, even though she had dismissed him and said that she never wanted to see him again, he knew that he still loved her. Carmel filled a space in his life, but he still yearned to be reunited with Marguerite.

He climbed the stairs to the second floor where Carmel had her apartment and knocked on the door. When she opened it, he could see that she had been crying. Her eyes were puffy, and her nose was red from constant wiping with the handkerchief she was clutching in her hand.

'What's the matter?' He reached out and pulled her into his arms. Her head sank onto his shoulder. She started to sob quietly.

'It's my parents.'

'What's happened?' He pushed her gently away from him, so he could see her face. She wiped her nose and then looked up at him.

'I got a telegram from my brother, José Enrique. He has travelled back from Morocco, where he is serving in the army, to return home. He says that Mother and Father are in great danger. The anarchists and reds are taking control of the pueblo where they live. He wants me to come down and pick up our mother and bring her back with me, so she can be safe. I don't know what to do. Can you help us?'

She looked up at him imploringly.

'Come, sit down.'

Antoine led her to the table. He poured them both a brandy.

'Can't your mother travel up from Seville to Paris? She can get the train, and we can meet her at the station.'

'No. She hardly ever leaves home. She is a nervous wreck. The only way she would do it is if I accompanied her all the way.' Carmel started to sob again.

Antoine reached across and stroked her shoulder.

'Can your brother meet us at the station in Seville if we travel down by train?'

Carmel looked up at him, her eyes bright with hope.

'Of course, he can drive in from the estate and pick us

up. Then we can stay there for a few days and return with my mother. Oh, Antoine, thank you, thank you.' Carmel put her arms around him and squeezed hard.

'Right. I will tell the Rodins where I am going. I am sure they will be all right with that. I'm due some time off. So, let's plan to set off in a few days.'

'Antoine?'

'Yes.'

'My brother asks if you could come armed. Just in case there is trouble.'

CHAPTER 44

Real de la Jara, January 1936

IT TOOK OVER two days to travel by train from Paris to Seville. On the way, they stopped at Biarritz, where Antoine briefly left the train to walk to the station entrance and gaze up towards where Marguerite lived on the hill overlooking the town. He realised what an empty gesture it was, but he felt better for in some way staying connected to her.

When the train arrived in Seville, it was early morning, just as dawn was breaking. The lights around the station platform were being extinguished. Even though it was January, the air was warm and damp. Antoine put up his umbrella to protect himself and Carmel from the light rain that was falling as they walked up the platform towards the ticket barrier. Carmel gave out a shout, dropped her bags and ran towards a tall young man who was waving at her.

'José!'

She leapt into his arms and hugged him tightly, showering his cheeks with kisses.

'OK, Carmel, enough. Put me down.' José was laughing, while he twirled his sister round. 'Let's have a look at you, then. The big city has turned you into a high-class *putana*, dressed all in silk and lace,' he joked.

Carmel gave him a playful slap across the face. 'José, this is Antoine.'

Antoine put the bags down and shook José's hand. José looked to be around thirty years old. He had the same black curly hair as his sister, but in his case, it was tamed by a short military cut. His face was lean and deeply tanned. He wore brown riding breeches and boots and a dark-green woollen tunic shirt. It was easy to see from the way he carried himself and from his dress that he was a professional soldier.

'It's good to meet you at last, Antoine. Carmel never stops heaping you with praise when she writes home. On behalf of our family, I want to thank you for coming all this way to escort my mother to safety.'

'It is the least I could do. Anyway, it gives me the chance to visit somewhere I have never been before.'

'Well, I wish you could have come when you could see our homeland at its best. But unfortunately, it is on the verge of being plunged into a civil war. It all looks and feels grim now. Come. Let's get going and we can talk on the way home.'

He led them to a Hispano-Suiza truck parked just outside the main entrance of the station.

'I'll put the bags in the back. You two get in the cabin. Antoine, before we set off, have you brought a weapon with you?'

'Yes, I've got a Mauser in the rifle bag.'

'Can you get it out and take it with you in the cab?' Antoine noticed that José was wearing a side arm on his belt.

'Yes, of course.'

'You can sit on the outside, with Carmel next to me.'

As they set off, José explained, 'When we drive through the pueblo, people need to see that we are armed. It will ward off any hotheads who might want to have a go at us.'

'That bad, is it?'

'Yes. I am sure that Papa will explain it all to you. But right now, it feels that the landowners round here are under constant siege.'

They drove along in silence for a while.

'Carmel says that you are serving in North Africa.'

'Yes, I am a captain in the Army of Africa. Have been since I left the officer academy. In Spain, we call ourselves the Regulares. Our troops are native Moroccans, mainly Berbers. We have Spanish officers and NCOs. Tough troops. Battle hardened during the Rif wars. Your lot helped us out with that one. How about you?'

'Veteran of the world war. Served three years in an infantry regiment as a corporal. Invalided out but still in the reserve. Have done bits and pieces as part of the reserve when I spent some time in Indochina.'

'He's being too modest, José,' chipped in Carmel. 'He's still involved with the military, but it is all hush-hush. He won't even tell me about it.'

'And so he shouldn't. Don't tell her anything you want to keep secret, Antoine. She is a real gossip, this one.'

Antoine gazed out of the window. They had left Seville and had started to climb gradually across a barren landscape where there were few trees or bushes. There were some patches of green, but most of the earth was a dry, light brown, rutted with small boulders and criss-crossed by ravines.

'This is the Sierra Morena. We are about to come to Real de la Jara. Our *estancia* is on the other side of the pueblo.

Antoine, can you prop your rifle on your knee, so it can be seen through the window?'

They turned right off the main highway and entered the town along a track, strewn with pebbles. The truck kicked up a cloud of dust behind it. White houses with red-tiled roofs pressed in on the track from both sides. Dominating the town, from a craggy escarpment, was a deserted medieval fortress. As they drove through the main square, they passed the church. Through its main door elderly women were leaving morning mass. A group of men were sat outside the one café in the square. They all looked up sullenly as the truck drove past. Antoine noticed that the few children on the streets appeared gaunt and famished. None of them were wearing shoes.

As they left the village, the track narrowed into a single lane surrounded by two high-sided walls. José slowed the truck. As he did so, a volley of bricks and stones came raining down on the vehicle from behind the walls. The front windscreen caved in, showering glass into the cabin. Carmel screamed. José momentarily lost control of the wheel and the truck veered towards one of the walls. He managed to swerve before the front collided with the wall. He then accelerated quickly, so the vehicle shot out of the lane. Antoine looked behind him to see a group of youths emerge from behind the walls, shouting and making obscene gestures towards the departing truck.

'Are you both OK?'

Carmel shook the broken glass from her lap. She checked her face in the mirror to see if she had any cuts.

'Yes, all OK. Just a bit shocked.'

'Well, that's what we deal with all the time. And it's getting worse.'

They drove on for a few more kilometres. Antoine noticed that fences had started to appear on both sides of the track. Behind them he could see livestock grazing among the sparse vegetation.

José pointed to both sides. 'Our *estancia*. Prime bull-rearing country.'

Before long, they turned off the track and drove down a long drive, shaded by palm trees. They passed under a stone arch that had a set of bull's horns mounted on the top and pulled into a courtyard. Facing them was a two-storey ranch house, with stables and outbuildings running from its sides to make an enclosed courtyard. As they stopped, two men ran out from one of the stables.

José barked out some commands.

'Pépé, take the bags inside. Juanito, sort the windscreen out so we can use the truck again.'

Antoine and Carmel followed José into the house. As they entered the hall, they were met by an older man. He was shorter than José, had grey swept-back hair and long sideburns that gave the appearance of a mane, but his facial features resembled those of his son.

'What's all the commotion about, José?'

'We were ambushed as we were leaving de la Jara. Nothing to worry about. Sticks and stones, but there is some damage to the truck.'

'Papa!' Carmel cut across her brother and rushed to embrace her father.

'Carmelita, my precious. Are you all right? No injuries?'

'I'm fine, Papa. But now I can see what you must put up with. Where is Mama, so I can introduce you both to Antoine here.'

'She is lying down upstairs. She is struggling with her nerves. Why don't you two get cleaned up and have a rest after your long journey? Then we can all gather for dinner this evening.'

When they got upstairs, Carmel pushed Antoine into a small bedroom.

'You'll have to sleep in here on your own.' She giggled. 'My parents are very strict. Don't worry, I will come and visit you in the night.' She pulled him to her and gave him a long kiss.

Antoine and Carmel dozed fitfully for a few hours in their separate rooms. Carmel was still in shock from the attack on the truck earlier in the day and was worried about her mother's condition. Antoine wondered what he had got himself into by agreeing to accompany Carmel to Spain. He could sense that the place was like a tinderbox. It only needed a few more sparks to explode. He also needed to get something practical out of the trip that he could take back to Eugène and the rest of the leadership of the Cagoule. He was hoping that José would have contacts in the Spanish military that he could use.

Just before eight in the evening, a female housekeeper came upstairs to tell them that the rest of the family were waiting in the dining room. When they got there, Carmel's parents and brother were already sitting round the table. Carmel greeted all three with a kiss on their cheeks. She buried her head in her mother's shoulders while her mother caressed her daughter's hair.

'Please, Antoine, sit next to me,' Carmel's father said. 'I need to make more formal introductions before we eat because it was a bit chaotic when you arrived. My name is

Rafael de Medina. José, you know. And this is my beautiful wife, Teresa de Medina.'

Antoine took Teresa's hand very formally. 'Madame, I am honoured to meet you. Your daughter has told me all about you. Only good things, I assure you.'

'Thank you, Monsieur Martinet. I hope I will come to call you by your first name in good time, but I am a traditionalist when it comes to these things.'

'Of course, Madame.'

Teresa de Medina was dressed in a long, black silk evening gown. Her greying hair was covered by a lace mantilla that made her appear taller than she was. Her face was pale, accentuated by the dark shadows under her eyes.

They were sat round a long table that was formally laid out for dinner with silver cutlery, linen napkins and crystal wine glasses. Antoine was placed close to Rafael at the top of the table. Carmel and José were sat opposite each other in the middle. Madame de Medina was at the bottom of the table. A male servant and the housekeeper stationed themselves by the door ready to serve the food.

Before the meal started, Rafael said grace. He then proposed a toast – 'Death to the Republic!' – a cry that was echoed round the table. As the meal progressed, Antoine found that his attention was monopolised by Rafael.

'I don't know what it is like in France, but here, the reds and the atheists have taken over. As soon as the new Republic was proclaimed, they started passing anti-landowner and anti-clerical measures that are leading to the extinction of traditional Spain. Under the first government, I was supposed to hand over some of my land to the landless labourers in the pueblo. I was told to provide them with paid work even if there was no work for them to do. When I refused, they sent round some thugs, called them *pistoleros*, to shoot up the place. In the pueblo, they ran the priest out of town, painted over the frescos in the church and banned anyone from going to services. Fortunately, a more conservative government got in at the last election and reversed some of those measures. But everyone knows that we could get a popular front government next. If we do, then everything will start up again but worse.'

Antoine thought for a moment that he was hearing a lecture from the Rodin brothers. He picked his next words carefully.

'What I would say, based on what I saw as we drove through the town this morning, is that the poverty looks much worse here than in France. The children I saw looked starved. They had no shoes. You rarely see that in France.'

Rafael fixed Antoine with a ferocious stare. He spoke with venom. 'Don't be fooled, Antoine. These people are lazy. Most of them are inbred. Plenty of gypsy stock. They don't know how to do an honest day's work. If they are poor, then it is their own godless fault. It is all they deserve.'

Antoine tried to catch Carmel's eye so he could extract himself from Rafael, but she was talking animatedly to her mother so did not see him.

'So, what is the situation like in France then?'

'We think that we will shortly have a popular front government like yourselves.'

'Well, what are you doing about it?'

'Like-minded people are getting together to organise resistance. I can't really say more than that.'

'Good. I badger José to put out feelers among his army

comrades to see if they are prepared to take up arms against the popular front when it comes. He says that something is stirring in that direction. But I don't know if he just tells me that to shut me up.'

Antoine finally managed to move the discussion onto Rafael's other main passion, breeding bulls, until the end of the meal. At nearly midnight, Carmel and her mother rose and said that they were both going to bed. They said their goodnights and left the room, leaving the three men with brandy and cigars. Rafael spent the next half hour goading his son about what he was going to do to tackle the reds. Antoine could feel himself becoming more and more drowsy until he got up and bade the others goodnight. Within seconds of laying his head on the pillow, he fell into a deep sleep.

'Antoine, Antoine, get up now!' José was pounding on the door.

Antoine stumbled out of bed and opened the door. He found a half-dressed José on the other side, grappling to get his shirt on.

'Quick, downstairs. We are under attack. Bring your rifle. I'll meet you outside.'

Antoine threw on his clothes, grabbed the Mauser and raced down the stairs and out into the yard. José was sitting in the front of the truck, peering through the still smashed windscreen. Juanito and Pépé, the two ranch hands, were saddled up on horses, with rifles slung over their shoulders. Before getting into the front of the truck, Antoine was stopped by a sound that he had never heard before, a bellowing of pain and rage that was coming from the fields behind the house.

'Get in, Antoine, they are mutilating the bulls!'

The truck raced out of the yard, followed by the two men on horseback. José had rigged up a makeshift lamp on the top of the truck's cabin. Its beam lit up the track as they bumped across it into the first field. Before long, it picked out two shapes lying spreadeagled on the ground. As they got closer, Antoine could see that they were bulls lying on their sides, their legs twitching convulsively in the air. The loud bellowing sound that he had heard in the yard had been replaced by that of stentorian breathing as the bulls fought for air. Antoine leapt out of the cab before the truck had come to a halt. As he ran across to the first bull, he covered his nose with the back of his hand as he was assailed by the smell of blood, mixed with animal faeces. The bull's throat had been slashed. Its powerful neck and shoulders were covered in blood, which was still pumping from an open wound. As the bull gasped for breath, it rolled on its back, revealing a large open wound between its back legs. Its testicles had been sliced off and left lying on the ground beside it.

'Shoot it!' José shouted at Antoine. 'Put it out of its misery.'

Antoine pulled back the bolt on the Mauser, put the end of the barrel against the bull's head and squeezed the trigger. The bull gave one more convulsion before slumping onto its side. Juanito jumped off his horse and despatched the other bull.

José was down on his knees stroking the side of the bull that Antoine had just shot.

'Look at what the bastards have done. See, they cut its fetlocks to bring it down and then cut its balls off.'

As he gathered his composure, Antoine could see José's face take on a look of icy calm. The muscles in his jaw and neck tightened, making his features even more angular.

'They won't have got far. They will have come on foot. Juanito, Pépé. You ride off to the left and circle round. We will take the truck and go right. If you see them, shoot first and ask questions later. I put a call into the Guardia Civil before I left the house. They should be on their way. But I want to finish this before they get here.'

Juanito and Pépé wheeled away on their horses and disappeared into the night. Antoine and José mounted the truck and set off in the opposite direction.

There was very little cover on the sierra, beyond a few rocks and scrub-like bushes. The only hiding places would be in the ravines that criss-crossed the land. José drove slowly while Antoine stood on the running plate on the side of the cabin, moving the lamp from one side to the other like a searchlight. After forty minutes, they came to the fence that marked the boundary of the ranch, without any sign of the intruders. They passed alongside the perimeter until they came to a point where the wire on the fence had been cut. José drove the truck through the hole, taking the rest of the wire with him. He turned left towards de la Jara.

'They will have come from the pueblo. There is nowhere else out here beyond some herders' huts. They will want to get back home before daylight.'

Ahead, some distance away, Antoine could pick out the faint beam of some headlights coming towards them, the light bouncing up and down as they reflected off the sky.

'The Guardia Civil. I want to get to them before they do.'

After another kilometre, José slowed down. Ahead were three shapes of varying height bobbing along the track. Just beyond them, Antoine could see two horsemen standing sidewise on to the track, blocking the route.

'We've got them!' José exclaimed.

As they got closer, the three shapes slowed down and came to a halt. They had stopped in the middle of the track, realising that there was no escape.

'Antoine. You stay here. This does not concern you.'

José jumped down from the truck. He had his revolver in his right hand. Juanito and Pépé dismounted from their horses and approached from the other side. They raised their rifles to cover the men to prevent them from running off. In the distance, the headlights from the Guardia Civil's vehicle were coming closer.

José got the men to kneel on the track. He ordered them to take off the sheaths they had on their belts with the knives inside them that they had used to mutilate the bulls and lay them in front of them. José then walked round behind them and with his boot pushed them forward so their foreheads were pressed to the ground. He signalled for Juanito and Pépé to come round the back of the men and stand alongside him. They seemed to know what was expected of them as they both raised their rifles, so they were pointing at the necks of the men in front of them. Antoine could hear José bark out a command. There was a loud volley of shots. The three men's heads slumped forwards but their bodies remained in a crouching position. José went down the line and pushed them forwards with his boot, so they became spreadeagled on the track. Blood started to pool around their heads and seep into the dust.

The Guardia Civil truck braked and stopped just behind the two horses. An officer wearing a grey-green uniform and a glazed black bicorne hat walked slowly across to where the bodies were. He bowed his head in front of José. They had a brief conversation. The officer inspected the dead men. He looked at the knives they had been carrying. He then shouted an order to his men. They dismounted quickly, wrapped the bodies in some blankets and carried them back to the truck. The officer saluted José before joining his men. The Guardia Civil truck turned round and drove back in the direction of Real de la Jara.

When José got back in the truck, Antoine asked him what the Guardia Civil officer had said.

'Not much. I explained what had happened. That we had caught them in the act and that we had administered justice. He was satisfied with that. He will take the bodies back to the pueblo and dump them in the square so their families can find them in the morning. He understands that examples must be made if we are going to stop the country going to the dogs. Right, let's go home and get some sleep.'

The mood in the truck next day on the drive into Seville was solemn. Carmel and her mother were anxious about leaving Rafael behind on his own. José was worried about how safe they would be as they drove back through Real de la Jara. As a precaution, he had Juanito and Pépé escort them in another vehicle. Antoine tried hard to dispel the vision inside his head of the mutilated bulls and the executed men.

They arrived at Seville station without incident. As the luggage was loaded onto the train and Carmel and her mother went to find their compartments, José pulled Antoine to one side.

'What you have seen here will happen to you in France unless you act now to stop it. I don't know what you are involved in, but I will do anything I can to help you. You said that you wanted a contact to help you get your hands on some weapons. I can give you the name of one of our army intelligence captains. He is willing to help.' José slipped a note into Antoine's jacket pocket. 'Now, just make sure that you look after my mother and sister. If you don't, I'll be after you.' With that he smiled, waved and walked back down the platform.

When they stopped in Biarritz on the way back to Paris, Antoine remained in the compartment.

CHAPTER 45

Rue de Reuilly, Paris, January 1936

CARMEL SHUT THE door of the only bedroom in her small apartment. She manoeuvred her way round the pile of bags that her mother had dumped on the sitting room floor to join Antoine sitting at the table.

'She's a bit weepy. I think she is already feeling homesick. Fortunately, she's so tired that she fell asleep as soon as her head hit the pillow.' Carmel looked round the room and gave a rueful smile. 'Oh well, it looks like we will have to go back to making love in hotel rooms. I hope you don't mind.'

'Don't be silly. Of course I don't mind.' Antoine took hold of both Carmel's hands. 'I need to tell you a few things. Now seems as good a time as any.'

Carmel looked up anxiously. 'You've met my parents and now you want to end it. Is that it?'

'No, no.' Antoine laughed. 'Nothing like that.'

'What then?'

'I need to tell you more about myself and what I do.'

Antoine hesitated. Carmel waited, stroking the back of his hands.

'You know that I work for the Rodins. That I am in charge of the security of their factories.'

'Yes, down in Clermont.'

'Well, that's not all I do.'

'I guessed that. Otherwise you wouldn't spend so much time in Paris. I just didn't want to pry too much.'

'You joked in Spain with your brother that I was still involved with the military and that it was all hush-hush. Well, you were right. Because of my military background and my status in the army reserve, I have been asked to do things for the Sûreté. The French security services.'

Antoine looked across at Carmel to check how she was receiving this information. She smiled gently to encourage him to go on.

'They have asked me to continue working with the Rodins. To keep an eye on some of the things they are involved in. One of those is a new organisation. A sort of secret society that is plotting to overthrow the French government, with the help of the army if they can get it.'

'And what do you do for them, this secret society?'

'It's early days. But they are going to start ramping up their activities soon.'

'Do you support what they are doing?'

'I come from the same sort of background as you. Not as wealthy, but my family are staunch Catholics. We believe in, and have fought for, our country. We hate communism and everything it stands for. I hold them responsible for the death of my younger brother in the war. Many of the people in the Cagoule believe the same things. But the way they are going about it makes me very uneasy. People like the Rodins are just merciless capitalists, only interested in their profits.

I worked for them in Indochina. I saw how they abused their workers. People they are associated with defrauded me of land. Some of the leaders of this new organisation have shady dealings with potential enemies of my country, such as the Italians and the Germans. I'm worried that by weakening our country they might make us defenceless if, or more like when, we go to war again. They think they are patriots, but their actions could lead to our downfall.'

'In Spain, we are faced with the same threat to our way of life from the Communists as here. My brother and his fellow army officers are talking about rising up and taking on the popular front government. I support that with all my heart.'

'If I was Spanish, I would too, as you are defending your country and your way of life. But the people I am involved with are potentially weakening our country so it can be taken over by someone else. Russia, Germany, Italy.'

'How dangerous is it, this work?'

'The only danger will come if they find out I am playing a double game with them. They won't take too kindly to that.'

Carmel got up from the table. She went through to the kitchen. Antoine could hear her getting some glasses from the cupboard. When she came back, Antoine searched her face for any clues as to what she was thinking about what he had just told her. He hadn't known her for long. Could he even trust her?

'I want to help you.'

'What?'

'I want to help you. You must need women like me in this organisation. I work in the dance halls. I'm always meeting army officers and policemen there. I can pry information out of them. As a concierge, I am often given letters to hand on to other people. It's like a secret postbox. I can go places and meet people that you can't, simply because I'm a woman.'

'I'm not sure, Carmel. I don't want to put you in harm's way.'

She reached across and placed a finger on his mouth. 'Sssh! It will be fun.' She giggled. 'Now, off with you. I need to get my beauty sleep if I am going to be a spy.'

CHAPTER 46

Le Balajo, Rue de Lappe, Paris, February 1936

IT WAS STILL early enough in the night for Le Balajo to be relatively quiet. There were only a few couples on the downstairs dance floor when Antoine and Carmel walked up the stairs to the large second storey where Jean Fignon had said he wanted to meet. Antoine had been surprised by the request as Jean was one of the leaders of the Cagoule with whom he had the fewest dealings. He spotted him on his own sitting deep in one of the alcoves that were usually used by the prostitutes that frequented the bals when they wanted more privacy with their punters.

Jean looked up at them as they approached. Antoine noticed that he was still shabbily dressed in a patched jacket. His face was heavy with stubble.

'What's she doing here?' Fignon looked up at Carmel with undisguised hostility.

'She has a name. Carmel.'

'I bloody know that,' snapped Fignon. 'She's always hanging round the dance halls, trading her wares.'

Antoine decided to ignore his belligerence. 'I brought her along because she has already given me contacts in Spain who are going to help us get our hands on some weapons. I also think that we need some female members to help with our undercover activities, particularly when we need to make contacts with army officers and the police. I can vouch for her.'

Fignon did not disguise his disdain as he ran his eyes up and down her figure.

'It's your call, Antoine, but she will have to swear her loyalty to the movement just like anyone else.'

'I'll see to that, Jean. Now, why did you want to meet?'

'I'm planning an action tomorrow and I need your help.'

'That's short notice.'

'I know. I've only just heard about it myself, but I think it provides us with the perfect opportunity to start spreading terror, just like Eugène was advocating.'

'Go on.'

Fignon leant forwards so he could get closer to Antoine and Carmel, who were sitting opposite him on a banquette in the alcove. His eyes were taking on the fiery intensity that Antoine was becoming familiar with whenever Fignon was thinking about violent action.

'Some friends from the Paris branch of the Camelots du Roi are going to infiltrate a student demonstration tomorrow that is being organised to commemorate the death of some right-wing writer, Bainville or some such name. They say he was being persecuted by members of the popular front, particularly that dirty *juif* Léon Blum. They've heard that Blum will be being driven past the demonstration after he leaves the National Assembly. They are going to jump him and give him a real good beating.'

'It's too risky. In broad daylight in a public place. Surely, he will have a police escort. Everybody knows that he is a target.'

'No. We go in fast. And we wear our masks. This will be our first major Cagoule action, so I want it to be dramatic. Make a real statement.'

'How so?'

'I'm not planning just to rough him up. We need to eliminate him completely.'

'What do you mean, Jean?'

'Assassinate him, of course!'

Antoine looked across the table to gauge how serious Fignon was. He had sat back with his arms crossed, smiling broadly at Antoine.

'This will make history, Antoine. We can stop the popular front in its tracks.'

Antoine knew he had to play along with Fignon to maintain his cover. He felt as though he was on a high wire, starting to lose his balance.

'Have you squared it with Eugène?'

'No. He has given me the authority to organise actions when and where I see fit. So, are you in?'

'What do you want me to do?'

'I want you to provide the handgun. When the Camelots go in, we will be one step behind them. When they have got hold of him, you hand me the gun. I will do the rest.'

'Where do we meet up?'

'On the Boulevard Saint-Germain at ten in the morning. That is the route he takes once he leaves the National Assembly.'

'OK.'

As Antoine and Carmel rose to leave, Fignon shot his hand out and grabbed Carmel's wrist.

'This information goes nowhere. We are the only three people who know about it. Understand!'

'Enough, Jean.' Antoine prised Fignon's grip free from Carmel's wrist.

'Touch her again, and you will be dealing with me.'

Fignon looked at Antoine as though it was an invite he was keen to take up.

CHAPTER 47

Boulevard Saint-Germain and Rue de l' Université, Paris, February 1936

THE GROUP OF student activists from Action Française and the militants from the Camelots du Roi were gathered on the intersection of the Boulevard Saint-Germain and Rue de l'Université. They were wearing black armbands in memory of the writer Jacques Bainville, whose death provided the pretext for the protest. Banners fluttered over their heads proclaiming, 'Death to the Third Republic!' and 'Restore the Monarchy!' A thin line of gendarmes had linked arms to keep them off the road.

Antoine and Fignon had met at the top of the steps leading out of the Alma metro station. They were both dressed in thick winter coats that had large pockets where they could conceal their masks and weapons. Antoine quickly showed Fignon the Spanish-made Ruby pistol that he had had since the war, along with the clip of ammunition he would insert in the butt of the pistol when the action started. He checked that Fignon was familiar with the weapon. He received a gruff nod of the head in return.

The clock over the entrance to the metro showed that it was 9.55am. They walked briskly towards the noise of the protest, which they had heard as soon as they had exited the metro. It was getting louder and more raucous as 10am approached. Antoine stayed behind Fignon as they reached the edge of the group of protestors, who were now surging against the line of gendarmes with the aim of breaking onto the road and blocking it.

A shout went up from the front.

'There he is, the *juif* bastard. In the back of the first vehicle.'

Those at the back of the crowd yelled and pushed. The pressure broke the chain of interlinked arms of the gendarmes. Before plunging into the crowd, Fignon pulled out his mask and slid it over the top of his head. He signalled to Antoine to do the same. While Antoine was reaching into his pocket to get his mask out, he slid the cartridge containing the bullets out of the bottom of the pistol. He quickly inserted another, empty, cartridge as a replacement.

Fignon put his arms out and cleared a passage through the melee, with Antoine following in his wake. When they got to the edge of the pavement, they could see that a black ministerial limousine was being rocked from side to side by a group of militants. Fights had broken out with the gendarmes, who were attempting to stop the protestors from opening the limousine's door. Within minutes, the gendarmes were overwhelmed. They fell under the feet of the surging crowd, which cheered as the back door was prised open and the occupants on the back seat were pulled out and manhandled to the ground. Fists and boots started to fly.

Fignon and Antoine arrived just when a young militant wearing the light-blue shirt of the Camelots du Roi was rolling over a middle-aged man with grey hair and a goatee beard onto his back. He started to kick him in the stomach. Fignon grabbed him from behind and pushed him away. He briefly looked down at the man on the floor, who raised his hands up to cover his already bloody face. Fignon pushed his hands away to get a good look at him.

'That's him!'

He reached back to Antoine, who slipped the small pistol into his hand. Fignon pushed it against Blum's head and pulled. There was a click but no other sound. He pulled the trigger again. Another click. The crowd surged again, knocking Fignon onto the floor. He let go of the pistol, which bounced across the ground. Antoine quickly scooped it up and threw it under the limousine. By now the gendarmes were regaining control and had started to push the crowd back. Antoine ripped off his mask. He grabbed Fignon's arm and shepherded him through the crowd. They ran back to the metro where they had agreed they would separate and travel in opposite directions.

As they came to the ticket barrier, Fignon put an arm across Antoine's throat. He hissed into his face. 'What was that about, Antoine? You deliberately sabotaged the mission.'

'No, I didn't. You know as well as I do that pistols often jam. You saw the cartridge with the bullets before we set off.'

'You're a liar. I've got my eyes on you.'

He increased the pressure on Antoine's throat for a second. Then he released him and ran down the escalator to the platform.

CHAPTER 48

Le Figaro, 18 June 1936

POPULAR FRONT GOVERNMENT BANS RIGHT-WING LEAGUES

THE POPULAR FRONT government has passed a decree to dissolve right-wing paramilitary leagues, as it had said it would do before it was elected.

The leagues that have been banished include the Croix-de-Feu, Solidaritié Française and the Francistes.

Prime Minister Léon Blum has taken revenge on the rightists, whom he sees as directly responsible for the physical assault on him last February. It has taken the prime minister many months to recover from his beating at the hands of the militants.

Sources close to the right-wing leagues say that the ban will only redouble their efforts to overthrow the popular front and stop the spread of Bolshevism. 'We are not going to let the country be taken over by communists, Freemasons and *les juifs*.'

CHAPTER 49

Café Dominique, Paris, June 1936

ANTOINE PARTED THE bead curtain to let Carmel enter the café before him. He was annoyed, and unnerved, to see that Gallopin had brought Bernard to the meeting with him. Bernard had delivered the contacts in the military as agreed, but the less Antoine had to do with him the better.

Bernard watched them as they approached the table. He made no attempt to disguise his appraising look at Carmel, which, as she got closer, turned into a leer.

'Who's your friend, Antoine? Bit of a downgrade for you, isn't she?'

Antoine ignored him.

'This is Carmel. I have recruited her to work with me. She is from Spain. She has some useful contacts we can use with the nationalists over there. She is also used as an informer by the gendarme. Again, it is something we can use.'

'Delighted to meet you, Carmel.' Gallopin stood up and gave a slight bow in Carmel's direction.

'Delighted to meet you, too, Monsieur Gallopin.' She pointedly ignored Bernard, who continued to stare directly at her breasts as she settled into her chair.

'Thank you for sending through your report on the Cagoule, Antoine. It was very informative. Now that the paramilitaries have been banned, they will have to stay underground. Essentially, they have become a criminal organisation. We will let them grow and become more established before we move against them. They can be useful to us in some ways. We will determine when they cross the line. Then we will crush them.'

'How do you mean?' enquired Antoine.

'They can do things that we can't, as long as we can control and contain them.'

Bernard intervened. 'Get on with it, Gallopin. Stop speaking in riddles. Tell him what you want him to do.' Antoine noticed the look of disdain that Bernard directed towards Gallopin.

'It's good that you have brought Carmel on board. We will need to stop our friends in the popular front government here in France from being too enthusiastic in their support for their beleaguered comrades in Spain. Our ally Britain does not want us supplying arms to the Republicans in Spain. Unfortunately, Prime Minister Blum is only too keen to help. We think that he will publicly support the arms embargo he has agreed with Britain but covertly ship arms to the Republicans. We want that stopped. The Cagoule could do that. It would fit nicely with their ideological position.'

'Do you have any details about where the arms are being shipped from?'

'Bernard will give you that information when the time is right.'

'Anything else?'

'Oh yes. Mussolini is blowing hot and cold with Monsieur Hitler in Germany. He thinks that Hitler is not the real deal, that he is not a true fascist like himself. He is jealous that Hitler is receiving all the attention from the other powers. So, he won't sign up to a pact with him and keeps threatening to go with us or the British. We need to lure him away from the Germans. Your organisation could do Mussolini a favour by dealing with some of his critics based here in France. That might make him look more favourably on us. Again, Bernard will furnish the details to you when the time is right.'

'What makes you think that the Cagoule will want to run with any of these?'

'They will, don't worry. The nationalists in Spain and the fascists in Italy will provide them with weapons in return for doing these favours. Also, they fit with their world view. Your job, Antoine, is to sow the seeds when we give you the information and then get them to act on it. Is there anything else?'

Antoine directed his next question at Bernard. 'We haven't heard anything back from the army contacts we met with. Deblonde is getting anxious about them. I need to reassure him.'

Bernard slowly slid his eyes from Carmel's breasts to look at Antoine. 'The message went back to the high-level military contacts. They are keeping a watching brief.'

'What does that mean?' snapped Antoine.

'It means that if the Cagoule can demonstrate that they

are an effective organisation, and if the situation here in France deteriorates further, then they will step in.'

Antoine and Carmel rose to leave. Gallopin stood to say goodbye, his Star of David coming loose from the front of his white satin shirt.

Bernard stayed seated, his legs firmly planted on the ground, his thighs spread wide.

CHAPTER 50

Rue Nicolo, Passy, Paris, July 1936

EUGÈNE DEBLONDE HAD called Antoine to a meeting at his apartment. He said it was urgent.

When Antoine climbed the stairs to the sitting room on the second storey of Deblonde's house, he could hear raised voices coming from behind the door. He recognised one of them as Jean Fignon's.

He gave a loud knock on the door before entering.

Deblonde and Fignon were standing toe to toe by the fireplace. Deblonde's face was red and blotchy, with beads of sweat standing out on his forehead. Fignon's pallor, by contrast, was white, offset by his usual days' worth of stubble.

'Antoine. Jean here is making some serious accusations about you. So, I want to hear your side of the story before I decide what to do.'

'What accusations?'

'That you sabotaged his mission to assassinate Blum by handing him an unloaded pistol. And that you have recruited some Spanish dancer as a member without checking her background. Jean thinks she is a police informer.'

'He's talking through his arse on both accounts. As usual.'

Fignon started to stride across the room towards Antoine. Deblonde stepped across him and grabbed him by the shoulders.

'Calm down, Jean! We are going to do this in a civilised way. Antoine, explain to me what happened.'

'The gun I handed to Jean jammed. Simple as that. He saw that it was loaded minutes before the action started.'

'So, how come you didn't have it with you when we got to the metro?'

'It got knocked out of your hands in the melee. You know that.'

'And the girl?'

'I can vouch for her. I've known her for two years. She is from a strong nationalist family in Spain. Her brother serves in the North African Army, for God's sake. At this very moment he will be crossing over to mainland Spain to fight the Republicans. She could be very useful to our cause.'

Deblonde turned to Fignon, who had retreated to stand in front of the fireplace.

'I'm satisfied with that. So, enough, Jean. We draw a line under this today. Understand?'

Fignon continued to stare aggressively at Antoine.

'Jean, I said that is the end. I want to hear you say that.'

'OK, OK!' Fignon waved his hand at Deblonde dismissively and slumped into the nearest armchair.

'Well, it doesn't end there for me, Eugène. Jean is a hothead. He is out of control. He is going to expose us to the authorities through his rash actions before we need to be. I want you to hold him in check. You can't just give him a free hand to do what he wants.'

'Fuck you, Antoine.' Fignon strode out of the room, slamming the door on his way.

'Seriously, Eugène, you need to get him under control. He is a liability.'

'I know. But he is ruthless. I rely on him for the heavy stuff that no one else is prepared or experienced enough to do.'

'Fine. But you need to direct him, not just let him do what he wants.'

'Agreed. So, tell me, how are our contacts going with the army high-ups?'

'Still working on them. They are not prepared to come out and declare open support, for obvious reasons. But they are still sending out positive signals.'

'Good. We won't be able to do it without them. How about foreign support?'

'I have made contacts in Spain, thanks to Carmel, so we can get our hands on more weapons. The Italians want to work with us. I am just waiting to see what that might involve. I might need you to front some meetings with them, possibly travel to Italy.'

'That's fine. I can do that. Just let me know. And, Antoine?'

'Yes?'

'I'll deal with Jean. I promise.'

CHAPTER 51

Des Barreaux Verte, Rue de Lappe, Paris, July 1936

CARMEL HAD TIPPED off Antoine that the upper floor of the bal musette where she worked had been hired for the night by the central committee of the French Communist Party. They were celebrating their victory at the recent national election and their place in the popular front government.

'I was thinking that I could make a few contacts with them. Find out what they are up to.'

'What do you mean?'

'Well, there are going to be high-ranking men in the party attending. I could try and get close to one or two of them. Gain their confidence. Pump them for information. That would help us, wouldn't it? We see them as one of our main threats, don't we?'

'Yes, we do. But it's risky, not to say dangerous, for you. If they think you are an informer, they won't mess about.'

'You said that I could help you by gathering information. This is a perfect opportunity. I know how to do this. I am an attractive woman, yes?'

'Yes.'

'Well, let's use that. Men are so gullible.'

'OK. But I am going to be there tomorrow. In the background. Just keeping a watchful eye.'

'Fine.'

The next evening, Antoine arrived a few hours after the event had started. It was swelteringly hot inside the building. Upstairs he could hear the band and the thumping on the floor that indicated the dancing had started. Carmel was nowhere to be seen. She was not at her concierge station, nor at the bar downstairs. He slipped upstairs and poked his head over the balustrade. The room was heaving with people. His view was obstructed by the cloud of smoke that hung in the air. When his eyes had adjusted, he spotted Carmel sitting at the top table. She was leaning in close to a middle-aged, balding man, who had his arm loosely draped around her. Just at that moment, he lifted his head and gave out a great bellowing laugh and then proceeded to nuzzle Carmel's neck. Antoine turned around and went back downstairs. He took up a position at the bar from where he had a good view of anyone coming down the stairs from the top floor.

After a couple of hours, Antoine's patience was beginning to wear thin. Some people from upstairs had already left the party but there still seemed to be some life left in it yet, judging by the clapping and singing that had started up. Ten minutes later, the balding man appeared at the bottom of the stairs. He stood and swayed from side to side before Carmel came up behind him and took his arm to provide support. She looked across at Antoine and signalled with her eyes that she was going to take him outside.

Antoine left it a few minutes before he followed them out of the door. He could see them making their way slowly down the road. The man had to stop every few paces to steady himself and gather his breath. Carmel looked back down the road to see that Antoine was following. After turning the corner, they disappeared into the door of the hotel that Carmel and he sometimes used when they needed to escape from her mother. Carmel gave one last backward glance and then shut the hotel door behind her.

Just before dawn Carmel crept quietly into the apartment so as not to disturb her mother. She found Antoine asleep on the couch in her sitting room. He woke as soon as she came in.

'Well?' he said groggily.

Carmel slipped in beside him on the couch. He put his arms round her. She wriggled her body against him.

'Fortunately, he was so drunk he couldn't do anything. Although he did have a good paw of me.' He could feel her body give an involuntary shudder.

'Who is he?'

'Vincent Duclos, no less. Deputy party leader. Member of the National Assembly. And recently elected to the Comintern, whatever that is.'

Antoine whistled.

'A big hitter.'

'Yes. He likes me. And he wants to see me again.'

With that, she fell asleep.

CHAPTER 52

L'Écho de Paris, 23 July 1936

POPULAR FRONT GOVERNMENT DARES TO ARM SPANISH REPUBLICANS

PRIME MINISTER BLUM and Minister of the Air Force, Pierre Cot, have made it very clear in public pronouncements that they want to send arms to their Republican allies in Spain. This despite the clear objections of their allies in Britain and the declared positions of the German and Italian governments that they are prepared to sign a non-intervention pact.

Minister of the Air Force, Pierre Cot, states that the government has several aircraft ready to be sent to Spain.

Other ministers in the popular front government, mainly Radical Party MPs, are vehemently opposed to arming the Republicans and dragging France into this foreign adventure. One minister told this newspaper that 'it would be the beginning of the European war desired by Moscow'.

CHAPTER 53
Tossus-le-Noble, near Paris, August 1936

ANTOINE AND CARMEL had arrived at the garage on the Boulevard Picpus before dawn broke. The garage was run by one of the Cagoule's members. It was used primarily as a depot for storing the weapons that were being smuggled across the borders of Belgium and Italy in large numbers. It also had a stock of vehicles of all sizes and makes that could be adapted for the use of the organisation.

Antoine needed a large saloon car that could pass for one used by a visiting government delegation. When he stepped through the door into the garage workshop, he saw a gleaming black Hispano-Suiza Cabriolet De Ville parked in front of him. On its bonnet, two small pennants had been fitted flying the colours of the popular front government of Spain. Sitting behind the wheel was Gabriel Jeantot. He was a passable speaker of Spanish and an explosives expert, skills that would be needed over the coming days.

The mission had come together quickly once Bernard had provided Antoine with information on where the planes that were on route to Spain were being kept. He had been contacted by a colonel in the Nationalists' Army Intelligence Unit to request that the planes be disabled or destroyed before they were shipped to Spain. In return, the nationalists agreed to supply the Cagoule with weapons as soon as they had conquered the areas of Northern Spain where the country's arms factories were based. Bernard had given Antoine forged letters of credentials for Carmel and himself. He had also sent through an official-looking communiqué to the airfield stating that a visit from representatives of the Spanish government was to take place.

Carmel was to act the role of a junior minister of the Republican government conducting a tour of inspection of the planes, while Antoine was to be her aide. Jeantot was to be the official chauffer. They had calculated that as the Republican government in Spain was so new, and as the normal channels of communication between Spain and France had been thrown into chaos by the war, there was a chance that they could bluff their way through the gates at the aerodrome and gain access to the planes. After that, they would have to decide how they could disable them.

The drive to the airfield at Toussus-le-Noble did not take long as it was only a few kilometres north-east of Paris. As they approached, they could see several large white hangar buildings located on one side of the landing strip. There were a couple of French Air Force planes parked up outside one of the hangars. As they approached the gate, Antoine turned to check if Carmel was prepared. She had taken hours before they had set off deciding what she should wear. In the end, she had chosen some loose-fitting black trousers, matched with a black tunic shirt and topped off with a beret. She had said dismissively that this is what a progressive Republican woman would wear.

Jeantot brought the car to a halt at the guardhouse at the entrance to the airfield. A member of the Garde Mobile, who provided security at government installations, came round to the driver's side window. Jeantot handed over the documents that Bernard had provided them with. After a cursory glance, he gave them back.

'Yes, we are expecting you. Please drive up to the main administration building where you will be met by the commandant for the airfield. I will phone ahead to say that you are on your way.'

The gates were lifted, and Jeantot drove the car through. As they approached the buildings, they could see a small welcoming party gathering on the tarmac. When the car came to a stop, Jeantot jumped out and opened the back door for Carmel. Antoine followed just behind her.

'May I welcome you on behalf of the French Air Force to Toussus-le-Noble airfield, Minister.' The commandant was a man in his fifties, most probably allocated to this backwater of a post to see out his days.

Carmel replied in heavily accented French to the commandant's greetings. She had decided to display a working knowledge of the language and only show ignorance if the discussion became technical.

'Thank you, Commandant. Can I just express my gratitude on behalf of the government of Spain for your support in our effort to stem the fascist threat in our country. We do not have much time as I must return as soon as we have concluded business here to report on what I have seen. So, please can you show me the planes that you are proposing to transfer to us?'

Antoine had a quick glance at the commandant to see how he reacted to being co-opted to the anti-fascist cause. His face betrayed no clues as to his inner thoughts.

'Certainly, Minister. Please follow me. I am afraid that we will need to walk towards the end of the runway, as we are keeping them in two of our smaller auxiliary hangars. Keeps them away from prying eyes.'

The commandant led them along the grass verge of the landing strip until they came to two small hangars, side by side. When they reached the first hangar, a member of the Garde Mobile unlocked the door and slide them open.

'In the first hangar, we have six aircraft that have been completely refurbished. As they are ready to go, we always keep this hangar locked. We can deliver them to you as soon as you say the word.'

'I am afraid I am not authorised to do that today. As soon as I get back to Spain and inform my other ministers of what we have here, we will contact you about the arrangements to transfer them. And, in the second hangar?'

They approached the second hangar. Its doors were wide open. They could see mechanics working on the four planes that were inside.

'Now, these four are not ready to go. They arrived in bits, and we are having to assemble them. It's taking longer than expected as our mechanics are having to work on drawings that the Americans left us with. They could be ready in a couple of weeks.'

'That is good to hear. We can do with as many planes as we can get our hands on. And the security for this hangar?'

'Well, our mechanics need access, so yes, it is not always locked, but we do keep it under surveillance.'

'Very good. If it is all right with you, Commandant, I would like my two aides here, who are more expert in this field than I am, to take a closer look at the planes. Just so we can report back in detail to my colleagues about what we are getting. Perhaps you could ask your mechanics to stop working for a bit, so my men can inspect these planes here. Then they can look at the others.'

'Of course, Minister. Please come with me. I have requested some refreshments. Your men can join us when we have finished.'

The commandant spoke quickly to the mechanics, who downed their tools and left the hangar. He then ushered Carmel back towards the administration buildings, leaving Antoine and Jeantot on their own.

Jeantot walked quickly inside the second hangar and did a tour of the building. He then inspected the four disassembled planes. Two of the planes were nearly complete. They just needed their wheels fitted. The other two still needed a lot more work to get them airborne.

'What do you think, Gabriel?'

'Well, I suggest that we forget about the planes in the other hangar. We are never going to get near them given that they keep them under lock and key. These, however, we can target. If the doors aren't always locked, we may get lucky. But, even if they are, the thickness of the walls at the back of the hangar are thin. They are only made of tin sheet. We can cut through those and get in. Depending on how long we've got, we could rig up some individual explosive devices for each plane or do something bigger for the whole hangar. The second option won't take as long.'

'OK. We come back tonight and head for here.'

'Agreed.'

They spent a bit longer in the hangar to give the impression that they had done a thorough inspection. Then they headed back to the administration buildings to find Carmel.

'Ah, here are your men. Everything to your satisfaction?'

Jeantot spoke to Carmel in Spanish.

'Yes, he says that all is good. We need to leave now. Again, I want to thank you on behalf of my government. We will be in touch as soon as we can about when and how we want the planes transferred.'

It was not long before they were back in the car and driving towards Paris. In the back seat, Carmel ripped off her beret and shook out her hair.

'How did I do?'

'Quite the actress,' Jeantot replied.

She giggled and draped her arms round Antoine's neck, pulling him back so she could kiss the side of his face.

Early the next morning, when the sky still held onto the darkness of the night, Antoine and Jeantot cut a hole in the perimeter wire at the airfield. They scuttled like crabs across the grass towards the two hangars. There was no sign of any guards posted outside either of them. Antoine quickly checked the doors of the first hangar. These had a sturdy chain and padlock threaded through the handles. He could also see the blinking red light of an alarm over the doors. Meanwhile, Jeantot was slowly pulling open the doors of the second hangar. As they guessed, and had hoped, these had remained unlocked.

Antoine stayed outside to provide a lookout. Jeantot went inside with a rucksack containing already made-up explosive devices and timers over his shoulder. Antoine could hear Jeantot moving around inside, securing the devices to the legs of the workbenches that the mechanics used to repair the planes' engines.

'Antoine,' he whispered, 'come in here and help me shift these benches.'

Between them they lifted the benches and placed them alongside each of the planes.

'That should do it. I've set the timers for two hours' time to go off before dawn. No one should be in here before then.'

'Right, let's go.'

Antoine slid the doors shut behind him, then joined Jeantot as he made his way to the fence. They ran back to the car that they had left parked in a narrow lane. Jeantot drove off slowly without putting the headlights on. After a couple of kilometres, they came to a small lay-by that overlooked the airfield. Jeantot parked up to wait.

At 4.30am, just as the first light was appearing over the airfield, there was a bright yellow flash, followed by a delayed booming noise that rolled across the countryside. There was a short pause before the next explosion went off, followed by two more in quick succession. Jeantot gave out an exultant cry and punched Antoine on the shoulder in delight.

'Just drive, Gabriel. Get us out of here!'

CHAPTER 54
Nice, September 1936

AS HE SWUNG his car into the haulage yard in Nice, Antoine could see Joseph Darnot coming out of his office to greet him. With each passing meeting, Antoine noticed that Darnot's image was changing. He had added to his bulk the dress and demeanour of a gangster, copied from the stars he watched addictively in Hollywood movies. Today, he was wearing a black leather jacket, pulled tight around his midriff with a belt, army-issue trousers and black ankle-length boots. He had cropped his black moustache so that it nestled under his nose like an exclamation mark. His hair was cut very short. It was smothered in pomade, so it glistened in the sun. Antoine had to steel himself not to laugh out loud when Darnot opened his mouth and spoke in the feminine, high-pitched voice that issued incongruously from his manly frame.

'Hello, Antoine. Good trip?'

'Yes, fine thanks, Joseph. How's business?'

'Booming. Both sides of it.' He winked towards the garage where he stored the trafficked weapons that he had shown Antoine when he first visited the yard. 'Floor to ceiling. Boxes stacked high.'

Antoine was about to follow Darnot across the yard to have a look when another car drove into the yard. Inside were Eugène Deblonde and Jean Fignon. Antoine had been expecting Deblonde as they were going to a meeting over the border in Italy the following day, but he didn't know he was bringing Fignon with him. The two men got out of the car.

'What's he doing here?' Antoine asked Deblonde angrily.

'Calm down, Antoine. He needs to do a job for me, with Joseph. Although you might need to go along to help them.'

'What job? I only came here for the meeting with the Italians.'

'Well, we need to pay a visit to one of our colleagues. I don't think you know him. Maurice Fily? He's a friend of Joseph's, or at least he was. He owns a shoe shop in Nice. Was useful to us when we started bringing in weapons from Italy. Unfortunately, he has become a bit careless and greedy. Some of the money we gave him to buy the weapons with has gone missing. There are rumours that he has been living the high life recently. Fancy meals in luxury hotels, accompanied by even fancier women. You get the picture. So, I've asked Joseph and Jean to call on him later today. Get his side of the story. And I need you to drive the car for them.'

'Why me? They can both drive. They don't need me.'

'I'm not asking, Antoine. I'm ordering. For what they need to do, they need a driver waiting for them outside. Understand?'

'He's chicken, Eugène. I told you.'

'Shut up, Jean,' replied Deblonde.

'At least his Spanish whore isn't here to act as an informer.'

'I said, shut up, Jean.'

Antoine stayed out of Joseph and Jean's way until the time came to drive into the centre of Nice later in the evening. Jean sat next to Antoine in the front seat, while Joseph lounged in the back.

They drove down the hill from the suburb where Joseph's haulage firm was based until they came to the Boulevard Gambetta. They passed the main railway station on the left-hand side, before crossing Rue Verdi. Just before they hit the Promenade des Anglais, Joseph told Antoine to turn into Rue de la Buffa. Halfway along, he asked Antoine to slow down and swing into a small alley that ran alongside the side of one of the shops.

'This is it.'

Antoine peered out of the window. Along the side of the wall was painted in large red scrolling letters 'Fily's Chaussures à la Mode'.

'Right, Antoine. You wait here. I'm not sure how long we will be. But we may come back with a load, so you need to be ready to open the boot so we can put whatever we've got in there. Understand?'

'Understood.'

'Have you got everything you need, Jean?'

'Yes, everything.'

With that he turned towards Antoine. There was a sharp clicking sound. Out of his jacket sleeve shot a long-serrated blade that stopped just short of Antoine's knee. Antoine flinched. There was another metallic click. The blade disappeared into Jean's sleeve just as fast as it had come out.

Jean and Joseph got out of the car and disappeared down the alley before turning onto the main road. Antoine sat and waited, thinking he would have to deal with Jean soon or Jean would surely kill him first.

Over an hour passed. The alley became almost pitch black apart from at the end where it met the main road, where there was a small pool of light from the street lamp. Antoine could hear them returning before he could see them. They were both panting heavily as they wrestled with a long bundle that was wrapped in what looked like a carpet. Antoine leapt out of the car, went round the back and opened the boot. Inside he could see that the floor had been covered with a tarpaulin. Jean and Joseph propped the bundle on the lip of the boot and then heaved it inside. Antoine caught a quick glimpse of the silver wire that had been used to tie the top and bottom of the rolled carpet together.

Joseph whispered urgently at Antoine. 'OK, let's get going. Drive normally. Not too fast, not too slow. We don't want to attract any attention. I'll direct you where you need to go.'

Antoine edged out of the alley and turned onto Rue de la Buffa. They dropped down onto the Quai du Midi and skirted round the sides of Port Lympia. Antoine could see a few lights blinking from the decks of the naval ships and yachts moored in the harbour. Otherwise, there was no sign of any other human activity. They carried on driving until they had left the port area. The tarmac road petered out and became a track. After two kilometres, Joseph ordered Antoine to pull into the side. They parked up at the top of a small, shingled beach. Joseph and Jean got out of the car, opened the boot and lifted out the bundle. Antoine watched them as they climbed down onto the beach and then stumbled across the pebbles until they disappeared into the dark. Twenty minutes later they returned. Their trousers below their knees were soaking wet.

'Are you going to tell me what has just happened here, or I am just going to have to make an intelligent guess?'

'Don't tell him anything, Joseph. He'll only blab to his police informer friend, the Spanish dancer.'

Antoine ignored Jean.

'Let's just say that the debt we were owed has been repaid. Now, drive us home. I need a drink.'

Antoine turned the car round. He looked across at Jean. His face had that same ecstatic look he had last seen at the bal musette in Paris when he had beaten the man's face to a bloody pulp.

CHAPTER 55

Grand Hotel des Anglais, San Remo, September 1936

ANTOINE, EUGÈNE AND Joseph had driven down to San Remo on the pretext that they were going to enjoy a few days' gambling at the casino. The real purpose of the visit was to meet representatives of the Italian government to explore whether, and how, they could benefit mutually from any relationship. Joseph already had well-established dealings with low-level functionaries in the fascist regime, mainly border officials and policemen, who had turned a blind eye to his gun running expeditions. Antoine had been assured by Gallopin and Bernard that there were senior members of the regime, including from the Italian secret service, who wanted to meet them. The cosmopolitan surroundings of San Remo were a fitting setting for such a meeting. It was the kind of place where it was taken for granted that Europe's businessmen, government officials and spies congregated together to spend their leisure hours while cutting deals and trading information.

Eugène had booked a private dining room in the

hotel for the meeting. As the head of the Cagoule, he had insisted that he would lead the negotiations. Joseph and Antoine were there to impress their military credentials on the Italians. The arrangements were so clandestine and last minute that they were not even sure who it was they would be meeting until the appointed hour arrived and there was a knock on the door of the dining room.

'Enter, please.'

Only one man came through the door. He was small of stature, early middle-aged, with receding black hair. He wore an anonymous lounge suit. His only distinguishing features were his long face and dark eyes. Antoine and Joseph exchanged covert glances that communicated they were less than impressed by this emissary of the Italian state.

'Good afternoon. Let me introduce myself. I am Filippo Anfuso. I work for OVRA, the Organizzazione per la Vigilanza e la Repressione dell'Anifascismo.'

Eugène walked briskly across the room to shake hands with the guest. He introduced Antoine and Joseph, making sure to explain their roles within the Cagoule and to provide a quick pen portrait of their wartime experience.

After they had all sat down and drinks had been served, Anfuso delivered a short statement.

'You must understand that I am not here in any official capacity, and I do not have any authority to make decisions. My brief is to listen to what you have to say, to ask questions and to report back to those above me. Only after that might they decide to move to some more formal negotiations.'

'Understood,' replied Eugène.

He paused. Anfuso signalled for him to proceed with a wave of his hand.

'We are here because we believe,' Eugène stopped, 'no, we know, that we share the same interests. The people of Italy have been far-sighted enough to give their support to an authoritarian regime that acts as a bulwark against the spread of Bolshevism, Freemasonry and Jewry. That is what we so desperately need in France, where we are misgoverned by a bunch of self-serving thieves, laughingly called the Third Republic. We set up our secret organisation, the Cagoule, to work with whoever we can find to overthrow this feeble excuse of a government and replace it with the kind of regime that you have here in Italy.'

'And how do you propose to achieve this?'

'We have built up a secret army across France that is ready to rise up and seize power, along with our allies in the armed forces. We think that the Communists will provide us with a pretext for doing this by starting their own insurrection. We, along with the army, will crush them. Then the people will clamour for a strong ruler.'

'How many men do you have in this secret army and how well trained are they?'

'We have nearly twenty thousand spread across the country, with a particularly heavy concentration in Paris, where we will need them when we seize power. Many of them are veterans so can handle combat. I have here a document setting out our organisational structure and where our men are deployed.'

Eugène slid a folder across the table towards Anfuso, who let it lie there.

'Do you have the support of the army? If so, who, precisely, in the army?'

'I am not at liberty to disclose their names. But I can assure you that they are serving officers of the highest rank, as well as veteran generals from the war who continue to hold much sway in the ranks.'

'At some point, you will need to share that intelligence with us so we can make the appropriate links within our own military.'

'We will only do that if these discussions bear fruit.'

'Understood.'

Anfuso took a sip of his drink.

'Well, gentlemen. That is all I need for now. I will report back to my superiors and then get in contact with you if we desire further discussions. Are you staying here for a few days?'

'We can stay if that helps.'

'Good. I will be in touch.'

After Anfuso had left the room, Eugène lit one of his Belga cigarettes and greedily sucked in the smoke. He looked at the others to gauge their reaction as to how they thought the meeting had gone.

'He's just the same as our lot. Patronising bastard. You would think we were handing him a turd on a plate the way he was looking down his nose at us.'

'Come on, Eugène. He's got to sound us out. Take the measure of us. See if we are credible.'

'I get that, Antoine. But why do they have to be so bloody high and mighty about it? It's not as if all of us in the room haven't served our country. We bloody understand how the military works. Most probably more than someone like that, some flunkey from intelligence, who looks like an accountant.'

'Well, we've put our case. There's not much more we can do now. I don't know about anybody else, but as we are going to be here for a few days, then I am going to spend a few hours in the casino. Are you coming, Joseph? Let us know if they get in contact, Eugène.'

The call for a follow-up meeting came through quicker than they thought. When they arrived outside the room in the hotel where the meeting was to take place just after breakfast the next day, they found two members of the Italian black-shirted militia guarding the door. Before they could enter the room, they were frisked for weapons.

'What's going on here?' protested Eugène.

The militia men did not answer. Once they were satisfied that the three Frenchmen were unarmed, they opened the door. When they entered the room, they could see two men seated at the table. One of them was Anfuso, still dressed in his lounge suit. The other was a man of medium height, but who looked smaller than he was due to his short arms and legs. He had black brilliantined hair, which he was obviously proud of as he involuntarily patted it as he stood up. He was wearing an elegantly cut white tunic shirt with matching trousers. On the lapel of the jacket there was a prominent Fascist Party emblem displaying the fasces axe and bundle of sticks.

Anfuso stepped forward to make the introductions.

'May I introduce His Excellency Gian Galeazzo Ciano.'

Eugène and the others tried hard not to look shocked. They were being granted an audience with Mussolini's son-in-law, who had just been appointed as the regime's new Minister of Foreign Affairs.

'Gentlemen, it is a pleasure to meet you. Anfuso here has provided me with a briefing. I want to say that we in the government are interested in collaborating with you, although it goes without saying that these discussions must be kept private. We would deny that they ever took place if questioned. Is that understood?'

'Absolutely,' replied Eugène, who had regained his composure after his initial surprise.

'I am sure that we can do business. But we have very precise needs as a regime that we want you to help us with. Your country, with its popular front government and democratic politics, is currently unfriendly towards us. It harbours and gives sanctuary to many of our home-grown opponents. They spread malicious propaganda against us, both here and abroad. And they openly fight against our troops in Spain, where we are legitimately responding to requests for support from our nationalist allies. If you can help us combat these enemies of the state, then we can help you realise your ambitions in France. I will leave you in the capable hands of Anfuso here, who will spell out our detailed requirements.'

Ciano stood, smoothed his hair, then left the room.

'Gentlemen, you heard what the foreign minister said. We have two people in mind, brothers in fact, whom we would like you to deal with for us. Carlo and Marco Bartali. They are currently fighting in Spain for the Republicans on the Aragon Front. We have intelligence that Carlo is unwell and may soon flee to France. When he does, we want you to make sure that he is eradicated, along with his brother if possible.'

'You mean, assassinated?' Antoine asked.

Anfuso inclined his head slightly.

'We can supply you with information on their movements as my organisation tracks them constantly. Is this within your capabilities?'

'Yes. But obviously, we want something in return.'

'Naturally. What would that be?'

Eugène replied, 'We need the latest semi-automatic weapons. You should be able to supply us with a hundred Beretta rifles.'

'Yes. We can do that. I will arrange delivery of these through Monsieur Darnot once you have successfully completed your side of the bargain.'

After shaking the three men's hands, Anfuso left. Eugène could barely contain his excitement. He hugged Antoine, with a huge smile lighting up his usually tense face.

He whooped. 'We've done it.' He punched the air with his fists.

CHAPTER 56

Gian Galeazzo Ciano's diary entry for 28 September 1936

UNUSUALLY BUSY DAY. Started early with a meeting with the representatives from the preposterously named Cagoule, which I think translates as the Hood. Anfuso from our intelligence service tells me they are a secret society hell-bent on overthrowing the Third Republic. Delusional, I am sure, judging from the three sorry specimens I met today. No matter. Our enemy's enemies are our friends, and we will use them as best we can.

We want them to assassinate the Bartalis, who are currently causing us problems in Spain. If we can get rid of them that will help us in our relationship with Franco. Who knows, maybe we can then trade them into the French authorities, so we can build our broken fences with the government there as well. The price? A few guns for their tin pot coup d'état. A good bargain, one that my ungrateful father-in-law would be proud to have made.

CHAPTER 57

Café Dominique, Paris, November 1936

'THEY ARE GETTING out of control,' Antoine protested. 'They have a stockpile of weapons that wouldn't disgrace an army. They've blown up planes sitting in an Air Force hangar. They are dumping bodies in the sea. And now they are going to assassinate someone on the orders of a foreign government. You've got to call a halt to this, now!'

Gallopin and Bernard sat opposite him. Gallopin was smiling benignly, while Bernard had the usual disdainful look on his face whenever he had dealings with Antoine.

'You say "they" all the time. You mean "you", don't you?' Bernard crowed.

'I'm in too deep. I need out.' Antoine tried to control his emotions. He wanted to shout obscenities at them as they sat there complacently drinking their coffees and issuing him orders.

'Not yet, Antoine. It's too early. But, I promise, we can get you out soon, when the time is right.'

'You mean, when these idiots have served their purpose, and you can close them down.'

Gallopin brushed aside Antoine's pleas.

'Listen, Antoine. This time you can help save some lives. The French state does not permit a foreign government to carry out extra-judicial killings on our sovereign territory, whatever we might think of the people at the receiving end. So, we want to stop it. Or, at least, we want you to stop it.'

'And how do you propose I do that?'

'Well, you make sure that you are part of the hit squad. Find out the place and time of the assassination and then let us know. We will have people ready to intervene and arrest those involved before they get the chance to pull the trigger. We will obviously arrest you at the same time as the others, just to maintain your cover. Then we will engineer your release through the judicial system. Don't worry, we'll make it look convincing.'

'Why does that not reassure me? I will let you know, through the normal channels, where and when they are proposing to act. Just make sure that the Sûreté are up to the task of disarming and arresting the Cagoulards, because they know what they are doing.'

With that, Antoine pushed back his chair and left the café.

CHAPTER 58

Bagnoles-de-l'Orne, Normandy, January 1937

THE ITALIAN GOVERNMENT, through Anfuso, tipped off Darnot that the Bartali brothers had left Spain and were now in France. The brothers were planning to take a short holiday in the town of Bagnoles-de-l'Orne in Normandy to recuperate after their role in the fighting in Aragon. They had booked into one of the town's hotels, known for its spa. As expected, Eugène had selected Darnot, Fignon and Antoine to make up the hit squad for the assassination. The plan was for them to enter the hotel and kill the brothers while they were taking a treatment.

Early on a wet, overcast Saturday morning, Antoine waited outside the Gare du Nord to be picked up for the trip to Normandy. After ten minutes, a Citroën Light 15 drew up alongside him, with Fignon at the wheel. Darnot was in the back. Antoine got into the front seat, and they promptly left. Darnot talked through the plan for the evening. He and Antoine would enter the hotel at 6.45pm. Fignon would stay outside in the car, keeping the engine running. They would go downstairs into the basement of the hotel, where the spa was located. Darnot had been informed by a veteran working at the hotel that the Bartali brothers were booked in for a treatment in the sauna room. After killing the brothers, they would return to Paris, before travelling on to different destinations across the country. Antoine spent the rest of the journey familiarising himself with the Mauser Broomhandle pistol that Darnot produced from a small suitcase stowed in the footwell of the car.

At 6.30pm, they drew up outside the hotel. Guests were filing in and out, on their way to treatments, dinner, or a brisk walk down the town's tree-lined avenues. Antoine scanned the street quickly, but he couldn't identify anyone that looked like they were a member of the Sûreté. Fignon took the car round the hotel several times to eat up the minutes and to prevent them from being spotted by any potential witnesses.

Fifteen minutes later, they stopped outside the hotel again. Antoine joined Darnot on the pavement and followed him into the hotel. They were wearing heavy winter coats in whose deep pockets they could conceal their weapons. They glided by the doorman without attracting any undue attention. Before entering, Antoine gave one backward glance to check if he could spot any men who looked like they were following him. If they were there, they were staying well hidden.

They headed across the hotel lobby, with its ornate chandeliers and gilded Second Empire furniture, towards the stairs to the basement. Again, Antoine could not see any backup in the lobby. His apprehension started to grow. They followed the signs for the spa. At the foot of the stairs, they were hit by the humid, steamy air that was billowing from the double doors in front of them. Darnot pushed them open, to reveal a small reception area with two young women in white smocks sitting behind a desk and a corridor running off to the right-hand side, where the treatment areas could be found.

Darnot took his pistol from his coat pocket, pointed it at the two receptionists and told them to stay quiet and remain where they were. He signalled to Antoine to come with him as he headed down the corridor. Antoine followed, pulling out his gun as he did so. What was he going to do now? If the Sûreté weren't hiding in the spa area, then the hit would have to go ahead, otherwise he would blow his cover.

Darnot burst through the door into the spa, with Antoine right behind him. The air was full of steam and smelt of some soapy substance that filled Antoine's nose and made his eyes water momentarily. There was the sound of a soft murmuring of conversation coming from the treatment area. Looking over, Antoine could see two men, naked apart from the towels wrapped around their midriffs, lying on their stomachs while two masseurs pummelled their backs. The sound stopped suddenly as the masseurs looked up. They started to back away, their hands held up, as Darnot approached the treatment benches with his pistol raised. Without uttering a word, he shot the man lying on the bench closest to him in the head. There was a deafening noise as the sound of the shot ricocheted around the room. The wall behind the bench was sprayed with blood and fragments of brain. The second man tried to scramble off his bench, but his feet became entangled in his towel. He fell forwards into a heap on the floor, his legs thrashing around to try and escape.

'Do it, now,' barked Darnot.

Antoine stepped forward, placed his gun against the back of the man's neck and pulled the trigger. Again, the noise of the shot vibrated around the room. Before it settled, Darnot and Antoine were walking fast across the reception area, through the revolving door, down the steps and into the waiting car. No one had tried to stop them.

CHAPTER 59

Café Dominique, Paris, February 1937

ANTOINE SPENT TWO weeks holed up in Carmel's apartment. He read the reports in the newspapers about the shootings. The headlines in the left-wing press screamed their outrage at the cold-blooded assassination of these socialist heroes. The right-wing papers claimed that they were legitimate targets, given their campaigns against the government's official policy of neutrality in the Spanish Civil War. None of them identified who had carried out the killings, admitting that this remained a mystery, although there was plenty of speculation.

Two days later, he pushed opened the door and passed through the beaded curtain of Café Dominique to find Gallopin and Bernard sitting at the same table and with the same pose as before, as though they had not moved since their last meeting.

This time, Gallopin did get up and offer his hand. Antoine ignored him and sat down.

'You bastards! Explain why you left me in the lurch. I had to kill him as none of your men were there, and I had to cover my arse. You had better have a good excuse or I am quitting. You think you have that war stuff hanging over me, but I don't think anyone cares about that now, so you can do your worst.'

'Calm down, Antoine. I didn't trick you. I promise. There was a last-minute change of plan. Those at the Quai d'Orsay in the Foreign Office had their own agenda, which they didn't share with me.'

Antoine glared at him. He felt like punching that smug, Parisian expression off his face.

'Mussolini's a tricky customer. We find him hard to predict. He lays claim to Nice and all that lovely Riveria coastline, based on some outlandish ancient territorial claim. He blows hot and cold about allying with us against the Germans and then hinting that he will sign a mutual defence pact with them against us. So, we let him know, through the usual back channels, that we would turn a blind eye if he wanted to eradicate the Bartali brothers. We hinted that we could provide some of the manpower to bring this to a satisfactory conclusion. It seems to have worked, as he is now making more friendly noises towards us. For now, anyway.'

Gallopin paused, expecting a response, but Antoine remained silent.

'And this is the best part. The government has decided that, due to the escalation in extremist violence across the country, the security service should be given additional powers and resources to spy on and crush the groups behind this violence. Which is rather ironic, don't you think, given that we fund these very groups to deal with the people who we think pose a real threat to the Republic.'

'Very ironic, very clever. The problem is, I am right in the middle of it, like the bait in a trap. I want out now.'

Bernard coughed to get Antoine's attention.

'We've already explained that the time for you to quit is coming, but it's not right now. Maybe you need another incentive.'

'Oh, yes? Bernard, I am sick of you telling me what I need.'

'How about this, then. Your close friend, Madame de la Souchère. Remember her? Of course you do. Well, we know she is harbouring and supporting members of the Indochinese Communist Party, a proscribed organisation as you know. We could arrest her and them at any time. So, I suggest that you carry on taking my orders, Antoine, if you want her to stay out of prison.'

Antoine put his head in his hands.

'We know that Carmel has infiltrated the French Communist Party through her liaison with Duclos. And please pass on our congratulations to her for a fine piece of undercover work.' Bernard sneered at Antoine.

'Our own intelligence work tells us that the Communists don't have any plans to mount an armed insurrection. They don't have the means, and it doesn't fit with Stalin's current thinking. But Deblonde and the other leaders in the Cagoule see that as their main means of persuading the army to support a coup d'état. You need to get Carmel to persuade Deblonde that the Communists are ready to stage a rising. That will bring the Cagoule out into the open where we can crush them. Do you think you can do that?'

Antoine looked up wearily at Gallopin and Bernard. He got up slowly and, without saying another word, walked out of the café.

CHAPTER 60

Rue Nicolo, Passy, Paris, April 1937

CARMEL TOOK OUT the compact from her purse to check the final application of the bright-red lipstick she had decided to wear this evening, to match her red silk blouse and satin toreador trousers. Antoine had advised her to dress more conservatively. She told him that she needed to feel bold and confident to enable her to carry off what she was going to attempt tonight.

Antoine watched her in the rear-view mirror as he parked the car outside Eugène Deblonde's house. If she had any nerves, she was not showing them. They had spent the afternoon rehearsing what she was going to say. They knew that what they were about to embark on was risky and dangerous. All the leaders of the Cagoule had been called together for the meeting, including Fignon, who was deeply suspicious of Antoine and Carmel. Antoine had tried to reassure Carmel that he would handle Fignon if he got rough. He impressed on her that she needed to persuade Eugène of the credibility of her evidence. It was he, at the end of the day, whose opinion carried the most weight in the leadership group.

When they entered the sitting room, Antoine could see that the chairs had been arranged in a circle around the fireplace, where the leaders of the Cagoule had already taken their seats. The air was thick with cigarette smoke. The hubbub of conversation stopped as soon as Antoine and Carmel arrived.

Eugène extinguished his cigarette and then cleared his throat.

'Good evening, everyone. I have called this special meeting because Antoine requested it so that we could hear from Carmel about the intelligence she has gathered on our behalf about what the Communist Party are planning. I am going to ask Carmel to give us her report, and then we can ask questions. Carmel, please start.'

Carmel had taken off her coat. She walked to the centre of the carpet, turned and faced the group of men. She held their gazes for a few seconds, before starting to speak.

'As some of you will know, I have for the past eight months been conducting an affair with Vincent Duclos, deputy leader of the Communist Party, a National Assembly member and the party's representative of the Comintern.'

Jean Fignon gave out a ribald cackle. 'A nice bit of horizontal spying.'

'Shut up, Jean. Show some respect. You are going to let Carmel speak without any interruptions. Do you understand?'

'Yes, yes, Eugène. But you know what I think of her. You can't trust a word that comes out of her mouth.'

Antoine had told Carmel to expect Fignon's interruptions and to ignore them. She turned to Deblonde.

'Shall I carry on?'

'Please, Carmel. I apologise for his uncouth behaviour.'

'In the time I have been with Duclos, he has shared with me many of the decisions taken by the party's central committee. He drinks too much, and when he does, his mouth becomes loose. The party is convinced that the right-wing leagues, along with the army, are preparing for a coup d'état. They are prepared to stop that by putting their own armed militants onto the streets. The current line is that they should make a pre-emptive strike by rising first and seizing power. They think that this will be supported by the public and create a fait accompli that the army will abide by. They are planning for the uprising to take place over the next few months, depending on the fate of the popular front government. When it collapses, which they think will be soon, then they will strike.'

A hushed silence had descended on the room as the leaders digested what they had just been told.

Eugène stood up.

'Thank you, Carmel. I will start the questions, if I may. Duclos has told you these things when he has been drunk. Not always a reliable way of extracting information. What other corroboration have you had that this information is accurate?'

'When he has been asleep in the hotel we go to, I have looked through his papers. I have photographed the most relevant sections, which I can share with you. These corroborate what he told me.'

'Do you have those with you now?'

'Antoine does.'

Antoine handed over an envelope of documents to Eugène. He had anticipated this line of questioning, so he had asked Gallopin to prepare some forged documents and have them photographed.

Henri Deblonde raised his hand to ask a question.

'I am not an expert on dialectical materialism or the warped thinking of the Comintern,' he chuckled, 'but why would they want to swing so quickly from their popular front strategy to a revolutionary uprising? It doesn't make sense.'

Carmel directed all her attention at Henri, who found it hard to look directly into the eyes of such an attractive woman.

'I'm no expert either, Henri. But Duclos explained that Stalin's popular front line was only a tactic to resist fascism. Once it fails, he will want all the Communists across Europe to take revolutionary action in defence of the Soviet Union.'

'Never mind that,' butted in Fignon. 'I don't believe a word she is saying. From day one, she has been a Sûreté plant in this organisation. And who introduced her to the organisation, but Antoine here, who I believe is also working for them.'

'What evidence have you got for that?' Joseph Darnot had left his chair and was towering over Fignon. 'I can vouch for Antoine. He's come on a couple of operations with me and always carried out his orders. He's supplied us with the contacts in the army that we asked for. And, Jean, he fought heroically in the war, which is more than I can say for you. So, if Antoine is prepared to vouch for her, then that is good enough for me.'

'Back off, Joseph. She is a Sûreté *putana*. I can smell her a mile off.'

'I've had a look at these documents,' Eugène intervened, 'they confirm what Carmel has been saying. I think we should accept what she has told us. The issue now is what do we do about it?'

'That's obvious.' The light reflected off the lenses of Gabriel Jeantot's glasses. 'We alert the army to the Communists' plans. We mobilise our battalions to be ready to come out onto the streets the moment we get confirmation of the actual date of the insurrection.'

'Is that agreed?'

All hands in the room, bar those of Fignon's, were raised in support. He stood up quickly and marched towards the door. Before he left the room, he turned and shouted, 'You will regret this, mark my words,' slamming the door behind him.

Eugène approached Carmel and took both her hands in his.

'Apologies, Carmel. He sometimes doesn't know what he is saying. Now, let's relax and have a drink.'

As the drinks were being served by Eugène's housekeeper, Antoine came up behind Carmel and put his hand on the small of her back. He could feel the warmth and dampness of the perspiration that had collected there. He leant in and whispered in her ear, 'You did brilliantly. Now, I need to do my bit.'

'Can I have everybody's attention, please?' Everyone in the room turned towards Antoine. 'Once we know the dates of the communist uprising, I think that we, the Cagoule, should put on one final display of our own to help stoke the temperature to boiling point, so our friends in the army come out in force on our side. I have planned some fireworks, so to speak, that should fit the bill. Along with Carmel, I will need Jeantot to help. I can promise you that we will light up the Paris skyline!'

Everyone cheered and raised their glass in a toast.

'Vive la France! Death to the Republic!'

CHAPTER 61

Rue de Presbourg, Paris, May 1937

ANTOINE DRUMMED HIS fingers on the steering wheel of the car parked on the kerb outside the Gare de Lyon. The trains from the Midi were running late. Carmel, leaning over the back seat, massaged his shoulders to ease the tension that was building there. He had phoned Édouard Rodin in Clermont the previous day to explain what he had planned. He asked whether he employed any chemical engineers with experience in creating controlled explosions.

'Yes, I've got just the man. Maxim Méténier. He would be very willing to help. Member of an extreme right-wing league here in Clermont. Hates Communists. One of my best engineers. I'll send him up.'

'I remember him. Small, timid man with spectacles. I didn't know he was a supporter.'

'That's him. He's become very active since the popular front government came to power.'

Although Antoine was still nominally head of security at the Rodins' factory in Clermont, he was hardly ever there, given the amount of time he was spending in his role with the Cagoule. The Rodins did not seem to mind. In fact, their financial support for the organisation had increased over the past few years. They were as determined as ever to bring down the Republic.

'There he is.' Antoine pointed at a man at the rear of the crowd of disembarking passengers who were pouring through the station's exit.

Antoine got out of the car and walked across the pavement.

'Maxim, isn't it? I'm Antoine. Come with me, I have a car parked over here.'

Méténier squinted up at Antoine, who towered over him, through the thick lenses of his glasses. He was carrying a small, brown leather valise, which he clutched close to his chest.

'Do you want to give me your case? I can take it to the car.'

'No. I will hold onto it, if that is OK.' Méténier spoke haltingly, with a slight stammer.

'Fine. Anyway, let me introduce you to the others. This is Carmel. And this is Jeantot. They are going to help us today.' He settled Méténier into the back seat next to Carmel.

'Did Monsieur Rodin explain the mission to you?'

'Yes. He said that I was to prepare some small explosives. That we would use them against the Communists. I have the materials here.' He pointed to his valise.

'Good. So, we are going to drive somewhere that you can prepare the explosives. Then Jeantot, Carmel and I will take them to where we need to use them. We will get you back to the station straight after that and you will return to Clermont. Clear?'

Méténier nodded.

Antoine drove across the city to the garage on the Boulevard Picpus that the Cagoule used as an arms depot. He took Méténier through to one of the workshops at the back.

'How long will you need?'

'About an hour. What time do you want it set to go off?'

'Ten tonight.'

'Right.'

After an hour, Méténier came through to the garage, carrying the valise.

'It's all ready to go.'

'Do we need to do anything?'

'No. Just place it where it cannot be seen. Then walk away.'

'Right. We will return for you in a couple of hours and take you back to the station. There is a bistro at the top of the boulevard. Get yourself a meal and a drink. You deserve it.' He pressed some money into Méténier's hands. 'And thank you. On behalf of the movement.'

Antoine placed the valise gingerly in the boot of the car. He signalled to Carmel and Jeantot to get in. They drove slowly to Rue de Presbourg and parked up outside the headquarters of the Confédération générale du patronat français. Antoine stared out of the window at the elegant four-storey building.

'We've rehearsed this. You know what to do. Let's go.'

Jeantot got out of the car, opened the boot and took out the valise. Carmel came alongside him and the two of them walked through the glass double doors at the front of the building. Antoine remained in the car, leaving its engine to idle.

Carmel and Jeantot walked up to the reception desk.

'Good morning. We want to enquire about how we can join the organisation. We are a new business, just starting up in Paris, and would like to make contacts with other employers.'

The receptionist produced some forms from her desk and told Carmel that she would need to fill these in, and then her request for membership would be considered.

'Excuse me, *mademoiselle*. Do you have a toilet I can use?' Jeantot enquired.

The receptionist pointed distractedly down the corridor.

Jeantot walked briskly in the direction she had indicated. He went through the door marked 'Messieurs'. There was no one at the urinals or using the hand basins. He checked the doors of the stalls. All of them were open apart from one. He went up to the stall and pushed its door gently with his foot. It swung back to reveal that no one was inside. He climbed onto the lid of the toilet and, using his arms, pulled himself up onto the top of the partition. Above it was a ventilation shaft covered by a small hatch. He pushed it up with one hand. The hatch shifted sideways. He levered the valise through the opening and pushed it inside. He replaced the hatch and climbed back into the stall. He flushed the toilet. He walked across to the hand basins. He dusted down the elbows of his jacket, washed his hands, looked in the mirror and straightened his tie.

Jeantot rejoined Carmel at the reception desk.

'Thank you for your help. Filling in these forms is taking longer than I thought. I will take them back to work and return them later. Many thanks for your help.' She looked at Jeantot. 'Are you ready to leave?'

He nodded.

They walked calmly out of the building.

CHAPTER 62

Le Temps, 16 May 1937

MASSIVE EXPLOSION DESTROYS EMPLOYERS' HEADQUARTERS – COMMUNISTS TO BLAME

AT 10PM LAST night, a massive explosion ripped through the headquarters of the Confédération générale du patronat français in Rue de Presbourg. Only one injury was sustained to the nightwatchman on duty at the time. The building has been completely destroyed. The street in front of the building is strewn with rubble. Windows in surrounding buildings were shattered by the blast.

No one has laid claim to causing the explosion. However, sources in the police and security services are laying the blame squarely on the Communists and other extreme leftists. One well-informed source told the paper, 'The truth of the matter is that the origin of the affair lies with the Marxists and Syndicalists who are against the established order of society.' The belief among the police and security services is that the Communists are trying to create fear among the population.

Vincent Duclos, deputy leader of the Communist Party of France, stated that the explosion was 'a provocation' caused by right-wing extremists 'who want to use this act to encourage their allies in the military to rise up and overthrow the Third Republic. The Communist Party will use all means available to resist this outcome.'

CHAPTER 63

Central Paris, 16 and 17 June 1937

GALLOPIN LET ANTOINE know that the time was now right to spring the trap on the Cagoule. The Sûreté no longer saw a need for them. The Cagoule's actions were increasingly dangerous and destabilising. A failed coup would add to the already substantial incriminating evidence to imprison the Cagoule's leaders for a very long time. Antoine would have to go to prison along with the others to preserve his cover, but the Sûreté would ensure that he would be released early.

Antoine arranged a meeting with Eugène Deblonde. He reported that Duclos had told Carmel that the long anticipated communist insurrection was planned for the night of 16 June. Antoine also told Eugène that he had alerted his contacts in the army to be ready to leave their barracks to seize control of the state. Eugène ordered all the Cagoule units in Paris to be mobilised on that night, ready to take to the streets to combat the Communists.

Antoine and Jeantot arrived at the garage on Rue Picpus early in the evening. Even before they opened the workshop doors, they could hear the excited chatter coming from inside. There were about fifty men milling around. They were dressed in the blue tunics, khaki trousers and black berets that the Cagoule had adopted as its uniform. Laid out in front of them were wooden cases full of the Beretta semi-automatic rifles that the Italians had supplied as the reward for the assassination of the Bartali brothers. The men were stripping down and cleaning the rifles before snapping in the magazines of bullets. At the back of the workshop were trestle tables loaded with food and drinks for the night.

'OK, men, fall in!' Jeantot ordered.

The men formed into lines and came to attention.

Antoine carried out an inspection, walking up and down the lines. He adjusted a few of the men's uniforms. He gave some words of encouragement to the younger members of the battalion, who had never experienced combat before. He returned to the front of the group to address them.

'This is the night we have trained for. The Communists are planning to mount an armed insurrection, most probably in the early hours of tomorrow morning. Our intelligence tells us that they will form up in the Bois de Boulogne. They will then send out two columns, one on the right-hand side and one on the left-hand side of the river. Their aim will be to seize key strategic points in the city, including the National Assembly building, the Préfecture de Police, the Hôtel de Ville and Radio Paris. We will be there to stop them!'

The men cheered and stamped their boots on the floor.

'We will not mobilise until we have word that the Communists are on the move. We fully expect elements of the army to respond to the communist threat, so we will support them in whatever actions they take. The

Communists are armed. You will be expected to use your weapons to combat them. Is that clear?'

'Yes,' the men roared back.

'Good. Remember, today you will act as proud soldiers in defence of your fatherland. Dismissed.'

Antoine pulled aside Jeantot. 'Come on. Let's check in on the other units and see if we can see any early signs of movement from the Communists. I also need to report back to Eugène, so he knows what's going on.'

They climbed into a Citroën car that the garage proprietor had supplied with false number plates for the night. Jeantot drove a circuit of central Paris, stopping at various locations, including on Boulevard Victor-Emmanuel, near the Champs-Élysées, Boulevard Sarrail and the Carrefour Auteuil-La Fontaine. At each stop, Antoine spent a few minutes talking to men standing on the pavements or sitting outside a café. These were all acting as lookouts for their Cagoule units, which were assembling in nearby garages and depots.

'They are all prepared and ready. Let's go off to the Bois de Boulogne and see what's happening.'

They first drove round the perimeter of the park to see if there were any unusual traffic movements. There was nothing out of the ordinary. Jeantot dropped Antoine off outside the main front entrance. Antoine walked down the central tree-lined avenue. Again, there was nothing out of the ordinary to see. It was now about 10pm. There were still plenty of people taking a stroll, enjoying the cool of the night air after a hot summer's day.

'Right, let's go to Eugène's.'

They arrived at Rue Nicolo to find Eugène staring out of the window of his sitting room on the top floor of the house, smoking nervously. Standing a few feet behind him, glowering, was Jean Fignon. When they entered the room, Eugène turned round quickly.

'Well, anything to report?'

'No. But it is still too early. All our men are in place and ready. We just need to wait for the Communists to make their move.'

'And what if they don't?' Jean Fignon walked up very close to Antoine, so he was only a few inches away from him.

No one responded.

'Eugène, what if they don't?' The volume of Fignon's voice had started to rise.

'Well, we fully expect them to. If they don't, then we will have to review the situation again.'

'Eugène, you always were a bloody coward. I'll tell you what I think. This communist uprising was never going to happen. Antoine and Carmel have set us up.'

'Oh, shut up, Jean.'

'No, you shut up, Eugène. You've been conned by these two. You just can't see it. But don't let this opportunity slip. Even if the Communists don't come out, we have mobilised our men across Paris. We can control the streets. The army may or may not support us. We have the strength to seize power on our own.'

'Don't be bloody stupid, Jean. We can't do it on our own. That's right, isn't it, Antoine?'

'Without the army, we are just a terrorist group.'

'Listen to him, Eugène. The man is a traitor to our cause.'

'Jean, I've heard enough from you. Go and do something useful like take charge of your battalion. Go on, leave.'

Jean stabbed his fingers into Antoine's chest. 'I know what you are up to.'

Antoine pushed Jean away.

'Come on, Gabriel, let's go. We'll come back when we have something to report.'

Antoine and Jeantot drove back to the Bois de Boulogne. They parked up just outside the main entrance. Antoine knew that it would be a long night, given that nothing was going to happen.

At 3am, Jeantot shook Antoine awake.

'What? Are they here?' Antoine asked groggily.

'No, nothing. Just some lovers sneaking in for a quickie. What do you want to do?'

'Give it another hour. If nothing happens by then, we will have to report back to Eugène.'

An hour later, they were treading wearily up the stairs in Eugène's house. When they opened the door, they found him still staring out of the window, cigarette in hand.

'Anything?'

'No. Nothing.'

'Let's call it a day,' he said resignedly. 'Disband the men.'

CHAPTER 64

L'Écho de Paris, 20 June 1937

GOVERNMENT ARRESTS THE 'HOODED MEN' AFTER PSEUDO PLOT TO OVERTHROW THE REPUBLIC

INTERIOR MINISTER MARX Dormoy has arrested and imprisoned the leaders of a right-wing group on the grounds that they planned to overthrow the Third Republic in an armed coup d' état.

Brothers Eugène and Henri Deblonde, Gabriel Jeantot and Antoine Martinet were all seized on the morning of 19 June and taken to La Santé prison in Paris. It is claimed that they are the notorious 'hooded men', or Cagoulards, who have been behind the assassinations and terrorist acts that have terrified the country.

Their *avocat,* Xavier Vallat, claims that all the men are innocent and will plead not guilty when they are charged. Right-wing commentators complain that this is a 'Fantomarx' plot dreamed up by Interior Minister Marx Dormoy to advance his socialist political campaign.

Other leaders of the Cagoule are still at large and being hunted by the gendarmerie.

CHAPTER 65

La Santé Prison, Paris, August 1937

ANTOINE WAS DOZING on the bunk in his cell when there was a rap on the door.

'Prisoner Martinet to report to the governor's office. Now!'

A prison officer escorted him down the corridor. He remained stony-faced and did not respond when Antoine asked why the governor wanted to see him.

'Just keep walking, Martinet.'

They left the main prison block and walked across the yard to the administration buildings. Antoine looked up at the sky and felt the warmth of the sun on his face. They entered the buildings and climbed up the stairs to the first floor. The guard knocked on the governor's office door.

'Enter.'

The guard opened the door and pushed Antoine into the room.

'Hello, Antoine. Good to see you again.'

Gallopin stood up from behind the governor's desk. He reached out and shook Antoine's hand. Sitting beside him was Bernard, who acknowledged Antoine with a reluctant nod of the head.

'How are they treating you?'

'OK. We are being considered as political prisoners, thanks to Vallat's plea. So, I get to wear my own clothes. I can read newspapers and books. But I am still a prisoner. How long is this going to go on?'

'We're working on it. We think that with the way the international situation is going we could be mobilising for war soon. When that happens, all of you lot will be released to return to military service.'

'What if we go to trial before then and I am found guilty? Then what?'

'That won't happen, I can assure you. The Sûreté views you as too precious an asset. We will need you when things get ugly, but right now we need to maintain your cover by keeping you in here. How are relationships with Deblonde and the others?'

'Fine. I don't think they suspect anything. Eugène involves me in all the discussions he is continuing to have with those in the organisation who remain on the outside. To be honest, there is not much of an organisation left after all the arrests. Is it right that Fignon escaped to Spain and Darnot to Italy?'

'Yes. Fignon is holed up in a Cagoule-owned apartment in San Sebastian, with several others. Darnot is living in San Remo, cosying up to the local Fascists.'

'And will you arrest them if they try and get back into France?'

'Why is that any of your concern?'

'Because, Bernard, Fignon is a psychopath and there are people whom I care about whom he might want to hurt.'

'You mean the delightful Carmel,' snickered Bernard.

'We are keeping an eye on her, don't worry, Antoine,' reassured Gallopin.

'Well, you had better keep her safe. She did you a great service by feeding Deblonde that fake intelligence.'

'We will.'

Antoine turned and opened the door.

'Guard! Take me back to the cells.'

CHAPTER 66

Daumesnil Metro Station, Paris, September 1937

JEAN FIGNON COULD see the back of the head of wavy black hair disappear down the escalator to the platform. He pulled the lip of his battered trilby more tightly over his eyes. His tiredness after the long journey up from Spain was being kept at bay by the adrenaline that was starting to course through his veins.

He had been surprised when he found the package of documents shoved through the door at his apartment in San Sebastian. It had contained a fake passport in another person's name, a travel pass to Paris that would get him across the nationalist-controlled border in Spain and an unsigned note stating that the 'person of interest' was still working nights as a concierge at the Des Barreaux Verte, on Rue de Lappe. The pass let him stay in France for three days.

The metro was winding down for the night, with the last of the revellers and workers from the Latin Quarter making their way home. Fignon hung back behind a drunken couple who were slowly lurching their way towards the platform, their arms wrapped around each other as they fumbled their way through an embrace. He could see Carmel look up distractedly as the couple entered the platform, but her weary eyes did not linger long on them or the shape skulking behind them.

A hot gust of air rushing up the tunnel heralded the arrival of the train. Carmel waited for the doors to open, then slipped into a first-class carriage, where she was the sole occupant. Fignon followed the couple into the adjoining second-class carriage. He sat where he could keep an eye on Carmel but far enough away so she would not become conscious of being observed.

Carmel rose as the train slowed at the stop for Daumesnil. Fignon now knew that she was on her way back to her apartment. She was one of the few passengers to get off. Fignon left it until the last moment before he left the train. Carmel was already halfway up the escalator by the time he arrived at the bottom. There was one other passenger between the two of them. Fignon took a couple of strides up the moving stairs so he was close to the other passenger but hidden from Carmel should she look down.

Carmel stepped off the escalator and walked towards the exit. She waved at the attendant on duty, saying something to him in Spanish before turning right onto Rue Reuilly. Fignon left the station and crossed the road so he could keep some distance between them but still stay close to her. He knew that her apartment was not far from the metro station. He recalled from what Antoine had said that she lived there with her mother. He only had a few minutes in which to act.

Carmel slowed to a stop. She opened her bag, took out a cigarette and lit it. She stared up into the night sky as she pulled hard on the cigarette one last time before dropping it onto the pavement. Carmel's hand went back into her bag again to search for the key to the apartment building. Finding it, she turned to unlock the door.

Fignon's gloved hand wrapped round her mouth. He arched her backwards, so her neck was fully exposed. Carmel heard the metallic snap of the mechanism unleashing the serrated knife from Fignon's sleeve. She tried to buck and thrash to throw him off. But Fignon's knee had her pinned firmly into place as he slid the blade across her neck. Blood spurted out as he severed her jugular vein. Her body convulsed several times before falling limp. Fignon lowered her to the ground. As he did so he leant down and whispered into her ear, with the last flickers of life leaking from her eyes, 'That, *putana*, is what happens to those who betray the Cagoule. I swear I will do the same to Antoine.'

CHAPTER 67

Le Temps, 24 September 1938

CAGOULARDS RELEASED FROM PRISON TO TAKE UP MILITARY SERVICE AFTER HITLER INVADES CZECHOSLOVKIA

AVOCAT XAVIER VALLAT has secured the release of the so-called 'hooded men' from La Santé prison to enable them to take up military service. This is in response to the international emergency brought about by Hitler's invasion of Czechoslovakia in the past few days.

All the best-known Cagoulards – Eugène and Henri Deblonde, Antoine Martinet and Gabriel Jeantot – are honoured veterans of the last war. Due to their previous service, they all remain part of the military reserve ready for call-up. The prison governor at La Santé has been bombarded with letters from the officers of these men, demanding their immediate release.

Minister of the Interior, Marx Dormoy, after agreeing to the release, stated that the men would still have to stand trial once the international situation had calmed down.

CHAPTER 68

Bois de Marfée, 13 and 14 May 1940

THE GROUP OF German Fallschirmjäger emerged from the wreaths of smoke as they scaled the citadel of the medieval castle that dominated the town of Sedan. Once they had got to the top, they lowered the French tricolour and raised the Reich's red-and-white flag with its defiant black swastika emblazoned in its middle. Antoine could see through his binoculars, but not hear, the paratroopers raising their arms in victory and shouting to their comrades below. Sedan had fallen. The crossing of the Meuse River was all that lay between the Germans and their headlong rush to Paris and the Channel ports.

Antoine rolled on his back in the observation trench on the Marfée Heights and raised his eyes to the sky. He thought back over what had happened to him since he had been released from La Santé prison. Gallopin had met him at the gates to tell him that Carmel had been murdered. The police were claiming they had no clues as to who the assailant had been. No arrests had been made. Antoine, and he suspected, Gallopin, knew that Jean Fignon was the murderer. Antoine decided that he would take justice into his own hands and hunt Fignon down. He contacted Carmel's brother, José, who was still serving with the nationalist army in Spain. They arranged to meet in San Sebastian, where Gallopin had told him that Fignon had fled to a Cagoule-owned apartment after the failed coup. When they burst into the apartment it was empty. There was no evidence to indicate where Fignon had moved on to. The trail went cold. Antoine vowed to José that he would exact revenge when he caught up with him.

Along with all the other leaders of the Cagoule who were released early from prison, Antoine returned to his infantry regiment, the 97th, to prepare for the coming war. He had not been there long before he received an order to transfer to army intelligence, the Deuxième Bureau. Antoine knew that Gallopin was behind the move to keep him within the security services, although they had not met since Gallopin had told him the devasting news about Carmel outside the gates of La Santé. In his new role he was attached to the staff of General Lafontaine's 55th Division as part of the French Second Army. Now that the Germans had finally invaded after the long-drawn-out months of the phony war, the 55th Division found itself spread across the west bank of the Meuse River, tasked with stopping Guderian's panzer divisions crossing the river.

Antoine crawled up to the lip of the observation trench and peered through his binoculars. From where he was positioned, shielded by the surrounding woodland, he had a panoramic view of the river valley below and the approach roads that led up to it from Sedan. The French had dug in their long-range artillery on the reverse side of the slope, to protect them from the Germans' air attacks. From here, they could see the panzers advance towards the Meuse and then pick them off when they tried to cross. This was their opportunity to bring the German invasion to a shuddering halt and then drive them back to the border.

It was early in the morning. The combined mist and smoke from the earlier artillery exchanges were starting to clear from the bottom of the river valley. Antoine could see a column of panzer tanks moving along the road from Sedan towards Wadelincourt, the small hamlet on the east bank of the Meuse. In front of them, he spotted a detachment of infantry pioneers running towards the riverbank carrying inflatable dinghies across their heads. He turned to the radio operator sitting alongside him and ordered him to instruct the commanders in the bunkers on the west bank of the river to hold their fire on the pioneers until they entered the water. Minutes later he could hear machine gunfire pouring out of the slits of the bunkers. Wave after wave of men were cut down by the enfilading fire, with many tipping into the river as their boats capsized. After thirty minutes of intense fire, the Germans gave up the attempt to cross and hunkered down under any cover they could find.

An eerie silence descended on the battlefield. Antoine could pick out through his binoculars the corpses of the pioneers floating in the river and lying prone in the bottom of the dinghies that nestled against the banks. The panzers had stopped on the road, their exhaust fumes pumping out behind them, unable to cross the river.

Antoine felt his leg being shaken from behind. He looked down to see his radio operator pointing frantically into the sky. Above Sedan and moving towards them were three columns of planes. They had the unmistakeable shape of Stukas, their black-painted fuselages emblazoned with swastikas and their upturned wings carrying two bombs underneath them. The first formation dived from the sky, looking as though they were in freefall. The sight of them was soon followed by the sound. A whine that soon turned into a bloodcurdling scream as the planes started to bank before releasing their bombs onto the French bunkers on the riverbank. No sooner had the first wave peeled off, than the second wave followed, dropping their bombs. There was a slight pause, while the pilots in the remaining Stukas assessed the damage, then they too put their planes into controlled dives, targeting those bunkers that had not been hit during the first two attacks.

The attack had been devasting. Smoke was pouring out of the slits of the bunkers. Some had taken direct hits, so their roofs had caved in. Others had suffered near misses, but the earth had been so churned up around them that the infantry within them no longer had a clear line of sight to the enemy collecting on the riverbank below. Antoine could see men from the bunkers clambering out the hatches at the back and running up the hill towards the road. He switched his attention to the other side of the river. While the attack had been going on, the pioneers had launched their dinghies again. Some had managed to get across and established a small bridgehead. Small groups of engineers were starting to build pontoon bridges to bring across the panzers.

Antoine told his radio operator to call in the co-ordinates to the artillery division stationed on the reverse slope. Within minutes the barrage from behind them started up. The first few rounds of shells were too long and ended up in the fields behind the river. The next rounds started to find their range. Antoine saw the first half-built bridge collapse into the water when it received a direct hit. The barrage continued until none of the bridges were standing. The few German infantry men that remained on the west bank had dug in and were concentrating their fire on the bunkers. No panzers had crossed the river.

Antoine heard the drone of engines approaching from some distance away. He scrambled up to the top of the observation trench. High up in the sky to the east he could see the black outline of a formation of heavy Dornier bombers approaching the Heights. Antoine prayed that they were flying past them towards another target. He craned his neck to see them pass above him. Then they turned and started a run towards them. They were heading towards the artillery positions. He pressed himself into the earth at the bottom of the trench, his hands covering his head. There was only a slight pause before the Dorniers released their bombs. The ground reverberated as the bombs crashed into their targets. Branches and bark from the shattered trees in the wood rained down onto the trench, followed by mounds of earth that shot up into the air before crashing down around the craters left behind.

The sound of the engines disappeared into the distance. Antoine uncurled himself, stood up and shook all the mud and debris from his uniform. He checked himself for any cuts or grazes. He was untouched. He scrambled back up the trench to look at the damage. The artillery positions had taken a pounding. He could see some of the long-range guns lying on their sides, their muzzles twisted out of shape. Stretcher bearers and medics were running from one position to another checking prone bodies to see if they were dead or could be saved. Antoine switched his attention to the river valley below. Once again, the German pioneers had taken advantage of the aerial bombardment to start building pontoon bridges across the river.

Antoine ordered the radio operator to contact General Lafontaine, whose headquarters were in a farmhouse at Bulson two kilometres behind the frontline.

'General, we need to get some air support to bomb the bridges they are putting across the river. They are making fast progress.'

'It's too late, Captain. They are already across the river.'

'No, they are not, General. I can see them. The panzers are still on the other side.'

'We have a radio report from Chaumont, a kilometre to the west of you at Marfée. They are reporting that the tanks have gone round your position. They are coming up the road towards you. You will need to evacuate your position straight away. We will need to remove the rest of the artillery and retreat to Chémery.'

'That's impossible, sir. No tanks have come across or gone round us. We mustn't retreat and give up this position. We have the advantage of height here.'

'Captain, I am ordering you to retreat. I have given the same order to the captain in charge of the artillery.'

Antoine threw the radio receiver onto the ground in disgust. He ran to the top of the hill and then down the bank until he came to the road to Chaumont. Coming towards him was a large group of infantrymen. Many of them had discarded their rifles. Some had removed their army insignia from their uniforms. They were running in a ragged formation, pointing behind them in panic. Antoine had a disorientating flashback to the Chemin des Dames and the mutinying troops refusing to fight and fleeing from the Germans over twenty years before. History was repeating itself.

Antoine stood in the middle of the road. He pulled out his pistol. As the first men reached him, he could see the fear and panic in their eyes.

'The tanks are at Bulson. They are everywhere. Don't go forward,' one of the soldiers shouted.

'Halt! I am ordering you to stop and return to your positions. No tanks have crossed the river. If you carry on running, you will be treated as deserters.'

The men at the front stopped for a moment. They could see that Antoine was on his own. The men coming up behind them swept past him, ignoring his repeated command to stop. Antoine grabbed hold of an infantry captain who was running alongside his men.

'Captain! What are you doing? Who gave you the order to retreat? Turn your men around, now!'

The captain shrugged off Antoine's hand and continued to run down the road.

Antoine stood there for a while longer. He was like a rock in a river being bypassed by fast running water. It was futile.

He looked down into the valley below. The first panzers were just crossing the pontoon bridges. The gunfire from the French bunkers had fallen silent.

EPILOGUE

Café Dominique, Paris, 12 June 1940

ANTOINE WATCHED THE two men on the road outside the café pushing and shoving each other. One had just driven his truck into the back of the other's car, bringing the rest of the traffic to a grinding halt. People were jumping out of their cars, arms waving wildly in the air, shouting insults. The panic in the air was palpable as families tried to flee the capital city before the German army arrived. The sound of approaching artillery fire could now be heard in the centre of the city.

Gallopin had asked to meet Antoine. He had not said what the meeting was about. Antoine assumed that he was going to be given instructions about what he should do once the country was defeated. He could see Gallopin coming down the street, weaving between the men who were now lifting the front of the damaged truck and pulling it to one side. Gallopin came through the door, asked the proprietor for a cognac and sat down opposite Antoine. For someone who was normally so controlled and calm in his manner, Gallopin looked ruffled. Although he was still clad in his normal outfit of unbuttoned white satin shirt and black trousers, Antoine noticed that he was no longer wearing the Star of David pendant round his neck.

'It won't be long now. They will be rolling down the Champs Élysée in a couple of days.'

'Then what?' Antoine asked.

'Well, first we get out. Then we regroup. Look, what I am going to propose, you don't have to do. You've served your dues for us. But, if you want to carry on, then we could really use you.'

'How, exactly?'

'To be honest, we are not too sure yet. It depends on what happens after the defeat. Our intelligence is that the government will sue for peace. The Germans will impose some form of occupation, but they will do it differently to how they have done it in Poland. They are likely to mix direct occupation, maybe in Paris and the north, with a collaborationist government in the rest of the country. The collaborators will mainly be drawn from the right-wing leagues and elements of the armed forces. We need people who are known to and trusted by them to provide us with information about what they are planning.'

'People like me, you mean?'

'Yes, people like you.'

'And where will you and the rest of the Sûreté be?'

'Possibly in England. Although some of us will stay here, some underground, some operating legitimately as part of the remaining French government. We really don't know until we see what the Germans have planned. What do you think?'

'I've got nothing more to lose. My brother is dead. Carmel has gone. Marguerite thinks that I am beyond the pale. I've got unfinished business with many of the people who will fill positions of power when the Germans take over. So, yes, I want to continue.'

'Good. I'm pleased. I know that we haven't always seen eye to eye, but you have become one of my most effective and trusted operatives, so I want to keep you on board.'

'So, you will communicate with me about what I do, and where I go next, when we get a clearer picture.'

'Yes, but, first, I want you to do something for yourself.'

'What?'

'Marguerite may not want to have anything more to do with you, but you need to get to her as quickly as you can and persuade her to leave the country.'

Antoine felt his body tense.

'Why? Is she in danger?'

'Yes. Bernard has put her on a list of those to be rounded up for internment as soon as the Germans take over. He has her down as a communist agitator, I think because of her known support for the Vietnamese Communist Party. If the experience of those who have been interned by the Germans in other occupied countries is anything to go by, then her life is in danger.'

'That bastard. He had his eye on her from the start in Indochina. How do I get her out?'

'There are regular sailings to England out of La Rochelle. Get her onto one of those. Here, I have some government authorisations for her.' Gallopin slid the papers across the table.

'Now, go.'

Biarritz, 23 June 1940

The roads were clogged completely with families deserting the northern cities for the south of the country and what remained of the fleeing army. Broken-down vehicles littered the sides of the roads, where people had abandoned them. Those who did not have trucks or cars had resorted to piling all their household belongings onto horse-drawn carts. Those without a car or a cart, pushed their pitiful belongings along in prams or on bicycles. The chaos was made worse when the Armistice was finally signed. Those who were heading south now turned round and headed back home. Antoine only managed to keep his car on the road as Gallopin had requisitioned additional cans of petrol for him to stow in the boot.

Antoine eventually arrived in Biarritz late at night on the third day of travel. He had only had a few hours' sleep, snatched during very brief stops on the roadside. His eyes felt gritty with fatigue and his face and neck itched from the unaccustomed stubble growing there.

As he entered the town, the car fell in behind a military lorry trundling along the avenue behind the Casino Municipal. When it got towards the end of the avenue, it slowed and came to a halt. A soldier dressed in a German field grey uniform got out of the passenger seat, followed by a man in a white tropical suit. The soldier went round to the back of the lorry and let the tailgate down. Four soldiers, also dressed in field grey, jumped down. As the man in the white suit came round to the back of the lorry, Antoine's headlight briefly lit up his face. It was Bernard. Antoine inched slowly round the lorry and continued along the avenue.

Through his rear-view mirror he watched as the soldiers went up to the door of a house just past the Casino Municipal. One of them knocked loudly on the door. When there was no answer, the soldier proceeded to kick it in. The other soldiers rushed in behind him. Antoine cut his lights and parked two hundred metres further up the road. Still looking through his mirror, he saw the soldiers coming out of the house pushing a barefoot man in his pyjamas in front of them. They frogmarched him up to Bernard, who said a few brief words to him, before the man was shoved roughly into the back of the lorry.

Antoine pulled away from the kerb slowly, drove to the end of the avenue, then accelerated up the hill to Rue Maréchal. He parked outside Villa Tan Loc, leapt out of the car and started pulling furiously on the chain hanging outside the door to the garden. He could hear the tinkling of the bell in the house. He looked at his watch. It was only 10pm, so someone should still be up. He pulled the chain again. After a few minutes, he heard the bolt on the gate being pulled back. The gate opened a crack. Antoine could see Marguerite's servant peering out, alarm in his eyes.

'You need to let me in now – your mistress is in great danger.'

'No. Mistress in bed. Too late.'

Without thinking, Antoine put his arm through the crack in the gate and pushed the servant backwards. The servant lost his balance and fell over. Antoine slid through the partially open gate. He put his arm under the servant's and hustled him to the front door, which was still open. Standing there, with the light in the hall framing her hair, was Marguerite.

'Let him go! What the hell are you doing, Antoine, barging in like this.'

'Marguerite, listen, we've got no time. You need to get dressed, pack a suitcase and come with me.'

'Why? No! Of course I won't.'

'Marguerite, in a few minutes, Bernard and some German soldiers will be here to arrest you.'

'I don't believe you.'

'It's true. Come with me. You can see them with your own eyes.'

Marguerite reluctantly followed Antoine to the gate and out onto the road. He pointed down the hill towards the avenue that ran along the seafront. They could see the lorry parked up at the corner before it swung up the hill towards where Marguerite lived. Bernard and four soldiers were standing at the back of the lorry smoking cigarettes.

'That's them. And they are on their way up here.'

'Where can I go?'

'I've got a passage for you on a boat leaving La Rochelle for England, first thing tomorrow morning. It's your only chance.'

Marguerite looked down the hill. Plumes of cigarette smoke hung over Bernard and the group of soldiers, who appeared to be sharing a joke.

'You need to know that I am not on my own. I need safe passage for someone else.'

'Who? Your servant.'

Marguerite looked at Antoine, weighing up what she was about to say next.

'No. Den Hieu is here with me. He escaped from Paris before the Germans got there. He knows that they will arrest him and most probably execute him.'

'Christ, Marguerite. You are taking a big risk harbouring him here.'

'Will you take him with us?'

'Come on, then. We've no time to lose.'

Without a further word, Marguerite strode back into the house. A few minutes later, she came outside, dressed and clutching a small suitcase, followed by Den, who did not make eye contact with Antoine. Marguerite turned on the doorstep and hugged her servant, who closed the door behind them. Antoine took the suitcase and put it in the boot. Marguerite slid into the front seat. Her face was wet with tears. Den climbed into the back of the car. Antoine told him to lie down in the footwell, so he wouldn't be seen as they drove down the hill past Bernard and his men.

La Rochelle, 24 June 1940

The boat was moored up next to the Tour de la Chaîne in the Vieux Port in La Rochelle. There was a queue of people waiting to board. Antoine scanned the anxious faces to check that there was no one among them that might be working for Bernard. Satisfied, he went back to the car and escorted Marguerite and Den to the quay.

They had hardly said a word on the drive between Biarritz and La Rochelle. Marguerite had spent her time staring out the window across the sand dunes of Les Landes and out to the waters of the Bay of Biscay. Den had remained crouched down in the back seat in case they passed any military vehicles on the way. Antoine did not know what to say to Marguerite, so remained silent. He was just grateful that she was sitting here beside him and that he had persuaded her to leave.

They joined the back of the queue. The passengers at the front were starting to embark. It was a slow process as their papers all had to be checked before they were allowed on board. They inched forwards.

When they got to the front of the queue, Antoine handed over Marguerite's papers to the naval officer checking them.

'And what about this one?' the officer said, pointing at Den.

'I have no papers for him. They didn't come through in time.'

'Well, in that case, he cannot board.'

Antoine pulled his Sûreté identification out of his breast pocket and held it up very close to the officer's face.

'You will make an exception for him.'

The officer hesitated, staring at Den. 'OK, get him on board. We haven't got time for this.'

Den filed up the gangway without a backward glance at Antoine. Marguerite held back.

'What are you going to do?' she enquired quietly.

'Not too sure yet, but I will still be working with Gallopin.'

'Why, Antoine? You don't owe them anything anymore.'

'You are right, I don't. What I do will be for me. Because of my background and the people I know, I can work from the inside to undermine those whom the Germans will put in control.'

'So, you're staying here.'

'Yes.'

They fell silent.

Marguerite took his hand in hers and squeezed it gently. 'Thank you, Antoine.'

Antoine waited on the quayside to watch the boat leave the harbour. There was no sign of Marguerite standing with the other passengers waving to their family members as they left.

Within twenty minutes he was driving back towards Paris and the years of occupation.

COMING SOON

Crossing the Line

Volume 2 of The Dark Years Trilogy

PROLOGUE

The Volost River Valley, near Smolensk, May 1942

IN EXASPERATION, ANTOINE blew the green mosquito netting off his nose and away from his mouth. It stuck to his face, plastered there by the sweat streaming from inside his helmet. As much as he wanted to rip it off, he knew that the netting provided him with some protection against the swarming mosquitos, who buzzed around his face and upper body in search of any exposed flesh to latch onto.

The heat and humidity, and accompanying insect life, in the swampy marshlands surrounding the Volost river, reminded him of the conditions he endured trekking down Chinese renegades in northern Indochina. Now he was hunting Soviet partisans, who were harrying the rearguard divisions of the German Army Group Centre as it retreated from Smolensk.

Antoine gazed down at the tricolour badge sewn onto the sleeve of his German infantry grey field uniform. His brain did its usual contorted dance trying to rationalise why he, a patriotic French man, who had fought hand-to-hand with

Germans in the trenches at Verdun, was now serving in the army of his bitterest enemy. True, he was an officer in a French regiment, the Légion des Volontaires Français, attached to a German security division. Also true, he was fighting against Bolsheviks, for whom he had a visceral loathing, holding them responsible for the death of his younger brother. And he reminded himself, the primary reason he was here was because he was still working undercover for the French Sûreté. But, even so, he was finding it hard to reconcile himself to being a soldier in Hitler's army. Under his breath, he cursed Daniel Gallopin, his Sûreté handler, for sending him here to this sweltering, mosquito infested swamp.

A rough shaking of his arm distracted him from his thoughts.

'You need to take a look at this.' Pierre Jouvin handed him a set of binoculars, pointing towards the horizon. Antoine looked across at Jouvin's outstretched hand, and then up into his face. Jouvin was wearing a helmet, but without the green netting draped around it. He never seemed to be bothered by the mosquitoes, the cloying humidity or the partisans. He had the same temperament and approach to life as when he had managed the rubber plantations in Indochina on Antoine's behalf. Mentally imperturbable. Physically indestructible.

Antoine peered through the binoculars at a smudge of black smoke rising into the sky about a kilometre away, where a track ran alongside the edge of a dense pine forest.

'That's about where the convoy was heading for,' Jouvin observed.

'Why the hell did they send them down there without any advance recon?'

'You know why Antoine. The Boche think we are expendable.'

Divisional HQ had put in a request to Antoine's commanding officer early that morning to send out a truckload of men to provide protection to a group of engineers repairing telephone lines that had been cut by the partisans. No-one had thought to send out an advance patrol to see whether the partisans were still in the vicinity. Judging by the wisps of black smoke curling up into the sky, the partisans had been waiting for them.

'We will go down on foot,' ordered Antoine. 'Split the men into two groups. I will lead the first. You lead the second. We will circle round and approach the track from either end. When we get there, I want you to provide us with cover when we go and look at the damage. If I know those bastards, they will have slipped back into the forest by now but be prepared for them to be still lying in wait for us.'

It took them about half an hour to creep up on the track. Although it was high summer, the ground was still boggy underfoot, with the men's boots being sucked into the marshy ground. Antoine could hear the men's breathing getting heavier as they slogged across the terrain.

Antoine's group was the first to arrive. He signalled to his men to halt, waiting for Jouvin's unit to appear. He raised his binoculars to his eyes and looked down the track. He could see two trucks at right angles to each other, as though they had been driven together to provide some rudimentary protection. Smoke billowed out of their engines. Spreadeagled out around them, Antoine could make out the bodies. A quick count indicated that the whole detachment had been killed.

Antoine motioned to his men to follow him. They walked slowly down the track, keeping a wary eye on the pine trees at the edge of the forest. They were clustered together so tightly, that it was impossible to see beyond the first rank of trees.

They reached the burnt-out trucks. The dead men were lying front down. They had been stripped of all their clothing. Their weapons had been taken. Nothing stirred, except for the flies that were buzzing around the patches of blood congealing on the exit wounds.

Antoine went over to a body on the ground. He gently rolled it over with his boot. The partisans had left their usual calling card. The man's genitals had been sliced off and stuffed into his gaping mouth. He had seen this so many times before that he no longer felt the urge to vomit. Instead, he started to bark out orders.

'Cover these bodies immediately. Radio back to base and get them to send down some more trucks. We will get these men back to the camp as soon as possible to give them a decent burial. Then, my friends, we shall come back and track down the murdering bastards.'

Two hours later, the trucks loaded with the corpses arrived back at the regimental headquarters. Antoine dismounted and started to give the orders for the men's burials.

'Captain Martinet, report to me!'

Antoine turned to see his commanding officer striding across the parade ground, dressed in the uniform of a major of the Waffen-SS. Nestled under his throat was an iron cross. He came to a halt and raised his arm.

'Heil Hitler!'

Antoine returned an orthodox military salute.

'Captain Martinet, I order you to return the Hitler salute to a commanding officer in the German army.'

'Sir, as you know, it is my right, as an officer in the volunteer French army, to provide a conventional salute.'

Antoine held Major Philippe Doriot's unflinching stare. This was the fascist fanatic that Gallopin had sent Antoine all the way to Russia to assassinate.